THE
GODS OF
GREEN
COUNTY

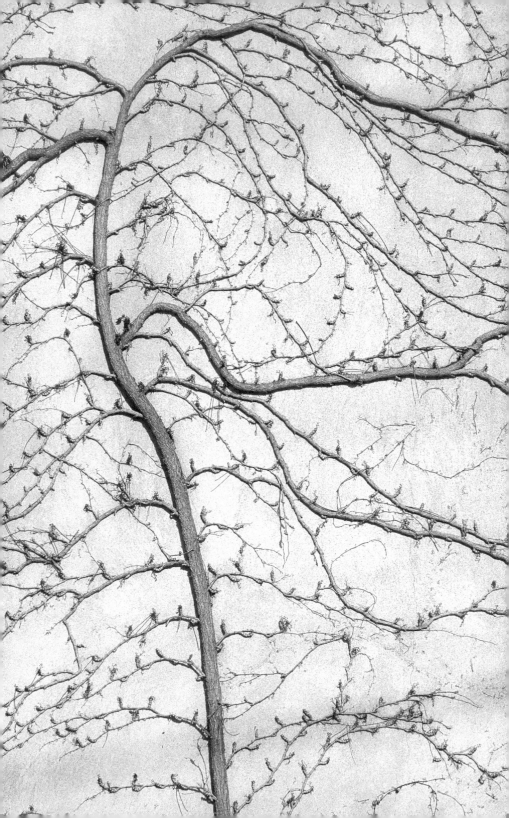

THE
GODS OF
GREEN
COUNTY

Mary Elizabeth Pope

— BLAIR —

Printed in the United States of America
Cover design by Laura Williams
Interior design by April Leidig

Blair is an imprint of Carolina Wren Press.

*The mission of Blair/Carolina Wren Press is to seek out, nurture,
and promote literary work by new and underrepresented writers.*

We gratefully acknowledge the ongoing support of general
operations by the Durham Arts Council's United Arts Fund and the
North Carolina Arts Council.

Library of Congress Cataloging-in-Publication Data
Names: Pope, Mary Elizabeth, author.
Title: The Gods of Green County / Mary Elizabeth Pope.
Description: Durham, North Carolina : Blair, [2021]
Identifiers: LCCN 2021024065 (print) | LCCN 2021024066 (ebook) |
ISBN 9781949467710 (hardcover) | ISBN 9781949467727 (ebook)
Subjects: GSAFD: Mystery fiction.
Classification: LCC PS3616.O65433 G63 2021 (print) |
LCC PS3616.O65433 (ebook) | DDC 813/.6—dc23
LC record available at https://lccn.loc.gov/2021024065
LC ebook record available at https://lccn.loc.gov/2021024066

For Matt Elliott
One day my laugh lines
will spell your name

And in loving memory
of my paternal grandparents,
Garl and Delia Pope

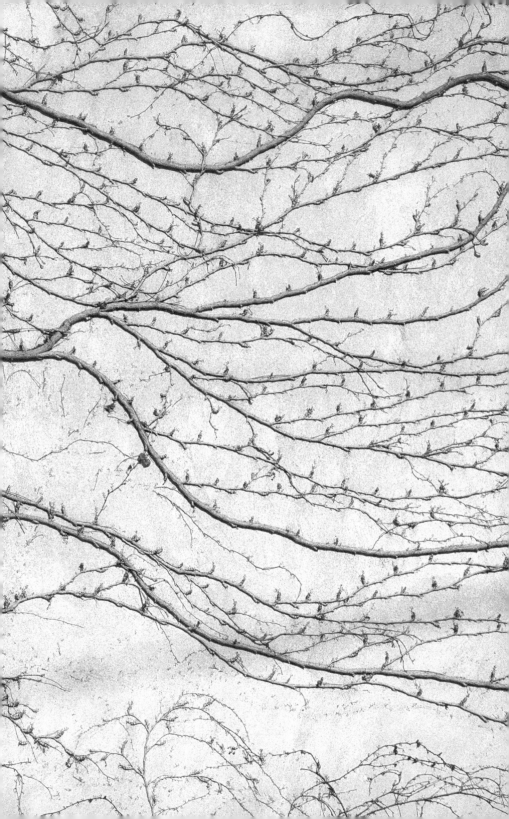

PART I

CORALEE

M y brother Buddy's blood stained the pavement of Main Street for weeks after he was murdered. In the drought of 1926, nobody was going to use what water they did have to clean up a sidewalk, so I passed that spot on my way to the Church of Divine Holiness to worship, or Merle's Grocery to pick up cornmeal, or Harvey's Hardware to buy a hinge I needed for Mama's cupboard since Buddy wasn't around to fix it anymore. That stain turned from bright red to dark brown, then faded to a dirty gray, until the edges began to flake away in the hot July breeze. I could've walked another way, I know. I could've turned down Oak Street or Linden Lane and cut over. But I just couldn't stop walking past that spot every chance I got, and I was really sorry when it finally washed away in the rainstorm all the farmers had been praying for because I was sure it was the last of my brother I'd ever see.

Turns out I was wrong. A month later I woke up to a moon so full I thought it was early morning, and when I lifted the curtain, I could see Buddy in the yard looking up at me.

"Buddy?" I called out. "Buddy? Oh, Buddy. It's really you." But the next thing I knew, my sister Shelby was on top of me, shaking me to keep quiet or I'd wake Mama.

"Buddy's out there," I said.

"Sure he is. Along with Daddy, I know," Shelby said. "Now quit talking nonsense and go back to sleep. You're just seeing things again, that's all." So I laid down and waited, but by the time her breathing evened out and I pushed back the curtain, Buddy was gone.

Truth is, I always could see things. Not every little thing all the time, but the full flower inside the bud of a rose, the fire inside a new green leaf that wouldn't show until fall, the old man inside the boy selling newspapers on the street. Sometimes I even knew the future. One summer when a hard frost killed the crops and everybody was hungry, I had a vision of Johnny Wilcox bringing us a wheelbarrow full of turnips, and sure enough, he showed up the next day. Another time, I saw Laverne Bishop take up a snake even though she'd never trusted the Lord enough to test her faith before, and the very next Sunday she did. Those times, Mama called me her little prophet. Most of the time she said it was Satan working through me.

Maybe my visions scared her. Maybe they were the reason she was so much harder on me than she was on Shelby. "Those are the neatest stitches I've ever seen," Mama would say when Shelby hemmed a tablecloth. Or if she put on a dress, Mama would say, "My word, Shelby, that gingham is so flattering on you." So I'd work real hard on my sewing and press my calico extra good hoping Mama might notice me too, but all Mama ever noticed were the places I'd missed when I wiped the supper table, or which dishes weren't dry when I'd put them in the cupboard, or that my hair was so curly it looked like a rat's nest.

She rarely had a kind word for my brother Buddy neither, no matter how many catfish he caught or rabbits he shot or how nice he'd fixed the post on the front porch, but for some reason Buddy didn't take it personal. Maybe it's because he always found ways to get Mama back: he'd hide a handful of toads in Mama's bed, or fill her sugar bowl with salt, or stroll through the living room in his drawers when Mama was holding a church meeting. I suppose I could've tried getting back at her too, but it wasn't in me. Still, whenever I'd get to feeling real low, Buddy would come sit beside me on the back porch where I'd go to hide my tears.

After a while he'd say, "Coralee, just because Mama can't see you're special don't mean it's not true."

"I know," I'd say. And for a while I would know, until the next time Mama was mean.

So when Buddy came home one day and told us he was heading to the Ozarks for a job laying tracks for a new railway, I knew I couldn't stay. I would've never left otherwise. It was the start of the cotton harvest, and I loved waking up in the mornings before sunrise and heading out into the fields before it got hot while most folks were still asleep in their little houses. I loved smelling the good earth, wet with dew, and seeing the light spread across the big sky, and watching the long lines of cotton stretch all the way to the horizon. I loved how something so light as cotton got heavier the more I put into my sack, and how, when I dragged it to the scale, Mr. Jenks always said, "Miss Coralee, I do believe that is your biggest haul yet."

Buddy had been gone a week when my cousin Darlene came home for a visit from Michigan and told me about her job waiting tables at Myrtle's Hotel in Flint, making twice the pay I made in the fields. She told me I could work there too, even board for free. When I told Mama I was going, all she said was, "Don't go getting above yourself, Coralee." But she didn't try to stop me. I hoped she might, right up until the day Darlene's daddy drove us to the station in Memphis. I was wearing my nicest dress and hat, and I'd already said goodbye to Mama and Shelby. I was about to step into the truck when Mama ran off the porch and hugged me so tight it near knocked the wind out of me. She said, "You look so pretty, Coralee, all ready for the big city." And I thought, *Oh, Mama, why now?* That was just like Mama, to push me to the point of giving up, only to reel me back in at just the moment it was too late to turn back.

When I came home a year later, I hoped maybe Mama had missed me, even if she never did return the telegram I sent her saying I was married. But when I walked in the house with my bags, she didn't even ask what I was doing there. She just looked at me like she'd told me so and said, "Shelby, put on another plate for supper."

See, Mama always said the only man a woman could truly rely on was the Lord. My own daddy drank himself to death, and before that Mama had a husband named Elbert who ran off after only a year. Maybe that's why she turned to the Lord. Maybe that's why she taught me that to love any man before Him was false. Which I had fully believed until the night Chess Collins walked into Myrtle's Hotel a month after I had moved up to Flint. That's when I learned it was a lot harder to love the Lord more than you love a man, especially when that particular man was seated at one of your tables, saying it just wasn't possible for a girl to look so fresh after the long shift I'd worked, and had I heard about the dances at Flint Park, and might I cut a rug with him one night? Chess had the gift for talk I'd never had, but he seemed happy enough just to have me listen.

But even though Chess and me was married in church, it didn't take long to know Chess was not a man of God. Not even a man of his own word. He'd promised to give up drinking, but I could smell the gin on his breath not two weeks after we'd said our vows. I pled with him for months. I begged him to stop. Then one morning before Chess came to from some bender he'd been on, I did something I do not know how

I ever found the strength to do. Must've been the Holy Spirit made me pack my bags. Must've been the Holy Spirit made me put on my coat. Because if it was only me deciding, I would've never left Chess. I could not imagine never waking up beside him again, never seeing his eyes crinkle when he smiled, never hearing him say, "Why don't you come on over here and give old Chess some sugar?"

The shame I felt living in Mama's house after a failed marriage was bad enough, but the shame I felt living back in Paradise was worse. It was a smaller town than I had ever noticed before. In Flint, if you didn't like one shop or bank or grocery store, you could always find another. But Paradise was only a few short blocks of small, shabby buildings that looked like they'd been dropped smack in the middle of a cotton field back before Mama was even a girl. Except for the sidewalks, Main Street wasn't even paved, so your shoes got either dusty or muddy if you crossed the street to get from one shop to another. And those shops were full of small-minded folks who wouldn't meet the eye of a woman who'd left her husband, so I had nowhere else to go when customers at the Dew Drop Inn looked away when I smiled, or seemed not to recognize me buying gloves at Miss Jane's Finery. Only place anyone met my eyes was the Church of Divine Holiness, where Brother Jeremiah Cassidy said the good Lord would forgive me. But folks in Paradise did not seem like they would ever forget.

Only person who ever made me feel any better about my time with Chess was Buddy, who'd come back from the Ozarks only a few weeks before I got home.

"So what? You married him," Buddy said one night when I shared my shame with him on the back porch. It was the coolest place you could sit, which is where you could find us most nights.

"You loved him?" And I said I did love Chess, but now I felt foolish about the whole mess, like I should've known from the get-go that he was trouble.

"How can you know a thing like that? Oh, that's right, tell the future, can't you?" Buddy teased.

"Sometimes," I said. Buddy always got a bang out of the things I could see.

But he just said, "You loved that man, Coralee. Ain't no shame in that. Trying *not* to love somebody you feel for, who feels for you, well, that'd be the real shame." Buddy's ideas about love made sense somehow, even if they didn't quite match up with what I knew of the Lord's, and what he said made me feel better whenever I thought of it that way.

But one day, helping Mama cook supper, she said, "I wouldn't put much stock in what Buddy says if I was you."

"You been listening to us, Mama?"

"You think I can't hear you crying Buddy a river over Chess Collins every night?"

"Buddy's just trying to help."

"That boy's full of the devil, Coralee."

"He's all right, Mama," I said. "He's just the same."

"People change, Coralee. You got a lot of learning left to do, and one divorce under your belt already." The papers had come in the mail just the week before, with Chess's signature on them. He had not even tried to get me back.

"You divorced Elbert," I told her.

Mama looked at me like she might kill me. She said, "Don't you ever say that name to me again." Then she turned and wiped her hands on a dish towel for a long time.

That night after supper, as I sat out in the cool evening air with Buddy, I said, "Why's Mama so mad at you?"

Buddy didn't say anything right away, and he didn't look at

me neither. Finally he said, "What happened between me and Mama is between me and Mama. You best keep out of it."

"Still," I started to say, but Buddy cut me off.

"I figure Mama's got a right to be mad if she wants to be," he said.

Now I didn't know what Buddy meant by this, but I didn't press the matter further, partly because without me really noticing it, we'd somehow begun to see less of Buddy and I was afraid if I brought up Mama again, I'd lose even those few nights I still got to spend with him. Mama was no company at all, and Shelby wasn't one for chitchat. All she'd said when I came home from Flint was, "There's more fish in the sea than ever came out of it." And for her it was that simple. She didn't have that way of feeling someone else's pain that Buddy had in him.

But holding my tongue did not stop Buddy from drifting away. Sometimes he'd turn up before supper and give Mama a duck he'd shot or a string of crappie he'd caught. After a while, though, he'd be out all night and I'd wake up and see his bed still made, and I began to wonder if what Mama said about him changing was true after all. And I knew wherever he was going was more than the usual trouble because Mama never mentioned Buddy's long absences. It was the kind of thing she'd have normally let loose on him for, and her silence worried me most of all.

Then a few months on, for a string of nights, Buddy was home again. He sat longer than usual out in the cool backyard with me, talking late into the evening. I had no idea where he'd been and no idea why he'd come home, but night after night, he seemed better than ever—no pranks, no fooling, just all grown up. And right before we went off to bed one night, he gave me one of his playful hugs and said, "You're a good girl, Coralee. I

want to see you smile again. You got to let go of Chess Collins
and move on with your life. Be happy." And looking across the
hall that night, seeing Buddy safe in his bed just as I tucked
myself into mine, I thanked the Lord and went to sleep with a
smile on my lips.

But early the next morning came a knock on the front door,
and for some reason I looked across at Buddy's room and could
see his bed already made. Which was strange for two reasons.
One, Buddy was always last up in the morning, and two, that
boy never made his bed. Mama always said that if cleanliness
was next to godliness, Buddy was going straight to hell.

Well, I ran down the stairs to answer the door but Mama
beat me to it, and there stood Buddy's friend Luther Jackson on
the little porch. He held his hat in his hand, respectful-like, but
he looked terrible. He stared at the floor for a long moment and
finally said, "I'm so sorry to be the one to tell y'all, but Buddy
was shot dead this morning."

Mama put her hand up to the doorframe, opened her mouth
to speak, then fainted straightaway. I thought I'd be next, the
way my knees were shaking, so I sank down on the steps and
leaned my head against the wall.

"Who done it?" Shelby asked. She'd broken Mama's fall and
was cradling her head.

"The Green County sheriff, Wiley Slocum. That's all I know.
Some scuffle next to the tavern. Y'all need get down to the
courthouse in Stillwater now."

Later, we heard Sheriff Slocum caught Buddy climbing out a
window of the Paradise Tavern with a pocketful of cash he'd
stolen, and when Buddy picked up a crowbar to defend himself, the sheriff had shot him. But my brother Buddy was no
thief. And I knew that boy would not hurt a fly. So I looked for-

ward to that hearing because I knew the law would clear things right up. But when the verdict came back that there was not enough evidence to charge Sheriff Slocum for killing Buddy in anything but self-defense, I could only watch that man let out a sigh of relief. I could only wonder how I'd ever learn to live with the sin of my despair.

"That sheriff was guilty," I finally said as we walked out of the courthouse. "There's no justice in it. No justice at all."

"You can't have justice if you don't have a trial, Coralee," Mama snapped, like Mama was some expert and I was nothing but a fool. Mama'd done a spurt of crying in the courthouse after the verdict was read, but right quick she was back to her mean old self again.

Luckily, Mr. Jenks had taken me back on his crew, and even if my job at Myrtle's Hotel had been high-class, I was glad to head out to the fields before sunup to start picking cotton again. I'd get so focused on finishing a row or making weight that I could all but forget that Buddy was dead and the law was a sham, or that I ever knew Chess Collins, let alone married him. Maybe that's why I worked so hard. Maybe that's why I took extra shifts until Mama said I'd ruin my health. But only work could keep those terrible thoughts away.

Then a few years on, Earl Wilkins asked me to dance at a social down to the gazebo. Shelby talked me into going. She was married by then with two kids and just dying for some grown-up talk, and maybe I was ready to move on in some way I didn't know yet, because even though I didn't want to go, I put on a dress and went with her.

Now, I'd known Earl all my life. Thought him a fine fellow, as everyone did. He wasn't flashy like Chess. He wasn't trying to charm or flatter me. He just brought me a Coca-Cola. Told me about his job at the cotton gin in Boone. Asked me what it was like to live in a city big as Flint. He was handsome in a way

I'd never noticed, maybe because he hadn't noticed it himself, didn't wear it the way Chess had always worn his good looks, polished up to a shine. Earl didn't need no shine: he was tall and broad-shouldered and square-jawed, and I liked his quiet way, the seriousness in his eyes when he looked at me. And the day Earl asked me to marry him, I felt happy in a way I didn't know I could again after believing Chess had ruined me for good and all. Earl even agreed to a church wedding, though he was not a church-going man, I'm sorry to say. But he cared about it because it was what I wanted. That was just how Earl was.

Still, there was one thing I had to ask Mama before I left home. I knew I'd never have the chance again. So the night before the wedding, after I'd packed my bags and set them by the door, I worked up the nerve to say, "Mama, why were you so mad at Buddy when he died?"

"Don't ask me to speak ill of the dead, Coralee."

"I'm not, Mama. I just want to know what happened is all."

"No, Coralee, you don't," Mama said. "You never would hear a word against that boy, and now it's too late." And it felt so much like losing Buddy all over that I cried myself to sleep.

But in the morning, Earl was waiting at Church of Divine Holiness with a smile on his face. I could still feel the hurt about Mama as we took our vows before Brother Jeremiah, but they say God never closes a door without opening a window. And as we drove past Mama's house on the way to start our new life together, I knew Earl was the window God opened for me.

LEROY

The lights were switched off and the courtroom empty as I gathered my notes from the case I'd won that day, but when I started for the door I noticed someone still sitting in the dark gallery.

He said, "You wouldn't be Caleb Harrison's son, now, would you?" When I said I was, he said, "I saw your daddy tear the britches off Banker Harlow when Billy Grimes sued him for fraud. One of your daddy's first cases, if I'm not mistaken, back when he was about your age."

"That's right." I smiled, and when he stepped out of the shadows, I recognized him.

"Leroy Harrison," I told him, and put out my hand.

"Wiley Slocum," he said. "County Sheriff." He had the fine, firm handshake of a man you can trust.

"How's your daddy these days? Haven't seen him around much."

"He's retired now," I told him.

"Glad to see you've taken after him," he said. "We could use another Harrison in the business." And by the time he tipped his hat to me, I felt about ten inches taller.

Now, in 1923 there was no one in Green County more respected than Sheriff Slocum, unless maybe it was his wife. Tillie Slocum came from a wealthy family in Jonesboro and donated to every charity and soup kitchen around. But the sheriff just had a way about him. After that first meeting, whenever our paths crossed, he'd say, "Now that was some fancy lawyering you did on that Wilson case." Or, "I don't know how someone so young could outmaneuver a veteran counselor like Lee Emmett, but you did it, boy, I tell you what." And even if we rarely stopped to talk, it was flattering to know he was following my career with approval. So it wasn't that surprising when, a few years later, he asked me to defend him after he killed a boy named Buddy Harper in the line of duty out in the little town of Paradise.

Now, at the time the sheriff approached me, my daddy was dying, and I was pretty cut up about it. He was a good man, my daddy, a good father, too. Never laid a hand on my brother, Cole, or me. Once, when I was ten years old, I stole a toy car from Gilbert Ray, and when Mama found it stuffed under my pillow, she locked me in my room. But when Daddy got home, he took me down to the five-and-dime to set up a layaway account so I could buy one of those cars a week at a time with what I earned from my chores. And the day that car was finally mine, he took me to Jefferson Park so I could drop it down the slide and show him how it flew.

Daddy said, "Now, Leroy, how many weeks of chores you reckon that cost you?"

"Eight," I said. And I felt proud having something to show for all that work.

Then Daddy said, "So if Gilbert Ray stole that car from you, what would he be taking?"

Well, I was filled with shame, because I understood then that what Gilbert would be taking was my hard work, my time, the moments my mouth watered watching other kids drink Coca-Cola or eat Good & Plenty while I saved up. And I never stole so much as a pencil again.

That talk with Daddy is probably the whole reason I grew up to become a lawyer just like him. And Daddy was always proud of me for it, every step of the way. So the sicker he got, the happier I was to tell him every bit of good news I could think of that might help him die in peace.

For instance, the streak of cases I'd recently won allowed Mabel and me to buy a house just around the corner from him and Mama, so he knew we'd be right there to care for Mama after he was gone. Even better, Mabel was expecting in a couple of months, after a stillbirth the year before, and when I told Daddy the good news, well, I didn't think anything could top that, he was so thrilled. But the day I told Daddy that Sheriff Slocum asked me to represent him in the Buddy Harper hearing, I swear the buttons on his pajamas nearly popped off, and I was glad I could still make him happy because by then we all knew it was only a matter of weeks.

"Leroy," he finally said, "You are the finest son a man could ask for."

Well, I nearly cried when he said that to me, but I didn't want to go soft on the man at a time when he needed my strength, so I said, "Cole's a good son too."

"He is," Daddy said, "but I worry about that boy."

"I know you do," I said. "But no one can say a word against him."

"I just wish I could see him settled, you know, before . . ."

"I know," I cut in. "But he's applied to open up that old cotton gin over in Paradise. There's no reason why that won't happen."

"He could still go running his mouth," Daddy said.

It turns out I wasn't the only son Daddy's lessons about fairness had rubbed off on. My brother Cole was as honest as the day is long, which I consider to be a good quality in a man, maybe the best quality. But even I know there are times when a lie helps keep the peace, like when your wife asks if the dress she already bought looks good on her, or your mama wants to know if her mashed potatoes are the creamiest you ever tasted.

But my brother Cole never could let a thing go if he thought it was dishonest. An argument over the price of cotton when he realized his boss in Dodgeville had rigged the scales. A public declaration against the way the hill folks were used for harvest, then sent packing when money got tight. Even early on, when he took a job as a barkeep in Stillwater and realized the liquor was watered down, he got the owner run out of town. So when Cole ran across that empty cotton gin for sale, we all knew this was his chance to be his own boss, to practice fair weight and pay and not answer to anyone. All that was left to make this happen was approval by the Paradise Village Council, which was headed up by Sheriff Slocum's brother, Virgil.

Now, I swear my daddy was not asking me to do anything wrong when, just as I was leaving his bedside that day, he said, "Leroy, if there's anything you can do to help Cole get that cotton gin, I would surely be grateful."

And I swear I did not agree to do anything wrong when I said, "Cole will get that cotton gin, Daddy. I'm sure of it." I simply felt confident that Virgil Slocum would naturally be inclined to look favorably on any kin of the lawyer who successfully defended his brother in a case that seemed pretty straightforward: Sheriff Slocum had caught Buddy Harper breaking into the Paradise Tavern, and the sheriff shot him in self-defense. Fourteen eyewitnesses had already gone on record saying they saw Buddy Harper charge at the sheriff with a crowbar—an open-and-shut case if I'd ever seen one.

I left Daddy's side that evening knowing that even if he died that very night, I'd done all I could to help him die in peace. On my way out, Mama hugged me tight for a long time, and when she finally pulled away, my shoulder was wet with her tears, but she just wiped her eyes with her apron and said, "Thank you,

Leroy. You've always been a real comfort to us." And when I got home that night, I told Mabel that I thought I was finally ready if it was Daddy's time, though my voice caught in my throat as I said it, and Mabel sat down next to me on the sofa and put her arms around me.

"For a lawyer, you're awful soft, you know that?" she said.

"*You're* awful soft," I said, patting her round fullness while she laughed. Then I wrapped my arms around her, and we rested our hands on her belly to see when the baby would kick.

After that bedside talk with Daddy, something inside me lifted. I woke up the next morning feeling better than I had in a long while. I could breathe a little deeper, see a little clearer, pay fuller attention to my work. Which is probably why, in putting together the paperwork for Sheriff Slocum's hearing, I began to see a few things I hadn't noticed before.

Take the eyewitness testimonies. Fourteen of them, all of which matched up with Sheriff Slocum's account of Buddy Harper charging at him with a crowbar, which wasn't unusual, except now I noticed the wording in each statement was almost identical. And any lawyer can tell you that nobody remembers things quite the same way. That doesn't mean their testimonies, even if they vary a bit, can't add up to something clear. It just means there's an honest margin of error in the way witnesses remember things, and when that margin isn't there, it looks suspicious to someone who expects it to be there.

Then, too, there were the photographs in the coroner's report that showed the bullet holes in Buddy Harper's body. The boy had been shot in the shoulder, hand, chest, and left eye. Which meant that Sheriff Slocum had shot a man holding only a crowbar four times. One shot made sense if it stopped Buddy Harper from advancing. Maybe two, to knock the crowbar out of his hand if he was carrying one. But four is going way beyond what was necessary for self-defense. And everybody knew Sheriff Slocum was a crack shot, so if he hadn't wanted to kill Buddy Harper, he knew good and well how not to.

Strangest of all, though, was the disappearance of a prostitute named Lorna Lovett the very day that Buddy Harper had been killed. She lived above the Paradise Tavern in a room with a bird's-eye view of the place on the sidewalk where the boy had been shot. Now, I didn't know a lot about prostitutes, but I did know that after they'd been arrested once or twice, they generally moved on to a new town where they could keep a lower profile. So it didn't strike me as odd that she'd moved. What struck me as odd was that she moved the morning Buddy Harper was killed, and when I went to see if this might have been prompted by a recent arrest, I couldn't find any record on her. Sheriff Slocum wasn't around when I went to his office to ask about this, but a young deputy named Lewis Hopkins told me he'd be back tomorrow.

"All right then, Lewis," I said. "Maybe you can help me. It says in this report that Lorna Lovett disappeared the day Buddy Harper was shot. But couldn't it have been a couple of days before that, or a week even?"

"The bartender at the tavern, Charlie Winters? He saw her head upstairs the night before. So she was still there that night, far as we know."

"Anybody tried to find her? Her testimony could be important."

"Sheriff Slocum says nobody'd put any faith in a prostitute's testimony."

It was a fair point. Still, it struck me as sloppy police work that nobody had even followed up on a missing prostitute who might have had the best view of Buddy Harper's death. It also struck me as more than coincidence that she'd been seen in the tavern the night before Buddy Harper was shot but by morning she'd cleared out with no word that she was leaving.

So that night I called Mabel and let her know I'd be home late. Then I went for a long drive, all the way out to Paradise, and took a seat at the empty bar inside the tavern below Lorna Lovett's old room. I knew the place, had sometimes gone there to drink a beer in peace, because as an increasingly prominent lawyer in Stillwater, it didn't seem prudent to be recognized in a drinking establishment.

When Charlie brought me my beer, I thanked him, took a few sips, and bided my time. Finally, I asked, "How are the farmers liking this drought?"

"Farmers," he shook his head. "Too much sun's bad. Too much rain's bad. No way to please them. Me, I prefer heat."

That's when I put out my bait. "In my line of work, you can just about predict a spike in crime with a spike in heat."

"Never knew that. Knew about a full moon, but not heat."

"It's nice and cool in this place," I tried again. "You live up top?" Barkeeps often lived above the taverns where they worked, so it was a natural enough question.

"Not yet," he said, "but soon."

"Somebody moving out?" I asked.

"Disappeared, more like."

I tried to sound surprised. "Disappeared?"

"Young lady lived upstairs went missing. Disreputable, you know, but a nice girl."

"You know her well?" I asked.

"Not like that," he smiled. "Just enough to say howdy do."

"Can't have been much of a life," I offered.

"Maybe not," he said. "But she seemed happy enough."

Now, *happy* was not a word I associated with prostitutes, and I was about to say so when the light from the door blinded me and someone walked in, so I held my tongue and finished my beer. That's when I saw a hand place a big silver lighter on the counter with the initials WS emblazoned in gold—a lighter I

recognized from all the times I'd seen it on my own desk lately—
and when I turned, I found myself face-to-face with Sheriff Slocum. I'd never seen him in plain clothes before. Out of uniform, he looked like your run-of-the-mill good old boy.

"You're a long way from home, Leroy," he said.

"I could say the same for you, Wiley." I tried to keep my tone
light, but I couldn't figure out why he was there. Buddy Harper's blood was still on the sidewalk outside, for chrissake.

"Beer?" Charlie asked.

"Make it two," the sheriff told him. "Have one on me, Leroy."

I needed to get home, but something in his friendly offer
held me fast to my seat. I wondered if Lewis told him I was
looking for him, but if that was the case, he didn't mention it.

Instead, he said, "Never seen you here before, Leroy. Come
here often?"

"Not often. Just to get out of town," I said.

"Stillwater's a small town," he agreed. "Too small. Too many
folks in your business."

"Paradise is even smaller if keeping folks out of your business is what you want," I said.

"What folks?" he said, looking at the empty tables.

"Me, for starters," I said.

"Aren't you supposed to be on my side?"

"I am on your side," I told him. "And I mean you no disrespect, Wiley. But while the case is ongoing, it would help me
do my job if you stayed away from this place."

"You don't need to worry about me, Leroy," he told me and
took a long drink from one of the beers Charlie had brought us.
"That brother of yours, now. That's another story."

"You know Cole?" I asked.

"Not personally," he said. "Just heard he wants to open up a
cotton gin out here in Paradise is all."

"Is that a problem?"

"No problem yet, but he's lost jobs too often to seem reliable," he said. "The Village Council has another application to open that same gin, and the other applicant looks like a better bet. I think the council just needs some reassurance that Cole will do what he says he'll do."

"Cole always keeps his word," I said.

Sheriff Slocum studied the bottles on the shelf behind the bar. He said, "People sometimes change their minds."

"Cole won't," I said. But by then I wasn't sure we were still talking about my brother.

My hands shook the whole drive back to Stillwater. I'd never even mentioned Cole's application to the Village Council to the sheriff. Sure, I'd hoped in a vague way that a positive outcome for the sheriff might mean a positive outcome for Cole. But what if it worked the other way around? It brought me up short to know the way I'd thought of defending the sheriff might be the same way the sheriff thought of his brother's approval of Cole's application. And the very idea that I might not be able to fully investigate Sheriff Slocum's case because I wanted something for myself, or my brother, well, it made me feel sick. It made me feel dirty. It made me feel like I'd been walking around in my drawers and didn't even know it.

I slept badly that night but got up early, sure of what I had to do and wishing like hell that Sheriff Slocum had asked any other lawyer in the county to represent him but me. Still, I put together a petition withdrawing from the case due to conflict of interest—something no lawyer ever claimed around here since otherwise he'd never do any business, we were all so tied together.

Still, I knew a lot was on the line. Cole might lose the cotton gin. Daddy might take his worries to his grave. And Mabel and I might have to leave Green County over the scandal of a broken contract with Sheriff Slocum. But I knew Cole would want no part of anything this ugly, and that Daddy of all people would understand. It really was Mama who might take it the hardest if Mabel and me had to move.

I was just finishing up my letter of resignation when the phone in my office rang, and when I heard the doctor's voice on the other end of the line, I braced myself for the words about Daddy I'd been dreading, though for a moment I felt relieved to think he had died peacefully believing the lies I'd unwittingly told him. But the doctor wasn't calling about Daddy. I was so sure he was that it took some time for me to realize it was Mabel he was calling about, and by the time I hung up and reached for my hat, my heart had already broken for the both of us.

We'd lost one baby already, and the sobbing that went on that time was so awful that I knew what to expect when I got home. Only this time, there was such a stillness to Mabel that I thought maybe some part of her had died too. The way she clutched that lifeless gray bundle just slayed me, so I let her sleep with it until we drove to the cemetery the next morning to bury the child, a girl this time, next to her brother's tiny headstone. When the undertaker left, Mabel laid down on that grave and wept, even after the rain came, even after the fresh dirt turned to mud that stained her dress, then my shirt and trousers too, trying to keep her from following the child into the grave, because that's what she would have done if pain alone could have killed her.

That is why, in the end, Cole got his cotton gin. That is why my daddy died in peace. But it is also why twenty years later, when Sheriff Slocum asked me to oversee a sanity hearing for Buddy Harper's sister Coralee, I couldn't help wondering if the justice I might have stolen from that boy's family was about to be visited upon me.

BIG EARL

First time I knew something was wrong with Coralee, I come home from my shift at the cotton gin in the spring of '45 and she was gone. I looked in the kitchen, the bedroom, the backyard. Looked in the work shed. Walked back to where Little Earl was sitting on the front porch, and said, "Son, where's your mama?"

"Don't know."

"When she leave?"

"Can't rightly say." He was sitting on the swing, little legs dangling, just a bitty boy, no sense of how time passed yet. So I sat down next to him and rocked. Waited. Put Little Earl in the truck and took a spin around town. Still no sign.

Well, I fixed a couple bowls of cornbread and milk for supper, tucked Little Earl in bed, and went out on the back porch. In the dusk, Wilber Higby was checking on his hogs, so I asked if he'd seen Coralee. Jonah McGinty came walking by, and I asked him too. Finally, I knocked on Jamie Gilman's door, and Jamie says he seen Coralee light out for town hours ago. Like she was in some hurry too.

So I went back home and waited. It was dark out by now. And finally, here she comes, walking up the street like nothing doing, her long stride steady and her brown curls blowing in the breeze, with only her housecoat to keep her warm.

"Coralee," I said, "where the Sam Hill you been?"

"Nowhere," she said.

"You left Little Earl alone for hours," I said. "I been sitting here waiting for you. Drove all over town. Now where you been?"

"Here and there," she said. "You know."

Now a man could get mighty curious when his wife cannot account for where she has been. Even suspect. But I swear that even though I could not begin to know where Coralee had been, what I knew in that moment was that the reason she couldn't answer me was not because she didn't want to. It was because she didn't know. I could tell by the look in her eyes she had no idea where the past few hours had gone.

You might wonder how I came to believe this without pressing the matter further. Funny thing is, at the same moment I realized something was wrong with Coralee, I also realized that I'd known it for some time. Just didn't want to know it, the way you don't see what's right in front of you because, seeing it, you can't go back to the way things were before. Like the time she came home from some sermon Brother Jeremiah preached on gluttony and went on this starving jag for days. Or the time I heard her laughing in the kitchen and thought maybe her sister Shelby'd dropped by, but when I looked in, nobody there but Coralee. Or the time she washed the floor ten times at least.

"Look, Coralee, that floor shines like the moon," I told her. But she cried all night, and in the morning she was at it again with the scrubbing.

At the time, I chalked those things up to one simple fact about Coralee: the deep hurt she carries inside from her brother Buddy's death some years back. She loved that boy, I know. But even if Coralee's problems started with Buddy, it was clear that they'd turned into something else entirely, and I can't tell you what it does to a man when he realizes something is wrong with his wife. Not Spanish flu or dropsy or ptomaine poison. Not whooping cough or yellow fever. I'm talking about things you can't tell nobody, not without scaring them half to death. Which is when I began to keep Coralee's secret. "A little too much sun today," I'd say if someone had seen something strange, or "Bad night of sleep, but thank you very much." And I just tried to keep a closer eye on her, best I could. And once I got used to the idea, it seemed sort of natural, just a part of who she was, same way most folks have something that sets them apart.

Then early one morning after I'd come home from my third shift at the gin, I walked into the house and found Coralee on the back porch, gripping the knife we used to slaughter hogs.

"Coralee," I said, "what's wrong?" The knife kept my tone gentle, but I could feel my heart jumping under my overalls.

"I must keep this house pure before the Lord."

"That's fine," I said, "but what're you doing out here?"

"Waiting for the devil," she told me.

She was rocking back and forth real slow, her eyes fixed on the dark cotton field behind the house, like that devil might appear any minute now. But the only thing that appeared was Little Earl, stumbling out of bed, and I swear she turned her eyes on him for a second like she couldn't tell if he might be the devil she was waiting for.

That was when I turned cold, right down to my bones. That was when I grasped just how sick Coralee might be. That was when I locked every knife, pair of scissors, and rifle we owned in my work shed and started taking little Earl to sleep at the gin when I worked nights. I'd lay him down on the pads under the furnace to keep him warm, and after a couple weeks I thought maybe I had things figured out, or as figured out as they were going to get, until one night my boss, Mr. Holmes, said, "Earl, that's a problem."

"Come again?" I said. But I was already scrambling to think where on earth Little Earl could sleep when I worked nights, and after what felt like a long moment, Mr. Holmes said those heaters were too unpredictable for a boy to be sleeping under, and why don't we follow him to his office? And when I carried my boy inside and saw the blanket and pillow he'd set out for him, I nearly bust out crying, and I hadn't cried since my mama died when I was thirteen years old.

After tucking Little Earl in, I closed the door behind me, and Mr. Holmes said, "Listen, Earl, I know you've got it rough right now."

"How'd you mean?" I asked. But it sounded like a lie, even to me.

"I just know you do," he said, "and I'd like to help if I can."

Now it is a hard thing for a man to admit he's got a nervous wife. I had never mentioned it to anyone except Doc English.

"Doc English says all women are nervous," I told him.

"Like hell," Mr. Holmes said, and then he really had my attention. I had never heard a single soul question Doc English. His word is law. If you went to see that man with a case of poison oak and he called it chicken pox, that's what it was.

"Look," Mr. Holmes said. "There's a hospital in Jonesboro might be able to help. I've got to pick up Bobby Lee from college in a few weeks and I'll stop in and talk to somebody there. I can't promise anything, Earl, but I'll see what I can find out."

Well, those weeks I waited to hear from Mr. Holmes felt like the longest of my life. But true to his word, the day he got back from Jonesboro, he called me into his office.

"I checked out that hospital for you, Earl."

"Yes, sir."

"It's a nice facility, good doctors, even sounds like they have patients who suffer the way Coralee does. Problem is," he said, "it's a private hospital."

"How much does it cost?"

Mr. Holmes folded his hands on the desk. He smiled at me.

Finally he said, "I mean you no disrespect, Earl, and I'd promote you if I could. But even then you couldn't afford it."

"What's it cost?" I asked. *I will pay every dollar I have except what it takes to feed Little Earl if somebody can help Coralee*, I thought. *I will starve for a solid year.*

"About seven hundred dollars," he said, "and that's just for the first year." Well, my stomach dropped right through the floor then. I'd have had to save for years to come up with that kind of money.

"Now, Earl, there might be another way. There's the state hospital in Little Rock, and if you could get the paperwork to admit her, it would cost you nothing."

A free hospital that can help Coralee, I thought. Then I asked, "What paperwork?"

"There would have to be a hearing with Judge Harrison first."

Now, I knew Coralee would want nothing to do with Judge Harrison, who'd been the young lawyer that got Sheriff Slocum off for killing Buddy. Still, I said, "What for?"

"To declare her insane." He said this carefully, because he thought it might be the first time anyone had called Coralee's problems what they were. And in fact it was the first time, but he didn't stop there. "If she's declared insane, she becomes a ward of the state, and then the state is responsible for protecting the public from someone who might be a danger."

"Most folks probably know it's true." It was the first time I admitted even to myself that people knew about Coralee.

"Be that as it may, Earl, it's got to be legal-like and documented."

"Documented?"

"It would probably mean testimonies."

"From who?"

"You. Her sister, Shelby. Her mama. Maybe Little Earl. People who know her well and can speak to her state of mind."

Well, my own state of mind started to whirling then. It was

one thing to have a private conversation with your boss about your wife, but it was another to go before a judge and have to say the things you try to keep secret so nobody knows how bad it is in your house. Not to mention I knew it would be a terrible thing to do to Coralee. But when I said this to Mr. Holmes, he just said, "Well, give it some thought. Meantime I'll look into it some more. But I have to tell you, Earl, I doubt you can keep a lid on this thing for very much longer."

CORALEE

I never thought I'd see my brother, Buddy, again after that night I'd seen him wandering around Mama's yard in the moonlight. For weeks and months and even years after his death, I prayed to the good Lord to bring him back to me. I'd go down to the cemetery and sit by his grave hoping he'd speak to me the way the dead sometimes did when I was down there on church business, tidying up the graves. Some days they sounded like a swarm of locusts, jabbering away at the same time, so I couldn't tell one voice from another. Other days it was the person whose grave I was tending who spoke to me. But unlike so many other folks buried there, after twenty years, I had still never heard Buddy.

So it like to knock me flat one afternoon when I saw Buddy walking down Main Street in broad daylight. I was on my weekly shopping trip when I saw him heading into Merle's Grocery, which is where I was headed too, so I followed him. I walked past the aisle where he stood, then doubled back to take another look. When he didn't notice me, I turned my cart down the aisle where he stood.

"Buddy?" I asked.

He looked at me then, and I felt myself stop breathing. It was him all right. He hadn't changed a minute. He was even wearing those same old overalls he always wore. Well, my whole body started to shaking and the tears sprang to my eyes. It felt like falling through time, like maybe twenty years had gone backwards and there was my little brother again, standing there in Merle's like it was just an ordinary day.

"Buddy?" I said, reaching out my hand.

But before I could touch him, Buddy moved down the aisle. I stood there for a moment in shock, then tried to follow him, but a woman with a cart blocked my way, so I turned around and tried to go down another aisle, but Sherwood was restocking shelves from a big pallet, so I left my cart and slipped past him, but by the time I made it out to the street, Buddy was gone. I went back inside.

"Did you see Buddy?" I asked Charlene. She was working the register.

"Who?" Charlene asked.

"My brother, Buddy," I told her. "He was just here."

Charlene looked up then. She had the kind of smile that made you feel like she understood that even if you never said so, you were really just as sad as you felt. "You better finish up your shopping, Mrs. Wilkins. Little Earl will be out of school soon. You want to be home for your boy, now, don't you?"

"I surely do," I told her. But I couldn't keep my head on groceries for the excitement. I was so wound up I didn't know what to do, so I left Merle's and walked up and down the street, peering into doors and down side streets, hoping to catch another glimpse of Buddy. When I didn't, I went straight to Divine Holiness and just thanked the Lord that he had come back from the dead. Like Lazarus. Like Jesus. Now my own brother, Buddy.

Brother Jeremiah must've heard me because he wandered in and sat down next to me.

"How are we doing this fine afternoon, Sister Coralee?" he asked.

"Brother," I told him, "I have witnessed a genuine miracle today."

"The Lord is good, Sister Coralee," he said, patting my hand. "The Lord is good. There ain't nothing he can't do. Nothing in this world," Brother chuckled, "except maybe fix this roof."

I looked up then and saw the water stains coming through from outside.

"Can't you fix it?" I asked.

"A roof is mighty expensive for a building so big. To be honest, it's been hard to pray for the rain we need when I know this roof cannot shelter us for long," he admitted.

I pulled out the money I'd taken to the grocery store then. I was so grateful to have Buddy back that I wanted to show my gratitude to the Lord with more than just words of praise.

"Brother, I want you to have this for your roof. The Lord is good, and I am so grateful."

Brother looked surprised. He said, "You are a generous woman, Sister Coralee. I will be sure to mention your generosity in particular Sunday morning."

I thanked him and headed on home after that. But I couldn't stop thinking about Buddy coming back. And I couldn't talk it over with Earl. I knew well enough what he'd say if I told him. And Mama and Shelby wouldn't hear it neither. So I kept it to myself. But I spent weeks looking for him. I walked every road in town, through all the fields and trees trying to find him. But just like the first time I'd seen him in Mama's yard all those years ago, he seemed to have vanished. I could not find that boy anywhere, and I began to realize that maybe he was gone again, that maybe he'd be gone again for a long time.

Then one day, I was headed to town to grocery shop, and suddenly, there he was again, standing in front of Miss Jane's Finery, looking at a dress in the store window. He looked sad, so I walked over to where he stood. I didn't say anything this time, just stood next to him, but closer up, he looked even sadder than he had from a distance.

"Buddy," I finally said. "I've missed you so much."

Things happened so fast then that I couldn't make sense of it. Because Buddy was simply gone. I looked around to see where he went, but it was like he'd disappeared into thin air, and I took off running then, down one street, then another. I would not lose him again. "Buddy!" I cried. I ran down the alley behind all the stores on Main Street. "Buddy, please!" By then I really was crying, the tears cold on my face, and I was just rounding a corner when I ran smack into something solid that like to knock me over. It was a sheriff's deputy, Lewis Hopkins, one I'd seen in town on occasion, chatting with Vernon Hartsoe outside his barbershop or keeping the older kids in line at the park where they gathered after school.

"Whoa, now," he said. "You all right there?"

"No," I panted. "No." And I began sobbing then at the honest kindness in his voice.

"Don't cry, now, ma'am." He handed me his handkerchief. "Tell me what's wrong."

"It's my brother, Buddy," I told him.

"Is something wrong with him?" the deputy asked. "I know a lot of folks around here. What's his last name?"

"Buddy Harper," I told him. "He was just here."

The deputy looked at me for a long time. Then he helped me over to a bench and sat down beside me.

"Ma'am, Buddy Harper died," he said. "Must have been twenty years ago, just about."

"I know that," I said, "but the Lord has mysterious ways."

He took a long, deep breath then, and I thought he was about to say something, but just then a police car pulled up to the curb in front of us and the driver motioned to him.

"Ma'am, I have to be going now," he told me as he stood up. "But I'll keep an eye out for him. What's your name, by the way?"

"Coralee Wilkins," I told him.

The deputy patted me on the shoulder. "Keep the handkerchief. And get yourself on home, ma'am, you hear?" So I nodded, but I had no intention of going home. I was going back to Divine Holiness the minute he drove away. But when he opened the door of the car, I saw the man behind the wheel watching me, and I squinted in the sunlight to get a better look. But with so many years come and gone since I'd last seen him up close, it took me a moment to realize I was staring straight into the eyes of Sheriff Slocum himself.

BIG EARL

Planting season is a busy time in Arkansas. The days get longer and lighter, the load heavier. But it is also a happy time, before anyone knows how the weather will affect the crop and everyone gets hopeful that soon we'll be in tall cotton. There is nothing like driving through that wide, flat expanse of new plants stretching as far as the eye can see, broken only by a church steeple here or a gristmill there. I never realized how flat it was in these parts until I worked in the Ozarks as a boy with my Daddy one summer. All hills and trees. I didn't like trees above me. Felt like I couldn't breathe. I never seen the ocean, but Mr. Holmes says that's what it's like here—nothing but the sky twelve miles to the horizon in any direction, he says. But only a fisherman could see the ocean the way I see these rows of little cotton plants nosing up through the soil—nothing but possibility every way you look. It is such a thrill when you can finally see what you'll have to work with, and your job is just to see it through to harvest, best you can.

Now, maybe it was this general feeling of possibility that affected me. Maybe some of that hopefulness rubbed off on me. But by the spring of 1946, I thought maybe 1945 had just been a bad year. Coralee wasn't wandering off so much. She wasn't on about the devil all the time. And on Little Earl's birthday, she even baked a cake, and me and Coralee sang to him, and it was happy there in our kitchen, just a mama and a daddy and their nine-years-old boy. That is when I started to slip back into that good place I used to be in when Coralee and me was first married. That is when I remembered how it felt to pull into the driveway after work with my pretty wife waiting for me and the smell of supper in the air. That woman could cook. And grow a garden too, full of beans and tomatoes and okra, peas and carrots and onions. Back then we even had ourselves a little row of strawberries. You name it, Coralee could grow it, even years when nobody could coax so much as a turnip from the ground.

Some nights after we'd put Little Earl to bed, we'd sit on the porch swing in the quiet that comes over a small town, and Coralee would lean her head on my shoulder, and I could clean forget there was ever anything wrong with her. Then one Saturday, I came home from work and noticed the cupboards were empty. Now, Coralee always shopped at Merle's every Friday. It was the one thing she always did, the one thing that never changed no matter how strange she sometimes acted. But that day I found her in the kind of stupor she'd slip into after those church meetings, and I knew to be gentle with her.

"You go to Merle's today?" I asked.

"Didn't have no money."

"Just yesterday I gave you four dollars."

"The church was in need," she said.

"Of four dollars?" I asked.

"Honor the Lord with your wealth," she said, "and your barns will be filled with plenty."

Now, let me say this: I got nothing against tithing. I was happy to give to the church because it gave people hope, and that's pretty much all folks had to hold on to after the crash of '29. The church even made Coralee better able to bear the burden of her brother Buddy's death. So I expected Coralee to contribute, even if it was all we had to spare.

Still, we had to eat. So I drove back to the gin and asked Mr. Holmes if I could have a two-dollar advance on my paycheck, and he didn't ask no questions, even if I knew what he was thinking. And on Monday Coralee went down to Merle's and stocked up, and I figured things would be tight for the next week, but we could get by on roots from the cellar.

I stopped by Divine Holiness on Monday to have a word with Brother Jeremiah. Now, Brother Jeremiah had married Coralee and me, and for that I was grateful, so when the church secretary, Laverne Bishop, led me back to his office, we talked about one thing and another. Finally, I said, "Brother, you know Coralee and me support the work of the church."

"I surely do know it, Earl. Y'all are most generous."

"Only I would appreciate it if you wouldn't take so much from Coralee," I told him, clearing my throat, "because right now we just don't have it to give."

Brother said, "Earl, you know we do not accept more than what folks can give."

"Yes, Brother," I said. "But just please do not take more than a quarter a week from my wife. I have my boy to think of, and it's going to be hard to feed him after Coralee's donation."

Brother Jeremiah nodded. He said, "The good Lord always looks after his flock, Earl, but we will not accept donations more generous than y'all see fit." He shook my hand, told me he was glad we saw eye to eye, and walked me to the door. But he did not offer me the money back.

Still, when a month of Fridays went by with the cupboards restocked after Coralee had gone shopping, I started to feel like I'd gotten through to her. Like things were going to be all right. Until I came home from work one Friday and those kitchen shelves were bare again.

"Where are the groceries, Coralee?" I asked when I found her pegging out laundry in the yard, even though I was pretty sure I knew good and goddamn well where the money went.

But Coralee just said, "The good Lord will provide for us, Earl."

Which was fine to say, but what it meant was that we couldn't eat for another week because I would not press my luck with Mr. Holmes again. And I did not want to get behind on the house. Five years after you missed one payment, people down at the credit union always thought less of you, even if you'd never missed a payment since. So I headed back down to the church to speak to Brother Jeremiah, and when Laverne Bishop led me back to his office, I tried my hardest to be pleasant, waiting for the opportunity to bring up my trouble to him.

"Brother," I finally said, "I believe my wife gave you four dollars today."

"No, Earl," Brother said after a time. "Sister Coralee gave a four-dollars donation to the church." He said *church* louder than the other words, like I was accusing him of taking the money personally, which I suppose I was.

"But I told you not a month ago we don't have that much to give."

"Don't you fret, Brother Earl," he told me. "The good Lord will provide for y'all."

That's when I reached over the desk and grabbed him by the collar. I gave him a little shake. I said, "That Lord-will-provide horseshit might work on my wife, but I got a family to feed, and how am I supposed to do that if you keep taking all my money?"

Funny thing was, he didn't even look surprised. Just said, "I am not taking all your money. Your wife gives donations to the *church*."

"Then the *church* can feed my boy, you sonofabitch," I said. "I'll be back with him, and whether it's *you* or the *church* that feeds him, one of you will until I can feed him myself."

I was still holding Brother Jeremiah's collar when he handed me four dollars from his wallet. But I could tell he didn't like doing it. I could tell he hoped I never set foot in church again, even though him and the rest of them holy rollers been on me for years about joining up.

On my way out Laverne Bishop looked at me like I'd stolen from Jesus himself, and I'll be damned if that didn't push me right over the edge. I sat Coralee down when I got home. Told her we had to eat. Told her I worked double shifts trying to make ends meet. But I could see it did no good. So, as if I hadn't enough to worry about already, I took over the grocery shopping myself that very day so I wouldn't have to give Coralee money that was just going to go right straight back into Brother Jeremiah's pocket.

LEROY

Now, I knew Virgil Slocum's approval of my brother Cole's application to open up that cotton gin had helped my daddy die in peace because *he* thought it was just the thing for Cole. But I still had my doubts. Someone like Cole can't help being Cole, and he'd lost so many jobs to his principles that I just felt sure there'd eventually be more trouble on that count: farmers who tried to haggle too much, workers who were dishonest, taxes that were too high. But it turns out Daddy was right. Once Cole didn't have to answer to anybody, he was just fine, and he got that cotton gin up and running like clockwork.

I can't say I've always understood his hiring practices—over the years, he'd employed ex-cons, women with bastard children getting underfoot, a couple of drunks who were such hard workers when they did show up that Cole was willing to overlook the days they didn't. Most recently, he'd hired a mute boy who couldn't tell Cole his own name, let alone write it. The only person in the world who'd have given that boy a job was Cole. Still, odd as his employees were, they were loyal as all get-out, and Cole paid them well and treated them with decency, and in the end I thought it was a shame that Daddy never got to see that he was right about Cole, because like me, he probably nursed his private doubts, even if he never said so.

Cole had been running the cotton gin out in Paradise for several years when he married a local girl, Bess Hargrave, and they had a daughter, Lulu, and then a son called Nicky Joe. It really looked like things had turned out well for Cole in the end. Bess was as calm and easy as Cole was high-strung, so whenever Cole got worked up about something, Bess would just say, "Oh, simmer down, Cole. It ain't so bad as all that." Then too, with a son who could work at the gin when he was old enough, well, I doubt it was possible that Cole could have been any happier.

Those little children were awful hard on my Mabel, though. By the time Nicky Joe came along, Mabel had lost four babies, and for a while she just couldn't stand to be near Bess, much as she liked her personally. I don't know what happens to a woman when she loses a child. It was hard on me, too, but for Mabel, knowing Bess had delivered two live babies into the world was just more than she could bear. With the first one, she tried to be magnanimous. But I guess the second was just too much. And a distance grew between me and Cole because Mabel just couldn't do our usual Sunday dinners together anymore.

Of course, after losing four babies, we'd both given up hope. Burying that fourth one in the cemetery just broke something inside me, and it was finally too much for Mabel. She got into bed after we came home from the cemetery and didn't get out of it for weeks. She refused to see anybody but me. Even Mama wasn't allowed in, but Mama showed up each afternoon with extra pork chops or greens or biscuits she'd cooked.

"Aren't we the ones supposed to be looking after you?" I asked her every single day.

And every single day, Mama waved me off and said, "I don't blame the girl if she's not up to cooking yet, but you both have to eat." But even then Mabel wouldn't see Mama, or eat the food she brought over. I couldn't even get Mabel to open her mail. When friends and neighbors sent notes, I'd take Mabel the envelopes whenever they arrived, but I always found them on the bedstand unopened the next morning.

Then one day an envelope arrived for Mabel that was unlike any I'd ever seen before. The paper stock was thick and creamy, the handwriting all curlicues and flourishes. And when I flipped it over, the sender's name was engraved across the flap: *Mrs. Wiley Slocum.*

Now, the Buddy Harper case was only a few years behind me at that point, and I still didn't know quite what to make of Sheriff Slocum, who never suspected I'd planned to withdraw from his case, and whose behavior toward me was friendlier now than ever. And I'd wondered on more than a dozen occasions if I'd simply misunderstood him that evening in the Paradise Tavern. Maybe he was just making conversation when he mentioned Cole's application for the cotton gin. Maybe the Paradise Tavern was simply his off-duty hangout. Or maybe I was taking things all wrong on account of my daddy's dying. So I had no reason to begrudge Tillie Slocum the desire to send a condolence, and left that fancy envelope on Mabel's bedstand.

It was funny, too, because the next morning I found that envelope torn open, and that evening Mabel sat up in bed and finished the first full plate of food she'd eaten since we'd lost the child. The next day when Mama arrived with her usual platter of food, Mabel even called out a feeble "Thank you, Mama" from the bedroom, and on her way out, Mama patted my hand and smiled. Then one morning Mabel even got up and drew a bath. When she came out of the bathroom, she had arranged her honey-colored hair loosely down her back. She was wearing lipstick and the pearl earrings she'd worn at our wedding, and I was so happy to see her doing anything approaching normal that I wanted to jump up and embrace her, but I was afraid of scaring her back to bed, so I stayed at the table, finishing my breakfast like it was any other day.

"Morning, Mabel," I said. "You look dressed for church." She went sometimes with her sister, Judy.

"Not church," she said, and a sheepish smile crossed her lips. "Tillie Slocum has invited me to join the Junior League."

Now, I loved my wife. She was a beautiful woman, even thin and washed out after a month in bed. But even I knew she didn't have the poise or pedigree of those Junior League ladies. She wore her pain too much on her sleeve, which is frankly what I had always liked about her. Still, she stood there looking a little embarrassed, waiting for a response from me. But even if it seemed like a silly thing, I couldn't bring myself to say so if joining the Junior League was what it took to get her out of bed.

"Well," I smiled, "Guess I'll need to start washing the car every day now. I wouldn't want to disgrace the Stillwater Chapter of the Junior League." But she just swatted me on her way to the door.

"You'll do no such thing," she said, picking up her purse. "But you might replace that moth-bitten overcoat of yours," she said, and she sounded so much like her funny old self again that I felt tears sting my eyes after she left, because I knew my wife was going to be okay.

But with Tillie Slocum's approval, Mabel wasn't just okay— she positively blossomed with the ladies of the Junior League smiling upon her. Cookbooks, charity drives, fundraisers— you name it, Mabel was all for it. And you'd have thought she was to the Junior League born the way she embraced it. Within a few months, she was so much better that when my path crossed with Sheriff Slocum's in the courthouse one afternoon, I even felt compelled to approach him.

"Please thank your wife for the kindness she's shown Mabel, Wiley," I told him.

"Think nothing of it, Leroy," he said. "Tillie can't stand suffering, that's all, and when we heard about Mabel, she just wanted to help."

"Well, I'm grateful in any case," I told him. "Mabel's much better."

"I'm glad to hear it. We've had our own troubles on that count too, you know," he added, and his candor surprised me. Folks didn't generally talk openly about that kind of thing, but I was grateful he had. It helped me know we weren't alone.

Now, with things back to normal at home and Mabel feeling so good, it shouldn't have been a surprise to me to discover that Mabel was expecting again. She never actually told me, but one evening when I laid my hand on her burgeoning belly as we were falling asleep, she looked at me and managed a sad smile, and I knew then that she was afraid to even hope.

Still, she was getting so far along that it became harder to wrap my arms all the way around her. And one day when she suggested we head out to Paradise for Sunday supper with Cole and Bess and the kids, I knew she was feeling optimistic, and I couldn't help but feel the same. Bess was expecting again too, and the two of them sat together, chatting away, bellies round and faces glowing. It was the first dinner we'd had with them in nearly two years, and I could tell how happy Cole and Bess were to have us there, how happy the kids were to see us again.

I still think about that Sunday afternoon we spent together. I can still recall where each of us was seated around their table, the laughter in the room, the way the kids let Mabel and me hold them, and mostly how clearly I could picture us all a few weeks on with Mabel's worries behind her, since she would have a child of her own to love, a child who would grow up with Bess and Cole's children, and we'd leave behind this long period of distance and become family again.

I still think about that supper, because it was the last time we saw Bess alive. A week later she died giving birth to another little boy. Bled to death. I didn't hear this from Cole, but from Doc English out in Paradise who'd called my office to let me know. By then Mabel had been in bed for three days after losing our fifth child, a tragedy I wasn't sure either one of us would ever recover from. But when I called to tell her about Bess, all her personal misery was eclipsed by the call of duty. Mabel was always good in any crisis that wasn't her own, and by the time I got home, she already had our bags packed so we could head straight to Cole's house.

Cole was wild with grief when we arrived, so wild and angry he couldn't speak to us or even look at the new baby, innocent as it was. He was pacing the room, kicking the furniture, gripping his hair in his fists like he was going to tear it out, the poor child fussing and crying something awful considering it was only a few hours old. It was lying in the cradle where presumably Doc English had left it before calling me. I thought Mabel might go right to it, but instead she went straight to Cole, put her arms around him, then rocked him back and forth until the dam broke and tears came rolling down his cheeks.

"I'm so sorry, Cole," she kept saying. "I'm so sorry." Which seemed to soothe him, even as the baby screamed louder and louder. I didn't know until that moment just what a racket a newborn can make.

Then Mabel did something I will never forget as long as I live. She pulled away from Cole, took his hands, and said, "Cole, will you let me feed that child?"

I didn't know what she meant at first, but Cole did, because he said, "I could never ask you to do it after all you've been through, Mabel, but I'd be so grateful if you're willing."

Which is when Mabel walked over to the cradle, unbuttoned her blouse, and lifted the screaming child. Big tears were streaming down her face, and then streaming down mine too, because that is when I remembered her body had readied itself for the child she'd lost, and hard as it must have been for her to do, she took Cole and Bess's child to her own breast and began to nurse him. And when the house finally grew quiet, Cole began to sob like a broken man.

At some point that evening I realized that if that baby was going to survive, Mabel and I were going to have to take over Cole's household for a while, which is what we did. Mabel cooked and cleaned for the visitors who came to pay their respects to Bess, whose body we laid out on the table where only the week before we'd eaten that happy Sunday supper. Mabel had brushed her hair and laid it out on the pillow she'd laid beneath Bess's head, all the while holding Lulu and Nicky Joe when she wasn't nursing the baby, cooking for them, helping them face the visitors who wanted to tell those children how sorry they were about their mama. And I understood then what we had lost in a fresh way, because Mabel was a natural-born mother.

I had to return to work a week later, but I brought our bed from Stillwater and set it up in the living room, and said we'd stay until the child could eat solid food. Mama disapproved of this arrangement, something she let me know one day after work when I'd stopped by her house to fix a leaky pipe under her sink on my way back to Cole's.

"I'm as sorry as anybody about Bess, Leroy, but Cole's got to take care of his own business," she told me.

"Mama, what else can we do?" I said. "Cole won't care for the baby."

"That boy," Mama shook her head. "I have never known what to do with him."

"Cole just needs some time," I said.

"Just be careful, Leroy. I'm worried about Mabel."

"Mabel will be fine," I told her.

But I was lying. Mabel already loved that child. I could see it. I don't know if it was because she was confusing it with her own lost child or if it is just that a baby is so easy to love, but I knew when the time came to return to Stillwater, it would be terrible leaving that child behind.

But despite Mama's protests, we stayed for the better part of that year, by which time Nicky Joe was in school and the baby could start on solid food any time. But Cole still couldn't even look at the child. A month after he'd been born, Cole had never even named him. So with his permission, I'd named the boy after our daddy, Caleb Dale Harrison, and filed the birth certificate at the county courthouse in Stillwater.

Mabel and I worried that Cole would neglect the child once we left. And Lulu and Nicky Joe weren't old enough to tend to a baby. Which is why I proposed Cole hire a nurse to look after Caleb until he was in school, which Cole agreed to do. Well, I couldn't bear the worry on Mabel's face as we waited, and to tell you the truth I couldn't bear my own worry, because by then I loved the child too. But when a month had passed and Cole still hadn't hired a nurse, I decided I had to settle the matter once and for all.

So one night after supper, when Lulu and Nicky Joe went outside to play and Mabel had gone to rock Caleb to sleep on the back porch, I said to Cole, "Have you looked into hiring that nurse?"

"Not yet," he said. He was looking out the window, his eyes fixed way beyond the fields.

"Mabel and me are happy to stay on, of course," I said. "But to be honest, I'm starting to worry how Mabel is going to leave the boy if we don't move back home soon."

"Take him with you," he said, and for a moment I thought I'd misheard him.

"Cole, he's your *son*."

Cole didn't hesitate. He said, "I don't want him."

This was a terrible thing to say, and a terrible thing to hear, but at the same time I could feel a surge of hope in my chest. Still, as a lawyer, I knew there were technical answers and then there were real answers, and if Mabel and I took little Caleb home with us, it had to be for good.

"Look, Cole, I know it's hard still," I said. "But he's Bess's son, too. He's half Bess."

"He killed Bess," Cole said, and I knew then that Cole's inability to lie, even to himself, made it impossible for him to move beyond Bess's death or even pretend to forgive the child.

"And you won't ever get over it?"

"Mabel is the only mother that child has ever known. Taking him from her is no good for anybody, leastwise the child. Even if I did get over it, I know that boy is better off with you all."

"Don't you think you might feel differently in time?"

"I doubt it," he said. "But if I do, I'll see him plenty."

"You'd better be sure, Cole," I told him. "Because if we leave here with Caleb and you change your mind, it will kill Mabel. She's lost too many babies already."

"You have too, Leroy," Cole said. "It's best for us all if you're the ones to raise him."

And so, although it wasn't the way we'd expected or planned, this is how Mabel and I came to have the child we'd been longing for after all. And you'd have thought Mabel had just given birth herself the way folks acted when we packed up and drove Caleb back to our home in Stillwater. Vicki Lee Jones brought over some baby food she'd canned, and Frankie Mack brought us a high chair that had once belonged to his grandson. Louise Smithers knit us a baby blanket when she heard the news, and

I swear Mabel's sister Judy bought out the boy's department of Burdick Brothers in her excitement.

And despite Mama's concerns, even she seemed to understand that things had all worked out for the best. She was the first to show up, waiting for us on the porch when we pulled in the driveway that first day back. Mabel, who'd hardly seen Mama while she was living out at Cole's all year, said, "Your mama's hair's gone white." And when Mama came down off our porch to greet us as we opened the car doors, it was then that I noticed Mama having trouble with the stairs. But when Mabel got out of the car, Mama called out to her, "Well, look at you, little mama!" Mabel just threw her arms around Mama, and something passed between them that had everything to do with women understanding each other and nothing to do with anything they said. Then Mabel carried Caleb inside, and I helped Mama up the stairs. And when we reached the porch, we saw that Mama had brought a week's worth of meals so that Mabel could have more time to get Caleb settled. It must have been an effort for her, all that cooking, but my concern about this was eclipsed by so many folks knocking on our door that it soon felt like the whole world was happy for us.

Even Wiley Slocum and his wife, Tillie, showed up on our front porch one evening with a giant vase of flowers from the Junior League and a fancy new crib wrapped up in a big bow. While Tillie cooed and clucked over Caleb's blond curls, Wiley set the crib up in the nursery and showed me how to work the levers on the side.

"Mabel's wanted one just like this," I told him.

"It's first-rate, Leroy. Tillie had one like it for our youngest, and when we heard the news, she insisted we get one for you and Mabel. We're just so happy for you both," he said, clapping me on the shoulder while we admired the crib, and before

I knew it, we were on the front porch, lighting the cigars he'd brought for the occasion.

"Goddamn those Cubans," Wiley laughed when he took his first puff. "What the hell do they put in these things?" And although I knew Mabel wouldn't approve if she'd seen us, when I took the first puff of mine, I really had to hand it to him. The man sure did know how to celebrate.

CORALEE

For weeks, I regretted talking to Lewis Hopkins about seeing my brother Buddy. Not because he was a sheriff's deputy. Not even because he got into Sheriff Slocum's car after we talked. It was more that I could never be sure people saw the same things I saw, or heard the same things I heard. Sometimes I felt like I lived in a world of fields and trees and spirits when everyone else lived in a world of bricks and clapboard and bodies. Maybe that is why I never could make conversation. There were rules about who talks first, and for how long, and about what, and also when it was your turn to say something funny. I never could get the knack of it.

The only really good conversation I ever had in my life was with Earl, after I had been feeling poorly. Couldn't stand in the kitchen without my ankles swelling. Couldn't finish frying the bass Earl caught because the smell made me sick. Couldn't even work the garden in the afternoon heat. Which is why Earl asked Doc English to stop by the house while he was at work to check on me. Doc English heard my complaints and asked about my bleeding and pressed the cold end of some contraption to my belly. He listened awhile.

"Do I have the appendicitis?" I asked him. My cousin Bobbie Jean had died from it, and I hadn't known until right then how afraid I was that I might die too. But he just smiled.

"Nothing wrong that six months won't cure, more or less."

He told me not to lift anything heavy in the meantime and to pass on his congratulations to Earl.

After he left, I put on a fresh dress—I realized now why they'd all felt so snug in the waist—and sat on the porch swing to wait for Earl to come home. Earl and me hadn't talked about children, except early on, but we'd never done anything to stop them coming, and we'd been so long without them that I just thought God had other plans for us.

When Earl finally pulled into the driveway and got out of his truck, he said, "Well, Miz Coralee, you're looking mighty pretty this evening."

"Thank you kindly," I said. It was just thrilling to have a happy surprise to tell.

"Now, what're you so tickled about, woman?"

"Nothing," I said. I had never played a joke before. I didn't know how. But somehow trying to pull a straight face brought the words to my lips. "Matter of fact, I got some bad news."

"You sure don't look like it," he said, studying me. "You sure don't look like it at all."

"Fact is, I need you to do me a favor," I told him.

"That burner go out?" he asked.

I shook my head.

"Back porch step give way?"

"No," I said, "but you'll need to buy some wood just the same."

"Wood?" he asked.

"I need you build me a chair," I said. By now I was enjoying my joke.

"A *chair*?" he asked.

"A rocking chair," I said. "So I can rock the baby."

He stared at me so long that I said a quick prayer: *Lord, let him be happy about the baby.*

But the smile that spread across his face was as wide as my own, and he hugged me clear off the ground. Then he brought me a glass of sweet tea, which he'd never done in all the years we'd been married. I didn't even know that man knew how to open the icebox, tell you the truth.

Before Little Earl come along, I did not know how much a child can love you. No one had ever loved me like that. Not Mama, not Shelby, not Buddy, not Chess. Not even Earl, though I knew he loved me in his way. No, Little Earl's love was like the Lord's, only it required no faith at all to believe in because his need for me was so plain. Even Earl seemed to love me more too for a while, like the boy was a present I had given him all by myself.

But eventually loving Little Earl started to wear me out. A child worries you every minute of the day. A child wakes you up in the middle of the night needing to be fed and cuddled and soothed. Also, I suddenly had so much to do. I'd always had the house to keep clean, and the garden to tend, and canning to do, and I enjoyed those things. But once Little Earl came along it seemed like there was no end of diapers to change, and food to mash, and laundry to wash and dry and press and fold, and after a while it was hard to imagine how I'd ever filled my time before that.

So you would think that when Earl took over the grocery shopping for me after I gave our money to the church, I would've been relieved. But somehow, I did not realize that even as a child grows your family, it shrinks your world. I did not understand how much my little exchanges each week down to Merle's meant to me. Just saying "Thank you, Sherwood," when he'd bagged up my groceries and hearing him say, "You're plum welcome, Mrs. Wilkins," made Earl's frustrations with me seem less important. Then too, if I could guess exactly how much I needed of every little thing, I would have a contribution for the collection plate at church.

This was more important than ever because Mama and Shelby had left Divine Holiness for First Baptist, saying I shouldn't let Brother Jeremiah come between me and Earl. But I couldn't see any harm in Brother Jeremiah's new fondness for me. Why, that man lit right up when he saw me walk in, as did the other members of the congregation, and came forward to greet me kindly.

But after Earl took over the grocery shopping, I felt a distance start to grow between me and the members of the church that I could not explain. It was the way the aisle seemed to clear when I walked into church, the little step back Laverne Bishop took when I spoke to her, the way Bev Harmon stared when she passed me the collection plate and I still had nothing to give.

That is why I hung back with Brother Jeremiah one morning after worship. I said, "Brother, my husband has taken away all my money, and now I have nothing to contribute."

"I am mighty sorry to hear that, Sister Coralee, but don't think we've forgotten your generosity. Why, we'd be worshipping under the hot sun without this new roof."

"It was the least I could do for the miracles I witnessed," I told him plainly.

"Sister, there are other ways you can show your faith, for the Lord recognizes a multitude of gifts," he said as we walked to the door. "But if you do happen to witness any more of those miracles, we sure could use some real pews. These folding chairs are downright undignified."

Now, right off I began to look for any opportunity to offer gifts the Lord would recognize. And on those Friday afternoons when I would've been shopping, I donated that extra time to the church instead, scraping and painting the siding, planting flowers in the church garden, washing the dishes after a social. I mopped the floor and dusted the altar and wiped the grime off the windows so the sun could shine in while we worshipped.

But even if the Lord recognized a multitude of gifts, I got the feeling that Brother Jeremiah and the congregation were not so appreciative. And I just wanted to find a way back into their good graces so they might take the time to speak to me. So I stayed for the healings that Brother Jeremiah performed. I spoke in tongues. I let the Holy Spirit roll me.

By then I was going to church every day, even though Sunday service was always the most special, because Sunday was the day for testing faith. Some Sundays none were willing, and then Brother Jeremiah would preach how our faith was false and our flock was cowardly, and we would all depart in shame for letting down our Lord, and Brother Jeremiah besides.

Now, I had always promised Earl I would not test my faith, but after taking away my time with my son and my shopping and my donations to the church, I didn't feel I owed that man anything anymore. So when the day finally came that not one single member of Divine Holiness would even greet me, I knew there was only one thing left to do.

All week I waited for Sunday. And when it came, I put on my best dress and walked to church, thinking of the glory to come. All through the service, I could hear the tails of the snakes rattling in their basket, and I waited for Brother Jeremiah to pull off the cover. And when he finally did, I was so eager that I stood right up.

"Come forward, Sister Coralee," Brother Jeremiah said, "so all can witness your faith."

I stepped forward to meet Brother Jeremiah, then turned around.

"Put your arms out," Brother Jeremiah told me, so I put my arms out.

Then he lifted one of the snakes from the basket and said: "In my name they shall cast out demons; they shall take up serpents; and if they drink any deadly thing, it shall not hurt them; they shall lay hands on the sick and they shall recover . . ."

I felt the cool slide of the snake on the bare skin of my arms then, and stopped hearing Brother Jeremiah's words. I could only feel the coil and writhe of the snake's long body as it moved through my fingers and over my arms. I watched that snake's cloven tongue as it flicked in and out of its narrow head, and a strange calm came over me then, because I knew if the snake bit me and I lived, that was His will, and if I died, that was His will too. I knew even if the congregation laid hands on me and couldn't save me, it was His will.

I could feel the Lord with me. And when I felt the Lord with me, I could feel the congregation with me. I knew they could see I was a true believer. I knew they could see I was a faithful woman of Christ. I knew it, even as I felt a sharpness in the fat part of my thumb. I knew it, even as the blood dripped off my fingers. I knew it, even as I felt their hands on me and saw their faces above me, whirling and blurring and fading into darkness.

BIG EARL

After Wilbur Higby found Coralee half-dead in his ditch one Sunday afternoon, there wasn't much deciding left to do about filing for that sanity hearing. I knew damn well how she got there the minute I saw her bruised, swollen hand with the fang marks in it. I was shaking so hard that Wilbur had to help me carry her to my truck so I could drive her to Doc English's office. Her breathing was labored, but we laid her on a cot and Doc English put her hand into a bowl of ice water to keep the poison from spreading. I told him I was sure that Brother Jeremiah had dumped Coralee in that ditch so it'd look like she'd been bit walking home in case she died.

"I don't doubt it," Doc English said. "My Aunt Marlena died from one of those snakebites. We found her in the grove of trees over in White Oak after she'd been to church."

"You proved it?" I asked.

"Never could. But we knew. Those holy rollers do what they can to cover their tracks."

When Coralee finally came to, she was still dazed, but she lifted her head and blinked.

"It's mighty good to see you with us again, Mrs. Wilkins," Doc English said. "You were bit by a snake." When Coralee said nothing, he asked, "Do you know what kind it was?"

"I don't remember."

Doc English said, "It would surely help me to know how

best to treat you if I knew the kind of snake." But Coralee wouldn't talk.

Doc English seemed to understand we weren't going to get much more out of her, so he bandaged her up once it was clear she was going to make it, and said, "Well then, Mrs. Wilkins, I think you're all set here."

I took Coralee home then and laid her down in our bed, then fetched Little Earl from Shelby's house. Shelby had seven boys by then, and although I personally found the chaos at her house a little on the noisy side, I was grateful for it because it had been a good distraction for Little Earl, who fell asleep the minute I put him in bed. No point scaring the boy.

That night, I sat on the porch swing for a long time. All this time I'd been telling myself that all I had to do was keep Little Earl safe and everything would be okay. But it hadn't occurred to me that I needed to keep Coralee safe too. She could've died of that snakebite.

So the next morning at work, I asked if Mr. Holmes still had that paperwork for me. I could read only a little, and write even less, but Mr. Holmes wrote down my answers to the questions. Whenever I wavered, he reminded me that this was the most loving thing I could do for both Coralee and Little Earl. Meantime it took all I had not to march down to Divine Holiness and string Brother Jeremiah up by his necktie. But when I said as much to Mr. Holmes, he put down his pen and buried his face in his hands.

"Earl," he finally said. "I know how hard all this has been on you. You damn near lost your wife. But I'm going to tell you something. You will have more trouble than you know what to do with if you lay a hand on that preacher. He's respected in this community, no matter what he might have done to Coralee. You do not want any suspicions raised about your own conduct going into this hearing. Understand?"

"Yes," I said.

"I'm not sure you do," he said. "If they find Coralee insane, they could take Little Earl from you if they think you're violent. You have to promise me not to touch that man."

"I promise," I said. I hadn't thought of losing Little Earl, and I knew then that I would not lay a finger on Brother Jeremiah. But my hands were still shaking as I said it.

"All you can do now is file this paperwork, you hear? You have to let the law sort out the rest."

"I know," I said. But I don't think he believed me, because he drove me to the courthouse in Stillwater himself, walked me inside, and sat in the hallway until it was done.

Until the day of Coralee's sanity hearing I had never been inside a courtroom before. I did not know a ceiling so high could make you feel so small, or how the blank faces of the guards could make you seem guilty of something you never even did. I did not know a courtroom looks like a church, with rows for sitting and a kind of pulpit for that Judge Harrison, who looked so grand in his long black robes that he might've been God himself up there, waiting to decide the path our lives would take. Which I suppose, in a way, he was.

It was strange after all those years pretending Coralee was just fine to watch all those folks file into the courtroom: Coralee's mama, Shelby, Jonah McGinty, Jamie Gilman, Wilbur Higby, Charlene and Sherwood Carter, Doc English, and other folks I'd hoped hadn't noticed anything wrong with Coralee. They weren't cruel about it when Mr. Holmes took me around to make my case to them. They weren't even surprised. They were kind. And knowing they were by my side to help me do what I had been putting off for so long made me feel less lonesome somehow.

Sitting there, I tried to remember what Mr. Holmes said about this being the most loving way of helping Coralee, best I could. It was this that helped me tell the lie that got her to come with me to the courthouse that morning, saying there were just some questions to answer about the snakebite. I'd been so focused on all the details leading up to that day I hadn't realized that this might be the last time I sat next to Coralee for a long time. And I suddenly felt empty in a way that made me wonder if all that held me together had never been real in the first place.

When the judge finally began to speak, it seemed like things were moving both too slow and too fast all at the same time. Too slow because I wanted it over. Too fast because almost before I'd had a chance to get my arms around what was happening, the judge called on me to take the stand, which I did.

"We are here today, Mr. Wilkins, because you have filed paperwork requesting an inquiry into your wife's state of mind. Is that correct?"

"Yes, your honor," I said. Mr. Holmes had told me to call the judge *your honor* when I addressed him.

"And you say here that you believe she is a danger to your son's well-being."

"Yes sir, your honor," I said.

"Can you demonstrate a moment when she behaved in a dangerous way to your son?"

I told him about the night I'd come home and found her with the butcher knife on the back porch. About how she said she was waiting for the devil, but she looked at Little Earl like she thought he might be that very devil, and how I was afraid she'd hurt him.

"Did she stab your son?" he asked.

"No," I said.

"Did she try to stab your son?"

"No," I said.

"Then why do you think she is a danger to him?"

"Because she looked at him like she might."

"Like she might?"

"Yes, your honor," I said.

"Has she ever harmed your son before?"

"No," I said, and I could hear my voice rise, "but I am afraid she might if I am not with him all the time."

Judge Harrison cleared his throat. He said, "We are a court of law, Mr. Wilkins. We do not speculate about what might or might not happen. We're here to determine what *has* happened and make a judgment based upon that." He shuffled the papers that Mr. Holmes had helped me file for a moment, then asked, "Have you ever witnessed any signs of neglect?"

"Yes," I said. "Sometimes she has left our son home alone and gone off for hours with no accounting for where she's been."

"Has any harm come to your son from her absence?"

"No, your honor, but she has twice given all our grocery money to her church, so we couldn't feed him."

"For how long?"

"Once I got an advance on my paycheck from Mr. Holmes, and once I went to the church and got the money back."

"So your son did eat, after all."

"Yes," I said, but I could feel a burning at the base of my skull. "But don't you see? At some point I may not be able to feed him if this keeps up. At some point she may hurt him, and I may not be able to stop her."

"But you've been able to feed him thus far?"

"Yes, your honor," I said, but I was getting angrier by the minute. "But it can't keep on this way."

"Mr. Wilkins, I can see that you are frustrated. But you must understand that establishing proof that harm has come to your son in some form from her behavior is essential to these proceedings."

"It is not just our son she might harm," I tried, though just as quickly as I had been angry, I was suddenly near tears. "It is harm to my wife herself that I worry about."

The judge looked down over his glasses for a while at the paperwork. He seemed so far above the danger I had been living with every day, so safe from the uncertainty that was always threatening to unbalance my family, that he could not possibly imagine how frightened I was. And I felt an urge to reach over that pulpit and give him something to be frightened of, but I kept thinking of what Mr. Holmes told me about losing Little Earl, which kept my hands in my lap.

"When you say she may harm herself," he finally said, "what are you referring to specifically?"

"She was recently bit by a poisonous snake," I said.

"Anyone can be bit by a snake," the judge said. "They're everywhere this time of year."

"She was bit by a snake at her church," I said. "It wasn't an accident."

"Has she told you this?"

"No sir, but my neighbor found her in a ditch after she'd been to church. They dumped her there in case she died."

"Are there any witnesses who can testify that she handled the snake in church?"

"No sir." I'd known better than to even ask. I knew about how far I'd get with that bunch.

"Any witnesses that saw members of her church dump her in the ditch?"

"No sir," I said, but I was some furious by now. "But they'd have made sure nobody talked."

"Which church does she attend?"

"The Church of Divine Holiness, back in Paradise," I said.

"Thank you, Mr. Wilkins," the judge said. "You may step down."

There were tears in Coralee's eyes when I sat down next to her, and I could feel the terrible thing I was doing to her as I heard the judge call Doc English to the stand next.

"You are Mrs. Wilkins's family doctor, is that correct?"

"It is, your honor," Doc English said.

"It says here you treated Mrs. Wilkins for the snakebite she suffered recently. Was there anything unusual about the bite?"

"Yes, your honor," Doc English said. "Most snakebites are on the foot or leg. But Mrs. Wilkins's snakebite was on her hand, which suggests she handled the snake that bit her."

"Is this your professional opinion?"

"Yes, your honor," Doc English said. "I've seen plenty of bites from church in my career, all on the hands and forearms."

"Have you ever seen a bite on the hands or forearms on someone who was bit outside a church setting?"

"Only on children, your honor, who don't know better than to touch them."

"Aside from the snakebite, have you ever seen Mrs. Wilkins behave in a violent or dangerous way, toward her family or anyone else, for that matter?"

"I have not, though Earl has asked me on occasion what I thought was wrong with her."

"And what did you think was wrong with her?"

"I didn't know."

"Did you think she was ill?"

"Yes, your honor, but not in any way I can treat. I only deal with illness of the body."

"Thank you, Doctor English," Judge Harrison said. "You may step down."

Well, I could feel hope rising up in me after Doc English's testimony. And when the judge began to call upon the other witnesses, I started to think that maybe, just maybe, I'd be able to get Coralee the help she needed after all.

"Strange-acting," said Wilbur Higby when he took the stand. He told of the altars she'd built of leaves and branches in his pasture, and of seeing her wandering all hours of the night. He told of finding her in the ditch after the snakebite.

"She's always seen things that weren't there," her sister Shelby said. "Right the way back to when she was a child."

"Over-religious," Coralee's mama said. "My daughter Shelby and me left Divine Holiness for First Baptist a while back. I raised my children to love the Lord, but lately Coralee's just taken things a step too far."

"She's a good woman," Mr. Holmes said. "But I have seen the toll her behavior has taken on her husband over the years. Their son has slept in my office for more than two years when Earl works nights because it's not safe for the boy to sleep at home."

"Sometimes she's still at the store long after she should be home to meet Little Earl after school," Charlene Carter told the judge. "And recently she claimed to have seen her brother Buddy in our store even though he's been long dead."

At this, Judge Harrison looked up from his notes, and well he might, since he was the lawyer who represented Sheriff Slocum in the hearing to determine if there was enough evidence to charge him with murdering Buddy, though maybe it was just the fact that Coralee claimed to see people long dead that caught his attention. But even before Charlene spoke, I could see that there was no way for Judge Harrison to believe that Coralee was sane. And the more this began to sink in, the more I began to realize what a relief it would be not to have to worry every minute of every day.

When the testimonies were over, Judge Harrison shuffled his papers. He ran his hand through his hair. And he was just about to speak when there was a scuffle outside the door of the courtroom, and the guard opened it and listened for a moment.

"We're in the middle of a hearing, Clancy," the judge said. "Is this relevant to the case?"

"Yes, your honor. Some folks would like to give testimony on Mrs. Wilkins's sanity."

"Why aren't they on my list of witnesses?"

"They say they only heard about the hearing this morning, your honor, but they know Mrs. Wilkins well and can speak to her state of mind."

"Very well, then," said the judge. "Send them on in."

And when the guard held the door open, that's when I saw them: Laverne Bishop, Charles Perkins, Sherman Lewis, and other members of the church whose faces I recognized. And last through the door, of course, was Brother Jeremiah Cassidy.

LEROY

It's not like I hadn't heard things about Coralee Wilkins over the years. I had never asked about her specifically, but aside from the weather and the crop report, the comings and goings of the folks who lived in Paradise was pretty much all the news there was to talk about on those Sunday dinners Mabel and I continued to have with Cole after we moved back to Stillwater with Caleb. POPULATION: 510, the Paradise Village sign read, but the place seemed so small Mabel said they must have been counting cats and dogs to reach that number. But whenever Coralee Wilkins's name came up, I took note. I'd heard when she married Earl Wilkins. I'd heard when she'd had a son called Earl too. I'd also heard she was a little on the odd side, but nothing to suggest there was any real harm in her.

But when Sheriff Slocum called me to his office about overseeing her sanity hearing, he handed me the paperwork and told me it should be an easy case.

"Why?" I asked.

"That woman's nuttier than a fruitcake, Leroy."

"You know her?" I asked.

"Not personally," he said. "But she told Lewis Hopkins she'd seen Buddy Harper walking down the street a few months ago. Her own brother, and she doesn't know he's dead." He shook his head like this was a real shame.

"She's got a son now, Wiley. It might not be that simple."

"Maybe not," he said. But something in his manner reminded me of our conversation in the Paradise Tavern about
Cole's application, and all the other times over the years I
walked away from him wondering if I'd just been told something he'd never said. Still, when you have that feeling as often
as I'd had it with Wiley, it starts to feel like more than a coincidence, so I was pretty sure he'd just told me to declare Coralee
Wilkins insane.

Now, I'd never known if Wiley had a motive for killing
Buddy Harper. We'd never talked about it since, and I'd never
looked into it further—something that had come to weigh on
me heavily over the years. But now, with Buddy Harper's sister's sanity case on my desk, I couldn't help but feel the weight
of the role I might have played in both their lives. I mean, if
the law telling you something is true when you know it's not
won't drive you crazy, nothing will. So if Coralee Harper was
insane, I might have had something to do with it, and this case
might just have been the opportunity to atone for any role I
played in suspending justice in her brother's death all those
years ago.

The problem was that I had more to lose now than I did in
the old days, because over the years I'd come to owe Wiley an
awful lot. It wasn't much more than a year after we brought Caleb home to Stillwater that he showed up in my office and asked
me to run for judge of Green County.

"I'm flattered, Wiley," I said. "But I'm a little on the young
side, don't you think?" I was just thirty-six years old, and once
on the bench, judges tended to stay there.

"Don't overthink it, Leroy," he said. "You'd just make a good
judge."

"Plenty of lawyers in Green County would make a good
judge, Wiley."

"Well, I'm grateful for what you did for me all those years

ago, Leroy, and I can't think of a better way to repay my gratitude than to nominate you."

But gratitude works both ways, and I could not deny that Wiley Slocum had often smoothed over my path in ways that meant the world to me and my family. His wife had helped pull Mabel out of the saddest time in her life, and they'd both been there to celebrate when we brought Caleb home. And Cole got his cotton gin, whether Wiley had something to do with that or not. Wiley had even put the word out about Cole's new cotton gin, which drummed up some business when he first got started. That's not to say that Cole wasn't a good ginner and that folks wouldn't have come to trust him of their own accord. It was just that Wiley had a way of dropping things into people's minds and bringing them around to what he wanted, all while thinking they'd thought it up themselves.

This talent of Wiley's to influence the way folks think became even harder to deny with the whole county clamoring for me to run for judge, and it wasn't a month later that the election was held and I became the youngest lawyer to ever assume the bench in the history of Green County. And I was glad of it on my own behalf, mainly because I felt I could do a lot of good in my role as judge. And in all my years on the bench I generally had.

It was when Wiley applied those unstated preferences that I felt his influence, the pressure beneath his casual demeanor. So I tried to satisfy him, mainly because the things he asked of me were small: overruling a minor piece of evidence to protect someone who had committed a misdemeanor, leniency in sentencing the son of a friend of his, ruling a particular way on a verdict, all other things being equal. But over time, complying with these unstated requests had begun to erode my sense of myself as a good man, so if there was a way for me to do some good for Buddy Harper's family, I was going to try.

———————

The funny thing was that by the time Wiley approached me about Buddy Harper's sister Coralee, I had just moved to Paradise myself. It was Mabel's idea. We were headed out to fix Sunday supper with Cole and the kids when she announced in no uncertain terms that it was high time we sell the house and move nearer to Cole.

Now, I'd kept my promise to Daddy of taking care of Mama. But the truth is she was never the same after Daddy died, and even having Mabel and me around the corner from her only slowed her steady decline. For the last few years we'd been at her house on an almost daily basis, turning off a tap she'd left on that flooded her bathroom, washing her clothes after she'd taken to wearing outfits that stunk to high heaven, cleaning up food she'd dropped that attracted all manner of rodents. And the truth is, the burden mostly fell to Mabel. Still, when Mama finally died of a bad case of pneumonia, it was a sad time for us all. But with Mama gone, our primary reason for staying in Stillwater was gone too.

But I knew Mabel had another reason for wanting to move to Paradise. It was getting near harvest time, and we both knew if any man was going to have a change of heart about giving up a son, harvest time was the most likely for purely practical reasons. Besides, Caleb was now ten years old and had been talking of nothing but helping Cole and Nicky Joe at the gin, and even I could see that this was a good thing for all of them. So in the end we bought a house a couple of miles from Cole in Paradise and had recently moved in, which meant we were spending more time with Cole than we had since Caleb was a baby.

Living so close, I had more opportunity to observe the rhythms of Cole's life. I could watch him interact with Lulu and Nicky Joe, and I was glad he was able to have a close relationship with them, even if I wished he'd been able to show Caleb a fraction of that kindness. I also had more opportunity to observe Cole interact with his employees, to whom he had always been extraordinarily kind. But I have to say, decent as he was to them all, it bothered me the way Cole was about that mute boy he'd hired, whom he'd taken to calling Sonny over the years. Because more than all his other workers, Cole had really taken Sonny under his wing.

Now, I understood that Sonny had always been especially needy. Over all the years Cole had employed him, he seemed to have no family or home, so eventually Cole put a bed in a storage barn and Sonny had slept there ever since. And after a while he was at the table on Sundays every time Mabel and me and Caleb drove out for supper. It wasn't even this that bothered me as much as the times I'd seen Cole lay his hand on the boy's shoulder or scruff up his hair as they headed in from the gin for supper. Because Cole had never shown half the tenderness to Caleb that he showed Sonny. Here Cole had his own son at the dining room table with him, and yet it was Sonny whose food he made sure was salted and peppered, Sonny whose corn he buttered, Sonny whose glass he kept full of sweet tea. I know it was partly because the boy couldn't ask for these things himself, having no voice, but still, over the years it was all I could do to watch him fuss over Sonny—who wasn't a boy any longer—without ever paying any mind to his own young son sitting right in front of him.

At the same time, I also knew that it was Cole's indifference toward Caleb that was the reason Mabel and I had a child of our own to raise. The light of our life too. I was proud of Caleb. Only ten years old but curious as all get-out about any manner of things. He wanted to know what made the grandfather clock in our living room tick, or the water come out of the faucet, or a bullet come out of my hunting rifle—questions I didn't exactly have the answers to, and ones I'd never thought to wonder about myself.

And kind too, that was Caleb's real gift. He had a way of sensing pain in other people. Like when I'd get to wishing I could talk a case over with my daddy and felt sad in a fresh way, even after all the years that had passed since he died, and Caleb would crawl up into my lap and say, "What's wrong, Daddy?" Or if Mabel would get to feeling blue about the lost babies. She'd never say anything, of course—we'd stopped talking about it long ago—but next thing you know, there'd be Caleb. It was like an alarm had gone off that only he could hear, and before you knew it, he'd be leaning his head against her side and stroking her arm. He was a special boy, and I suppose all I wanted from Cole was some acknowledgment of that.

The problem was, Caleb was getting to the age where he was going to start asking questions, and Mabel and I had been racking our brains trying to figure out what we were going to tell him when he finally asked the one we'd been dreading. One Sunday walking home from supper at Cole's, the boy piped up and said, "Who's Aunt Bess?"

Mabel shot me a look that said, *Here it comes.*

"Aunt Bess was your Uncle Cole's wife," Mabel said. "Why do you ask?"

"We always pray for her at Uncle Cole's," he said. "Why do we pray for her?"

"We pray for her because she passed on some years ago, and we all still miss her," Mabel said, and that seemed to satisfy him. And I was proud of how even Mabel kept her voice in that moment. Here the boy was asking about his own mama and didn't even know it.

That night, after Mabel had put Caleb to bed, she closed his door behind her and said, "We're going to have to tell him, Leroy."

"Why?" I said. "Cole doesn't want him to know."

"Lulu or Nicky Joe could tell him," she said. "He sees them more often now."

"They were probably too young to even remember," I said.

"But they're not the only ones who might. Other kids, older kids, ones who knew the family. Frankly I'm surprised it hasn't happened already."

"But it hasn't," I said, "so why worry?"

"Bess died giving birth to him, Leroy. Do you want someone else to tell him that too?"

"Mabel, how is the boy going to feel knowing his own father has no interest in him? Cole shows Sonny more kindness than he's ever shown Caleb."

"It's going to come out, like it or not," she said. "We have to be the ones to tell him."

"Can't we at least wait until he asks?" I said.

"In case you didn't notice, Leroy, I think he just did."

Now, living in the same town where Buddy Harper had been killed, I felt a new sense of urgency to know more about what happened to the boy. Maybe it was that I had never looked into the matter further after that conversation with Wiley in the Paradise Tavern. Maybe it was that I drove past the same tavern on my way to the courthouse in Stillwater every morning and again on my way home at night. Or maybe it was that, each time I did, I couldn't stop remembering Buddy Harper's blood still red on the sidewalk the evening I drove over to look into Lorna Lovett's disappearance.

Whatever it was, I felt it especially keenly on my way to Coralee Wilkins's sanity hearing. It was strange being in the same room with her again, all these years later, in part because I hadn't seen her in person since. Still, I recognized her as soon as I walked into the courtroom, not just because she looked much the same as she had twenty years ago, but because she had the same dignified posture, the same placid defiance on her face that she'd worn all the way through Sheriff Slocum's hearing.

Now her husband Earl sat beside her. I recognized him too because I'd met him once when he stopped by Cole's on a Sunday to determine who was going to take what farmer's haul during a particularly busy harvest. I also knew Cole held both Earl and Earl's boss, Wally Holmes, in high esteem. They were the only other cotton ginners in the county that Cole trusted not to steal business from him after they'd helped one another out, and for this reason I had trouble believing that Earl Wilkins would file a sanity hearing for his wife unless he had reason to, though I was pretty sure he'd never seen the inside of a state asylum or else he'd have thought twice about doing so.

Of one thing I was very glad, and that was the fact that their little son, who was just ten years old, was too young to attend the hearing or take the stand, though it was possible he might be questioned privately if the hearing was inconclusive. I'd recently been reminded of their son because Caleb had just started school in Paradise and was in the same class with the boy.

But pretty quickly I was sure it wouldn't come down to that, because as I began to question Earl Wilkins, he seemed unable to give evidence that his wife was a danger to him or to their son. In fact, Wally Holmes's testimony that their boy had been sleeping in his office at the gin for two years because of Earl's fear that Coralee might hurt him was as close as it came to proving anything.

Then again, I also couldn't deny that Coralee Wilkins was not what you'd call normal after listening to testimony by the family and friends who'd come to speak to her state of mind. She wandered, they said, talked to trees, built altars in fields and prayed to them, even claimed to have recently seen her dead brother, Buddy, in Merle's grocery store. This bit of testimony hit me particularly hard because it suggested that Buddy Harper's death was, as I suspected, in some way tied up in what had gone wrong for Coralee Wilkins over the years. And for the first time, I started to fear that I might be looking at a pretty clear-cut case of insanity, which was terrible to contemplate knowing I might bear some responsibility for her illness.

But when those folks from the Church of Divine Holiness showed up, everything about that hearing changed. Coralee Wilkins was a fine woman, they said, who attended church daily and donated money when the church was in need, who cleaned and painted and helped run Bible study. She was an upstanding member of the community, they said, married to a man who had once threatened Brother Jeremiah physically. A woman named Laverne Bishop claimed to have witnessed this herself, but Brother Jeremiah Cassidy simply said that in his many years as pastor of Divine Holiness, he had never had a more dedicated member than Coralee Wilkins and that this hearing was an attempt by Earl Wilkins to rid himself of a wife he'd grown tired of.

When they had finished giving their testimony, I decided that, though it was not required, I needed to question Coralee Wilkins herself. This isn't always necessary—sometimes in sanity hearings, the subject is so visibly agitated that you can't deliver a verdict fast enough. But when I called her to the stand, she stayed seated.

I said, "Mrs. Wilkins, I'm asking you to take the stand. Are you refusing?"

"Yes," she said.

"Why, if I might ask?"

She drew herself up then and said, "Because you are not fit to judge me. Only the Lord can do that, and in His eyes I am a righteous and holy woman."

"And how do you know this?" I asked.

"Because He told me," she said.

Now, this gave me pause, not only because it explained so much of the testimony against her, but also because if you declared everyone insane who claimed to have spoken with Jesus or Satan personally, you'd have to lock up half of Green County. And despite the fact that I was not certain I believed Brother Jeremiah Cassidy, who claimed the Church of Divine Holiness did not handle snakes even though most of the other Pentecostal congregations in Green County did, I did not believe that just because Coralee Wilkins might have endangered her own life to handle one was a reason to declare her insane. I was not a particularly religious man myself, but I did respect the mystery of faith. So if we were holding a hearing to prosecute a woman for observing her faith, we were moving into tricky territory, legally speaking.

This was not just my position on the matter. The Constitution guarantees religious freedom. I could not declare anybody insane simply because of their preferred method of worship, and I could not declare Coralee Wilkins insane even if her preferred method was a danger, so long as that danger was only to herself.

It was a relief to me, when all was said and done, to declare Buddy Harper's sister sane, not simply because I wanted to, but also because I had firm legal ground to stand on in doing so. Still, I knew the risk I was taking. This was the first time I'd defied one of Wiley's unstated requests, and I understood then that beneath my deference to Wiley's backslapping congeniality was a nagging suspicion that I could end up dead on the sidewalk like Buddy Harper if I crossed him. But when a month had gone by and nothing happened, I soon forgot all about Wiley in the lightness I felt for having repaid any debt I might have owed Buddy Harper's family. I hadn't realized how much my role in that case had weighed on me. But it was like being able to breathe again after all those years. Like being able to see how blue the sky gets in October or feel the summer air on your skin. And I realized just how much my unwillingness to look into the matter had really kept me from feeling fully alive.

One night while cooking supper Mabel even said, "I swear, Leroy, you look like a younger man the way you move lately."

I said, "What do you mean?"

"I mean, you look ten years younger."

"Young enough for folks to believe you're my wife?" I asked her, circling her waist with my arms while she fried up some hush puppies and green tomatoes and walleye that Caleb had caught fishing with Nicky Joe. It was my favorite meal, and I was inhaling Mabel's perfume mixed up with the smell of that good food, thinking there was no better smell in the entire world, when I heard a knock on the door.

When I didn't let go of Mabel's waist, she said, "Get that, Leroy."

"Let them knock," I said, nuzzling her neck.

"If I have to answer that door, I'll burn the food," she said, so I let her go. I was looking forward to that supper. But when I swung the door open, I knew I wasn't going to eat a single bite, because I found myself on the wrong end of the barrel of a gun, and after all my suspicions, the man with his finger on the trigger wasn't Sheriff Slocum. It was Earl Wilkins.

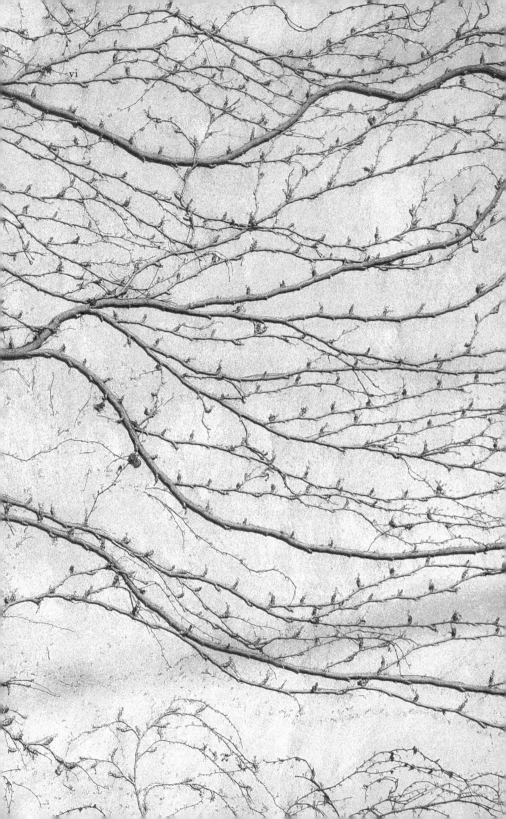

PART II

BIG EARL

Coralee could be a hard woman. Hard to reach. Hard to read. But that whole long drive back to Paradise after her sanity hearing, she didn't say a single word. And when we got home, that house was just as silent as it would've been if Coralee'd been taken away, only in some way, quieter still, maybe because I knew she was there. You could hear every cricket and tree frog and leaf in the breeze. You could hear Jonah McGinty's phone ring two doors down, and his wife answer it. Finally, after Little Earl fell asleep, I went out and sat next to her on the back porch steps.

"Coralee," I said. "I know you're some angry with me. But that snakebite could've killed you. What I did today was try to stop something worse from happening."

"Brother Jeremiah is right," she said. "You're tired of me."

It made me sick that she thought Brother Jeremiah was some kind of hero when he'd left her to die. All he'd done that day was make sure she kept quiet about that snakebite.

"Coralee, you're my wife, and I'd be lost without you," I told her. "I'm just trying get you some help so you can go on being my wife."

"I'm fine enough for folks at the church," she said. "Just not fine enough for you."

"Folks at the church who left you to die in a ditch?" I asked. "Them folks?"

"You're the one wants me to die in some asylum," she said.

She got up then and let the screen door slam behind her, and I knew I wasn't going to get anywhere with her. My last hope for Coralee had been that hearing, and with that gone, I knew what it meant to run out of rope. I thought I already knew what that felt like, but the truth is I didn't know it until then. And as I thought through the days and weeks and months ahead, I could feel tears hot in my eyes. Could feel my hands tremble with terror. Could feel the hate I felt in my heart for that goddamn Judge Harrison, saying my troubles with Coralee weren't real.

It might have surprised Brother Jeremiah and his holy rollers to know I said my very first prayer that night, lying next to Coralee, who had her stiff back turned to me. *Please Lord,* I said, *forgive me for hurting Coralee so bad. Help me keep Little Earl safe, and help me keep Coralee safe from herself.* And it was funny, because after all those years of refusing the church, I felt a kind of relief just thinking I was telling all this to someone who might have the ability to make things better. It was like talking to Mr. Holmes when the cylinder on the gin got stuck, knowing he'd be able to fix it.

Only as it turns out, my prayers were for nothing, because as the days passed, Coralee seemed worse than ever. Down to the church every day, the minute I left for work, so I'd have to wonder if she'd be dead of a snakebite by the time I got home. And when I did get home, she was always gone, so I had to search the fields until I found her. At first I felt relief because she wasn't dead, but that relief was always followed by more worry, because she always looked deep in conversation with folks who weren't there, and I couldn't help but feel jealous that she seemed to have so much to say to thin air but couldn't spare a word for me.

I also had to do my best with our meals after the hearing,

but even if I didn't think much of my own cooking, I'd have known it was bad by how much was left on Little Earl's plate each night. Maybe I could've done a better job, but with working two shifts and shopping and cooking and keeping Coralee from wandering too far, I just didn't have it in me. And I had given up on trying to keep the house clean. I was already worn to a nub.

Luckily, Mr. Holmes let Little Earl help out at the cotton gin after school since he was old enough, so at least I knew he was safe. And working alongside Little Earl made me feel so proud I could sometimes forget my troubles. He really hustled for Mr. Holmes, especially when we began work on building a new storage facility for the gin. One day I saw Little Earl drawing on some paper as Mr. Holmes watched, and after I'd punched my card for the night in the office, he said, "Earl, that boy's real bright."

"I know it," I said, feeling proud.

"No, I mean *real* bright. He just worked out the angles on the corners and roof of the new storage facility. He did it in no time at all. That's trigonometry."

"Come again?" I asked.

"It's college math, Earl."

Now I had no idea what trigonometry meant, but I knew what college was. And as we headed home after work my face felt kind of funny, and I realized, for the first time in a long while, I was smiling. A real smile. Not the kind you put on for other people. *College math*, I thought. And I understood that in spite of everything, Coralee and me were raising a boy to be proud of, and it was worth it if Little Earl came out of all this with a good head on his shoulders.

By the time we turned onto Oak Street, I was almost looking forward to seeing Coralee, even if I knew I might have to track her down. But when the house came into sight, I could see smoke pouring out the kitchen window, and I raced up the driveway.

"Stay in the truck," I told Little Earl as I climbed out. "Stay in the truck no matter what happens." And I ran inside then, calling for Coralee, but there was no sign. Still, I knew she'd just been there, because the fire was coming from a pot on the stove, and the flames were climbing up the walls.

I filled buckets of water and threw them at the stove. I wet down a blanket and beat the flames climbing the walls. I do not know how long it took me to put out that fire. I couldn't have said if it took me one minute or ten, or even an hour. Everything I'd worked for all my life was in that house. It was my home, the home I paid down on every month, and I almost lost it. If I'd stayed at the gin five minutes more, it would've burned to the ground in that weather, it was so dry. And I felt the weight of chance closing in on me.

My whole body shook. My knees felt weak. I mopped the sweat on my face with one of the towels, but it was wet again a moment later, and that's when I realized I was crying. So I sat myself down inside and let the sobs shake me. And when they finally passed, a calm came over me because I knew then what I had to do.

It was the only way. And maybe I should've been more scared than I was, but I was beyond all that as I walked out to the work shed, unlocked it, and got my gun.

"What happened, Daddy?" Little Earl asked me as I climbed back in the truck. "Are we going hunting?"

"Hush, now," I said as I backed out of the driveway and pressed hard on the gas. I hated the idea of him seeing what might happen if things went wrong, but I wanted him with me in case I had to make a run for it, though where we'd run to, I had no idea.

I told Little Earl to stay put when I pulled into the judge's driveway. Then I knocked on the front door, and when he opened it
and saw me pointing the gun at him, he stood still and stared.

"If you don't come with me right now and see what it's like to
live with my wife," I told him, "I will kill you."

To his credit, he didn't say a word. Just reached over to a
coatrack and grabbed his hat.

"Leroy," I heard a woman protest, "supper's almost ready."

"I'll be back, Mabel," he told her. "Don't worry."

He closed the door behind him and climbed into the truck
then, and Little Earl scooted over by me. I had the gun on my
lap, still cocked.

"Do you mind putting that away?" the judge said, so I put
the safety on and mounted it on the rack behind me. I figured
he wasn't going to run if I'd got him in the truck without a fight.

"Who're you?" Little Earl asked him.

"I'm Mr. Harrison," the judge told him. "And you're in
school with my boy, Caleb."

"You're Caleb's daddy?"

"That's right," I cut in, but I was speaking to the judge when
I said, "He's going to help us find your mama."

I drove up and down the roads outside Paradise, looking in
all the usual spots. Then I thought maybe she'd gone home and
pulled onto Oak Street and up our driveway.

"Coralee?" I called in the door, but there was no answer, so
we walked through to the kitchen.

"That's what I came home to tonight," I told him.

The judge looked at what was left of the walls around the
stove. "She's not here?"

"No," I said. "But there's one more place I could try."

We drove out to a field with a patch of woods in the middle, and there in the dusk I could see her moving through the trees. She still had on her white apron, or I might've just missed her. I turned off the engine, and we watched her for a while as she talked and gestured.

"Somebody out there with her?" the judge asked.

"No sir," I said, and I could see him taking this in.

"Mind if I go have a word?" he finally asked.

"Knock yourself out," I said.

He opened the door then, and I watched him walk through the fields in his nice polished shoes. I'd never seen a man dressed like him in a field before, but he seemed comfortable enough, and I remembered then that his brother Cole was a cotton ginner like me.

He moved toward Coralee slowly, and when she saw him, she turned toward him and spoke.

He kept his distance, but I could see him speak to her and see her answer. After a bit he took a step closer to her, and she pointed to something on the ground.

"What're they doing, Daddy?" Little Earl asked.

"Just having a little talk is all," I told him. Like Little Earl, I wondered what she was saying to him, but I'd heard it so many times myself I had a pretty good idea.

He stayed out there with Coralee for a good long while, even took a seat on a fallen tree and let her talk. Finally he stood up, tipped his hat to her, and walked back to the truck.

"I'm real sorry about this, Earl," he said as he climbed in. "I'll file the paperwork tomorrow morning. Have her ready to go by noon."

CORALEE

Mama always told us the only man a woman could rely on was the Lord, but when the law came calling, turns out you can't even rely on your own mama neither. Over-religious. That's what she told that judge, the same one who defended the sheriff who shot Buddy. Mama, who sometimes called me her little prophet. Mama, who taught me to love the Lord more than any man. And don't think I didn't see her praying when she thought nobody was looking. At least I wasn't ashamed to love my Lord and listen for His call. I wasn't afraid to heed His word. And now I knew He was the only one I could trust, because that hearing couldn't have been more proof that God is good.

In the end it was Brother Jeremiah and my brethren from Divine Holiness who stood by me in my hour of need. I had tested my faith, so they stood with the Lord and freed me. But I could not stand going home to Earl anymore. I did not want to live with him. I did not want to clean his house and do his laundry and only see Little Earl for twenty minutes together in a day. So one day after worship, I took my troubles to Brother Jeremiah.

"Now what can I do for you, Sister Coralee?" he asked me.

"I am most grateful for what you did to protect me from my husband," I began.

"We only did what was right," he said. "It is a crime against the Lord to lock a woman up just because she believes."

"I surely do know that," I told him. "But I do not want to live with Earl anymore. I need someone to take me in."

Brother Jeremiah said, "What about your boy?"

"Earl doesn't let me see him," I told him.

"Have you asked your mama? Surely she would take in her own daughter."

"She testified against me," I told him.

"Your sister, Shelby?"

"I will never speak to Shelby again," I said.

Brother Jeremiah let out a long sigh. He scratched his head. He said, "Sister Coralee, I can understand why you might feel that way. But Jesus teaches us to forgive. He forgives us all, every day. We must take his example."

"Isn't there anyone can take me in?" I asked. Tears pricked my eyes.

"The Lord will take you in, Sister Coralee. He is your shepherd. He will protect you."

And right then I could feel that Brother Jeremiah wanted me to leave. His words were kind, but he was using them to send me away. I could tell he thought I was too much trouble to bother with anymore.

I walked out of the church that day knowing that the only person left who loved me was Little Earl. That child was the best thing I ever did. He was always happy to see me in the mornings before school and again at supper, before Earl took him off to the gin. It was late harvest, which meant I slept alone in the house. Alone all day, alone all night, and now without even church to go to. I prayed to the Lord for relief. I prayed for succor. Most of all, I prayed for someone to keep me company. I was so lonesome.

And sure enough, one afternoon I looked out my window and saw my brother, Buddy. He was walking past the house, and I ran right out into the street.

"Buddy," I called after him. "Buddy!" But when he saw me chasing after him, he took off running, so fast I could never've caught him, especially once he cut through a cotton field. Still I tried to keep up with him. I ran and ran, tripping over clods of dirt and cotton husks and stalks until I could not run any further. I stopped to rest in the shade of a clump of trees and let the tears come.

Having Buddy back would've done so much to ease my pain. I don't think I could've wanted for anything if I had him back in my life. But he didn't want me neither.

After I'd cried myself out, I lay down on a soft patch of grass under those trees and slept. When I woke up, rays of light were shining through the leaves, almost like God was reaching out to me with His own hands. And I decided that if I was not going back to church anymore, I could worship right there. The thought was so powerful that I got right up. I didn't need Brother Jeremiah to preach to me. I could preach myself. And I set to picking up broken branches and gathering fallen leaves and began to make myself an altar. A squirrel watched me from a tree, so I preached about the fish and loaves. A sparrow landed in the grass, and I preached about Jesus making the blind see. Even a man appeared at the edge of the wood, so I preached about Judas's betrayal of Jesus.

"What're you building there?" he asked me.

"An altar to worship the Lord," I told him.

He seemed in no hurry, so I went on gathering leaves and sticks.

"How did you get out here?" he asked.

"I followed my brother, Buddy," I told him.

After a minute, he said, "Your brother died twenty years ago."

I turned and looked at him then, and I realized that without his robe, I hadn't recognized him. He was the judge who declared me sane, the same judge who'd defended the sheriff for killing Buddy.

"There's a lot you don't know," I told him. "Buddy's back. He was just here."

"How is that possible?" he asked me.

"Everything is possible with the Lord," I told him.

"It is indeed," the judge agreed. He took a seat on an old tree trunk and settled in. "But why do you think He sent your brother back?"

"He's probably trying to make things right with Mama," I told him.

"Make things right?" he asked me. "Now, how's that?"

"Mama thought he was full of the devil, but it wasn't true," I told that man.

"How do you know?" he asked.

"Because I could see all the way inside him, and I knew he was a good man."

"You see inside people?"

"Sometimes," I said, and he seemed to think about this for a moment.

"Where's Buddy now?"

"I don't know," I said, and I could feel the tears coming again. I did not want to cry in front of that judge, but I couldn't stop. "He won't talk to me. It's been twenty years, and my own brother won't talk to me."

"Why not?" he asked.

"I don't know why not," I said.

That judge let me cry for a while and didn't interrupt. Finally, when the tears had spent themselves again, he asked, "Shouldn't you be getting on home?"

"I am never going home again," I sniffed.

"Where are you going to live?" he asked me.

"I am going to live right here," I told him. "I will make a bed of leaves, and the Lord will watch over me." I broke off to pray then, that the Lord could bring Buddy back to me again, that He might be my shelter as I slept. I began laying leaves on the ground next to the altar for my bed and went to get more. I was about done with that man anyway, and he must've known it, because he stood and brushed off his slacks. Then he looked at me for so long I couldn't help but stare back.

"Mrs. Wilkins," he said. "If you can see inside people, what do you see inside me?"

I didn't need to look long. "A coward," I told him.

"Fair enough," he said, and tipped his hat. "Fair enough."

After he left me, I lay down on my bed of leaves and fell asleep, but it wasn't long before I came to. Somebody was shaking me gently, and when I opened my eyes, I saw Earl.

"Coralee," he said. "Come on home, now. You can't sleep out here."

"Yes, I can," I told him. "The Lord is the only shelter for me now."

Earl sat right down on the ground with me then. His voice sounded kind when he said, "Coralee, I want you more than anything. Please come on home. It's too cold out here."

I was shivering too much to argue with that, and I wasn't sure I wanted to. There was a kindness in Earl's voice I hadn't heard in a long time that lulled me into obeying him, into leaning on him as I walked, into letting him pick me up and carry me to the truck. Little Earl was there too as Earl set me inside, and that boy laid his head down on my lap and snuggled up tight to me, and I felt welcome and glad in a way I hadn't in years. Earl carried me into the dark house and put me to bed. He pulled the covers over me so tenderly. And I went to sleep that night and slept better and longer than I could even remember.

But when I opened the bedroom door the next morning that nice sheriff's deputy, Lewis Hopkins, was sitting in our living room, and Earl had packed two cases of my clothes and was sitting on the sofa next to Little Earl with his hands folded and his head bowed.

"Morning, Mrs. Wilkins," Deputy Hopkins said.

"Earl?" I said.

But Earl just sat on the couch with Little Earl as the deputy stood up.

"Mrs. Wilkins, I am here on behalf of the State of Arkansas to escort you to Little Rock. There's a hospital there that can help you."

"I let the Lord help me," I told him.

"Well, now, ma'am, it doesn't look like he was much help to you last night when you almost burned your house down."

"I didn't do that," I told him.

"You did, Coralee," Earl said. "You left a pot on the stove when you took off last night."

"Come on now, ma'am," Lewis Hopkins said. He took a step toward me.

"You keep your hands off me, you hear?"

But he moved closer. He was holding some kind of contraption.

"Mrs. Wilkins, all I want is for you to come with me peaceably and get into the car. We're going to take you to see some doctors, get you some help." But he'd taken another step closer, and suddenly I was punching and scratching and kicking him where my mama said to kick a man if you were really in a pinch.

He let out a howl and let me go, and I started to run for the back door, but Earl was on me by then, and they wrapped me inside that contraption.

I couldn't move then, and I began to cry. I heard Little Earl sobbing and wanted to comfort him, but Earl and Lewis Hopkins were already carrying me out the door.

"Say goodbye, Mama," Little Earl cried, and ran out on the porch. "Say goodbye."

I didn't want to say goodbye. I didn't want to leave him. But I knew they were going to take me away no matter what and this might be my only chance.

"Goodbye, son," I said. I watched him over my shoulder as they carried me to the car, tears rolling down his face. Funny thing was, when I turned to look at Earl, tears were rolling down his face, and down Lewis Hopkins's face too.

When they had me in the back seat, Earl said, "Coralee, I know you don't understand this, but I'm just trying to help you. Where you're going, they can make you well again."

"There's nothing wrong with me," I told him.

Lewis Hopkins shook Earl's hand before he climbed into the car.

"Thank you for your help," Earl said to him.

"I'm real sorry, Earl," he said. "Worst part of my job."

When we pulled out of the driveway, Earl put his arm around Little Earl and walked him into the house so he didn't have to watch me drive away, even if all the neighbors were standing on their porches with their mouths hanging open.

For a long time, I couldn't stop crying, which gave me hiccups, and when they finally stopped, Lewis Hopkins met my eyes in the rearview mirror and said, "I can't undo those stays, ma'am. But if you'll let me, I can use my handkerchief to wipe your face."

I didn't want to let that man help me, but I needed to blow my nose. I was having trouble breathing. I nodded then, and he pulled onto the shoulder of the highway and opened a small window between the front and back. First he dried my tears.

Then he held the handkerchief to my nose. His concern for me was so plain that he reminded me of a mother with her child as he wiped my face clean, then closed the screen between us and pulled back on the road.

"There now," he said. "That better?"

"Some," I said.

"Look, ma'am," he said. "I'm real sorry about what I had to do to you this morning, but it's my job."

"You work for Sheriff Slocum," I said, remembering him climbing into the sheriff's car after the first time I'd seen Buddy again.

He was quiet for a long moment. Finally, he said, "Yes ma'am, he is my superior."

"Then you work for the devil," I told him.

"I work for the State of Arkansas," he said. "Sheriff Slocum is just who I report to."

"Same difference," I said. And after a while I knew I had won that fight, because that man said not one single word after that, all the way to Little Rock.

But when he finally stopped driving and got out, he shook hands with two men who came to meet the car. "Jimmy, Sherman, nice to see you again," he said.

"Nice to see you too, Lewis," said one of the men. I thought he'd let me out of the back seat then, but the longer they all stood there asking after each other's wives and kids and jobs, the more I had to wonder just how many times Lewis Hopkins had been down there before.

LEROY

After filing the paperwork to declare Coralee Wilkins insane, any lingering fear I felt about Sheriff Slocum coming for me receded. In the end, I'd done what he wanted, even if I'd tried to do differently. I'd also dealt with him on a couple of cases since, and I could tell no difference in his demeanor at all. It was like I'd only imagined there was any harm in him, and I found myself second-guessing my sense of Wiley, the way I always had.

Then one day Mabel went to her Junior League meeting after making a Bundt cake for the table and returned home with the whole cake—not a single slice taken from it.

"Guess it was too humid for all that butter," Mabel said.

"More for me," I said, trying to make light because Mabel looked so hurt.

But a week later she found the meeting hall locked. She knocked on the door, checked her watch, finally walked home, bewildered. Later that day, she ran into Tillie Slocum, who said, "Oh, I'm so sorry, Mabel. We had to move the meeting to Charlotte Burnham's house on account of an electrical problem. Did no one call you?"

But at the next meeting, when Mabel found out she'd been replaced as secretary in a vote taken at the meeting she missed, she sat down with me when she got home and said, "Leroy, something's going on."

"Might just be an oversight," I said, because there was no

way to prove Wiley was behind it. I doubted he talked business with his wife. He didn't seem the type. And for a while, nothing more came of it, which made it seem like more of a coincidence.

So again, I didn't make much over it when Cole mentioned at Sunday supper that despite a bumper cotton crop, business seemed to be down at the gin.

"There's that new gin over in Black Oak," I said. "Maybe that's cutting in on the business."

"Maybe so," Cole said. "We've got more than enough work as it is, so it's fine for now," he said, and because I hoped that's all it was, I let it go.

But I didn't know for sure until the day I pulled into my driveway and saw Wiley sitting on the porch with Mabel, whose face was like a stone, and Caleb, who was crying on her shoulder, that Mabel was right. Something was going on.

"What's happening here?" I asked as I walked up.

"I'm real sorry, Leroy," Wiley said. "I thought the boy knew Cole and Bess were his parents, what with you all living right down the street from your brother."

It took me a long moment to realize what he was saying, and when it finally sunk in, I knew right then and there that my suspicions about Wiley were right. He'd known there was no better way to hurt me than to hurt my boy, and truth be told, I probably should have known all those years ago as I watched him set up that crib for Caleb that I was in trouble.

I also knew, in some way that I couldn't explain, that this wasn't the end of it. It was a test. If I let this pass, said it was understandable, that he couldn't possibly have known we'd never told Caleb about Bess, well then, we'd go on the way we had all these years, because the sheriff would know he could do the worst possible thing to me and I'd let it pass just to stay in his good graces. If not, he'd ruin me. I knew this for sure.

"Mabel," I said, "take Caleb inside."

When the door slammed behind them, I said, "Wiley, don't you ever set foot in this house again."

"It was an honest mistake, Leroy. That's all. I meant nothing by it. You're blowing this thing way out of proportion now," he told me, and he sounded so sincere that for a split second I doubted myself the way I always had with him.

"You leave me and my family alone," I said.

"Just what are you trying to say?" he asked.

"I'm saying get off my porch and get busy doing whatever it is you've got planned for me next. Just go ahead and get it over with."

"I don't know what on earth you're referring to, Leroy," he said.

"Like hell you don't."

"Come on, Leroy. We're old friends, you and me."

"No, Wiley, we're not."

"All right then," he said as he stood and put his hat on. "But this is all a big mistake."

"You can say that again," I told him.

Mabel told me afterward that Wiley had come on the pretext of discussing a case with me, and when I wasn't home, he said he'd sit on the porch and enjoy the fine afternoon while he waited for me. And though Mabel was in the middle of canning peaches, Caleb went out to keep him company on the swing, and the next thing she heard was Caleb crying.

After the sheriff left, we sat Caleb down in the living room. Mabel said, "Honey, I know what the sheriff told you must be confusing. I'll bet you have some questions you might want to ask us, now, don't you?"

Caleb had stopped crying, and his body was limp with exhaustion. He stared at a spot on the floor and didn't lift his eyes when he said, "Is it true?"

"It is true that your Aunt Bess gave birth to you," Mabel said. "But your Uncle Cole was too upset after she died to take care of a tiny baby. He was so upset that your daddy and me moved in with him for a while to take care of you. And the truth is, we just fell in love with you. And since your Uncle Cole wasn't any good with babies, when the time came for us to move back to Stillwater, he felt he was doing best by you to let you come with us. And that's what happened."

Caleb was still staring at the floor. He finally said, "So he's my daddy?"

"In a way," I said, though the question sliced through me. "But I'm your daddy too, because I'm the one who raised you. Me and your mama."

"And we love you," Mabel said. "We're like just any family, Caleb. Just because your Uncle Cole is your daddy in another kind of way doesn't change anything between us. Do you understand that?"

Caleb looked up finally and said, "I guess so."

And Mabel said, "Good. Now come give your mama a hug." And Caleb went to her slowly, like he wasn't sure she was his mama after all, and Mabel wrapped him up tight in her arms. Finally, Caleb put his arms limply around her. But the tighter she held him, the tighter he held her. She kissed him on the forehead after a while and looked him in the eye, then she kissed him again, more playfully, and pretty soon he was smiling.

"How about some fried chicken for supper?" Mabel asked him, which was his favorite, and he nodded and followed her into the kitchen.

I sat there in the living room alone. I could hear the pace of Mabel and Caleb's chatter start to pick up, and eventually I heard Caleb laugh at something Mabel said. And I was frankly astonished at Mabel's ability to love that boy through something so hard, to know when to be direct and when to let her hugging do the talking, and just how to kiss him to make him smile again. That woman had always been guided by her heart in a way I never was, and I wished I could be as composed as she was at such an awful moment. Because all I felt in that moment was a rage so gigantic it threatened to overtake me.

"I could kill Wiley," I told Mabel as we were getting ready for bed.

"I told you the boy was going to find out, Leroy," Mabel said. "If it wasn't Wiley, it would have been somebody else." And I knew she blamed me for not telling him when she'd wanted to, even if she didn't say it. So I didn't say anything more about Wiley after that, just got into bed and turned out the light. But those feelings were so powerful they rumbled around in my dreams and kept waking me up all through the night. And when I got up in the morning, the worse for wear, I knew for the first time in my life what it was to want to murder somebody, and I understood a lot more clearly all those folks I'd seen in my career who actually had.

For months, we watched Caleb closely. We wondered how the news about Cole and Bess would settle, and how he might feel about Cole at Sunday suppers, where I sometimes caught Caleb sneaking glances at him, and I could see the boy trying to put together the pieces of what he'd learned. I wondered if the attentiveness Cole always showed that mute boy Sonny would get to Caleb now too, the way it always got to me, but after a few weeks, I could see no difference in Caleb and things went back to normal, for the most part. Even so, to distract him I took him fishing on the St. Francis. I took him to a carnival down in Jonesboro. I took him down to the gun shop in Stillwater and bought him the shotgun he'd been begging me for so he could hunt rabbit and squirrel and duck with Cole's son Nicky Joe.

"An eleven-year-old with a gun?" Mabel asked over supper when we'd come home that afternoon. "That's crazy, Leroy."

"I was hunting by age nine," I said.

But Caleb said, "Mama, what's crazy mean?"

"Crazy is what your father is," Mabel said. "It means you don't think straight."

"Is it catching?" he asked.

"Better hope not, son," I said, "or we're both in trouble."

But Mabel said, "Now, Caleb, why would you ask a thing like that?"

"At school they say Earl Wilkins's mama is crazy. They say Earl might have caught it from her, and we can catch it from him."

Now this stung me. And I realized that it probably wasn't just the kids who believed this. Superstitions could run deep and got passed from generation to generation.

I said, "Does Little Earl seem crazy to you?"

"No," Caleb said.

"How does he seem?"

"He seems sad. Nobody eats lunch with him."

"Are you afraid of him?" Mabel asked.

Caleb didn't answer, so I said, "Son, answer your mama."

The boy hung his head. "I just don't want people to think I'm crazy too."

"And you think if you ate lunch with him, people would think you're crazy too?"

Caleb poked his fried okra around on his plate. "I know they would."

"So it would just be you and Little Earl eating lunch together?" Mabel asked.

"I suppose," Caleb said.

"So you'd have somebody to eat lunch with and so would

Little Earl. Seems like a pretty good situation, everybody having somebody to eat lunch with, now, don't you think?"

Caleb was smiling now. "I guess."

"Don't you listen to those kids, Caleb," Mabel said. "If you like Little Earl, you go on and be nice to him, just like you would to anybody, you hear me?"

"Yes, Mama," Caleb said.

"That's my boy," Mabel said, and she planted a kiss on his forehead as she stood and started clearing the plates.

Still, even if things at home seemed fine with Caleb, I knew the other shoe hadn't fallen yet. Wiley wouldn't stop at telling Caleb who his parents were or ostracizing Mabel from the Junior League. He'd get his revenge in his own good time. All I could do was wait.

BIG EARL

When word spread that Coralee had been declared insane, it was like the whole town of Paradise avoided me. Folks didn't meet my eye at the filling station, refused to make small talk in line at Harvey's Hardware, gave me a wide berth when they passed me on the sidewalk. The person who stood by me the most was Mr. Holmes. He called me into his office after work one day just to ask how I was doing.

"I've been better," I said.

"At least Coralee will get the help she needs now. Maisie Cooper went down to Little Rock a few years ago, and she's much better now. I think you have reason to feel hopeful," he told me. "How's Little Earl taking it?"

"Hard to know how it will settle," I said. "But it's been hard on the boy." Little Earl had gone quiet after his mama left. And I knew the reason too. It wasn't just that he missed her. It was that folks avoided him too. As a man I understood why, but it was harder on Little Earl. Some days I could tell it had been so bad I wished we could move somewhere else and start over in a place where nobody knew about Coralee. But you'd have been a fool to leave a stable job with a good boss. I had to pay the bills, repair the fire damage to the house, put food on the table after all, though lucky for us, Coralee's cousin Trudy came in to cook for us now that Coralee was gone.

Still, there are things that are just about as important as food, and after a while I began to understand that Little Earl was starving in a different kind of way. I would see kids from school going past the house playing and see Little Earl watching them so longingly, like one friendly word from them would just make his day, but they'd pass like they never even saw him there—even cross the road just to keep more distance—and Little Earl would turn his back on them and pretend to be real interested in something in the grass. Then he'd see me watching and he'd smile, and I knew then that the face he showed me was just the one he knew I wanted to see.

I also worried that he wouldn't remember his mama the longer we went without seeing her, so I put a framed photograph of her on a shelf in our living room so he wouldn't forget what she looked like. Then one day I got an idea. And even though I didn't know how to write myself, I said, "Son, would you like to write a letter to your mama?"

"Can I?" he asked.

"If you'd like to," I said. So he got some paper and a pencil from his room and said, "What should I say?"

"How about *Dear Mama*?" I said. I knew most letters began with *Dear* from listening to Mr. Holmes read off the ones he got from his creditors. So Little Earl wrote it down.

"What next?"

"Why don't you tell her what you've been up to lately?" So he wrote for a while, but I had no idea what his scribbles said, and I was too ashamed to ask him.

"What else?"

"How about school?" So he wrote a while longer.

"You done?" I asked when he was finished writing.

"Yes," he said.

"Then you need to sign it."

"How?" he asked.

"Do you love your mama?" I asked.

"Yes sir," he said.

"Then say that." So he scribbled some more.

"Now sign your name."

So the boy signed his name, and the next day I bought an envelope and stamp from Mr. Holmes, and Little Earl copied the address from a letter from the hospital, and I mailed it. I honestly didn't know what to do after that.

Then one afternoon, Mr. Holmes sent me on an errand over to Cole Harrison's gin. They were competitors, him and Cole, but they supported one another too. If Mr. Holmes ran out of baling bands, Cole Harrison would send some over, and if Cole ran out of burlap, Mr. Holmes would let him borrow some, which is what I had gone there to deliver that day, and I took Little Earl with me. When we pulled into the gin and I climbed out, Cole came out and shook my hand, and we let down the bed of the truck and eased the rolls of burlap off it.

Just to clear the air, I said, "Cole, I'm real sorry about what I did to Leroy. I just wasn't myself."

"Listen," Cole said. "If I'd known all it took to get through to my brother was a gun, I'd have pulled one on him long ago." And I had to smile at that.

"Thank Wally for the burlap, Earl," Cole said. "And give him my best."

Now, I was so relieved to know that Cole didn't hold what I'd done to his brother against me that it took me a moment to realize Little Earl wasn't in the truck. He wasn't in the gin either, so I walked out back and looked around, and that's when I first heard it. My son's laughter. It was a sound I hadn't heard since Coralee left, and it made my heart soar and my chin tremble and my eyes start to watering. I followed that laughter until I spotted him crouched in the grass with what must've been Cole's son, Nicky Joe, prodding a frog with a stick. And I felt so grateful to that child because Little Earl was talking so natural and jumping and screeching with so much joy as that frog hopped along that I just leaned against a fence post and watched for a while. I didn't want to interrupt him, happy as he was. I wanted him to be a child again for as long as I could let him, and I knew Mr. Holmes would understand if I was a little late. But when Little Earl spotted me, he waved me over to see the frog, and it was only when the boy playing with him turned and stood up that I realized that it wasn't Cole's boy being kind to my son. It was Judge Harrison's boy, Caleb.

CORALEE

Time is a funny thing. Most of my life I never felt like I had enough of it. But in that hospital, I had nothing but time. Time to wonder why Daddy drank himself to death. Why Mama was so hard-hearted when I knew she had feeling inside her. Why the Lord had blessed Shelby with nine boys but it took Earl and me ten years to have one child. Why Buddy got up so early the morning he was shot and bothered to make his bed if he was just going to rob the tavern like they said. Why Mama was so mad at Buddy when he died. Why Brother Jeremiah defended me so well that Judge Harrison let me walk free, but when I went to him in my hour of need, he didn't even try to help me get away from Earl.

Or why, if Earl ever loved me, he sent me to that terrible place where I was locked in a bare room with a tiny barred window that looked out on nothing but another wall, where the doctors poked and prodded me, where they fed me slop you wouldn't let your hogs eat, where they shocked me like the devil running through me, and afterwards it felt like I'd picked two thousand pounds of cotton in twenty minutes, I was so tired.

Only time I ever got to see grass or trees or fields was when the guards marched us around the grounds. It was real pretty out there, but sometimes it was hard to smell the goodness of the grass or notice how fresh the air felt on my skin because none of it meant the same thing with those nightsticks the guards carried banging against their legs. And it was all Earl's fault, setting me up for that hearing, testifying against me, leading me home like he was going to take care of me that last night, only to hold me down the next morning while Lewis Hopkins tied me up. But about the time I'd start to get angry they'd bring me another pill.

When I first got there, I was glad those pills made me feel nothing. I'd felt too much all my life. Fear of my daddy's whippings when I was a child. Anger at Mama for being so hard. Jealousy over the way she favored Shelby. Heartbreak when Chess wouldn't stop drinking. Grief when Buddy was killed. Joy when Little Earl was born. Sorrow watching him howl on the front porch when Lewis Hopkins took me away. Rage knowing Earl put me here.

I'd always been full to bursting with those feelings. They just spilled out all over the place, no way to keep them in. Only, I didn't know it could be any other way, not really. Just thought it was the way I was made, and that only the Lord could help me with it. But now I knew He must've had His work cut out for him, because even He could never do for me what that little pill did. I never knew a pill could be more powerful than the Lord. Maybe because I only ever took bicarbonate of soda after eating too many green tomatoes. Those pills were like swallowing peacefulness, the kind of peacefulness I've only ever prayed for but never once felt, especially after Buddy died.

But after a while, I started to miss all those feelings. I hadn't felt anything in so long—I didn't know how long—and I understood then that feeling is being alive. I never knew feeling was as important as seeing or hearing or touching. Just like hunger told me it was time to eat, or sleep told me it was time to rest, feeling helps you find your way through places and people, who to move toward and who to move away from. Without feeling, you can't get where you need to go, or find what you need to say, or figure out who you need to tell it to.

Not that I had a choice who I talked to. Not like I could go looking for anybody in particular. Only folks I'd talked to in months were my nurse, Miss Etta, or Doctor Garvey, who only asked me questions and wrote things down. When I told him I didn't like my pills, he said, "Take them anyway." When I asked him when I could see my boy, he just said, "We'll see." And it was then that I got to missing Doc English real good, even though he also testified against me like practically everybody else I knew. That man was kindly, at least. This one looked right through me.

Then, out of the wild blue yonder, the best thing happened to me that could possibly happen. Miss Etta came in one morning and said, "You have a letter, Coralee."

"A letter?" I said. "From who?"

"Someone named Earl," she said.

"Which one?" I asked.

"It's just signed *Earl*."

And when she handed it to me, I stared at it, realizing it was Little Earl's handwriting. I recognized it from his schoolwork, even if I didn't know what it said.

"Miss Etta," I said. "Can you read it to me? I can't see so well." This wasn't true, but I was ashamed to admit I didn't know how to read.

"All right," Miss Etta said. "It says, 'Dear Mama, Daddy took me duck hunting. I shot four ducks. Mr. Holmes says I can drive the tractor at the gin one day. I love math class. Miss Cooper is my favorite teacher.' It's signed, 'I love you, Mama. Earl.'"

I hadn't felt anything in so long, but now I was on the edge of tears thinking of my boy writing me this letter. I wished I could see the words and know what they meant. I wished I could've read it in private instead of having to hear it in Miss Etta's voice, which made it harder to imagine my son's sweet voice saying those words. But just knowing my son cared enough to write me a letter perked me up for days, and it wasn't long after that I met with that young Doctor Garvey. And I must've said something right because they changed my pill then and put me to work in the laundry after that, and soon I wasn't quite so fuzzy-headed as when I first got there.

Now, I always liked something to keep my hands busy, but even if I wished more than anything it could've been my garden, I was happy to have a task to complete. They let a few women do it with me, and I got to know them by name eventually: Ruth, Ester, and Libby. Ruth and Ester didn't say much— we all moved pretty slow—but Libby moved quickly and smiled and asked questions like which building we were in and which doctor did we see.

We were all about the same age, but Libby seemed younger somehow. Had a pretty smile. And she never got flustered or made mistakes. I made them all the time. Once, when I got behind, she just walked over and helped me fold.

"I'm slow today," I told her.

"It's the medicine," she told me. "They were late with it today." And it took me a while to realize she was right. I couldn't really tell how time passed in there, and I wondered how she could. I also wondered why she wasn't slow like the rest of us. She was just the same as anybody I ever knew.

"Miss Libby," I finally told her one day. "You don't seem like you should be here."

"None of us should be here," she said. "This place ain't fit for pigs."

"Maybe so," I told her, "but you seem just fine to me."

"I am just fine," she said.

"How'd you get here, then?" I asked.

Libby sighed and looked out the window. "I guess you could say I crossed the wrong man," she said.

"Your husband," I said. But for some reason this made Libby laugh.

When she stopped for breath, she said, "I don't got no husband. Golly." Then she said, "You're funny, Coralee." And I realized that without meaning to, I'd made a joke, and underneath all that numbness I felt a bubbling up of something bright.

Still, even when the medicine came on time, Libby folded three loads for every one the rest of us did, and I knew a shame over my slowness that must've been left over from my days as the fastest cotton picker who ever worked for Mr. Jenks. So one day, when Ruth and Ester left early and it was just me and Libby, I asked her how she was always so quick.

Libby looked at me for a long time. Finally she said, "Can I trust you, Coralee?"

"Yes, you can," I said.

"Because if I can't, they could hurt me," she said. "They could even give me the shock."

"I would never want that for you, Libby," I told her. "The shock is terrible."

"Oh, Coralee," she said, and wrapped her arms around me. "I didn't know they was doing that to you." And Libby just held me and started to cry.

Nobody had held me in so long. Nobody'd hardly touched me in kindness since the night Earl carried me out of the woods to his truck, and even then he betrayed me the next morning. So I didn't realize until Libby's arms were around me that the touch of another person mattered so much, let you know that folks saw you, let you know that you were there.

When Libby stopped crying, she wiped her eyes and looked around to make sure nobody was nearby. Then she lifted up the top of the pajamas we all wore, reached inside her brassiere, and pulled out the exact same pill I'd taken just that morning.

"I hide it between my cheek and gum, up top, way in the back of my mouth, so when they check to see if I've swallowed it, it looks like I have. Then I flush it down the toilet."

"Well, I'll be," I said. I had never thought of that. I was never one to break rules unless I felt it was a rule that went against the teaching of the Lord. And although I wasn't sure if taking medication was right or wrong in the eyes of the Lord, just the question brought me up short.

"Don't keep it in your pocket where it can fall out," she told me. "And don't throw it out your window, or they'll find it. You have to flush it down the toilet."

Just then we heard footsteps. An orderly walked in.

"Bathroom break," he said. "One at a time."

"Coralee," Libby said, real casual-like, as she picked up a pillowcase and started folding it. "Why don't you go first?"

LEROY

It took me some time to process what had happened between Wiley and me. But I was sure what he'd done to Caleb was no accident, just like all the slights to Mabel by the Junior League had been no accident. Still, I hoped maybe Cole's comment that business was down might have been made at the end of a slow week, and nothing to do with Wiley. So when the harvest was over, I made a point to drive over to Cole's after work the day his crew had baled their last to see what Cole had to say about the final tally. But when I arrived, Cole was loading everybody into the bed of his truck to head down to the Paradise Tavern to celebrate, so I followed him even though I knew I'd catch hell from Mabel if I was late for supper.

The Paradise Tavern had changed hands recently, and everybody in town had an opinion about what the new owners had done with the place. I hadn't been inside it but five times in twenty years together, partly because of my association of it with the death of Buddy Harper. And although from the outside it looked the same, I must say it was pretty fancy on the inside. The bar was in the same place, but they had new tables, and bright lamps suspended over them, and lots of framed pictures on the wall of local sports teams and graduating classes, even old photos of the tavern itself. It was just a beer joint when I'd last been inside, but now it was more like a restaurant, and before we'd even got settled at a table, Cole told the waitress to bring us two pitchers of beer and a platter of chicken and some fried potatoes and a big bowl of collards—and even though I knew Mabel would have supper ready by the time I got home, I ordered myself a plate of hush puppies and figured I'd just keep that to myself.

When the beer came, Cole poured us all glasses and raised his own. "To all your hard work, boys," he said. "It was a good harvest."

"And to many more," I added. But that must have been the wrong thing to say because Cole looked serious then.

"I hope so," he said. "Profit's still down. Can't figure out why."

I was about to ask by how much, but just then the waitress came out with the food and all Cole's workers dug right in to that meal, and everyone seemed so happy to eat and drink and settle into the ease that follows a harvest that I dropped all talk of profits and let them enjoy the evening.

On our way to the register, Cole walked over to those old photographs of what the tavern had looked like and showed them to Sonny. "That's the old bar there. See these little tables here? Hey wait, Leroy, is that Clive Jones in that picture? And look at those hats. Haven't seen one like that in years. Me and Leroy used to wear those things, Sonny," Cole told him. "And check out the old oil lamp on that table. When we were kids, we didn't used to have electric light," he told Sonny. "Now wait a second, is that Floyd Wetherbee's father in this picture?"

But Sonny's eyes hadn't moved with Cole's. He was still staring at the photograph of the table of folks with the oil lamp on it, and all the color had drained from his face. But Cole just kept chattering away about those photographs and didn't notice Sonny wasn't listening anymore.

Now normally, I let Cole take the lead with anything to do

with Sonny. He wasn't real comfortable with anybody else. But when I noticed the peculiar look on his face, I said, "Everything okay, Sonny?"

Sonny could nod *yes* or shake *no* if you asked him a question, and that's all I expected him to do. But to my surprise, he opened his mouth and made a sound. It was so soft it was like he was blowing out a candle.

"What was that, Sonny?" I tried to sound calm, like it wasn't just about the biggest surprise I'd ever had to hear a sound come out of a boy who'd never made a peep in all the years I'd known him.

"Muh," Sonny said.

"Sorry, Sonny, I still didn't catch that."

"Muh," he said. "Muh."

"Muh?" I said.

"Muh. Muh," Sonny said again.

"Muh muh," I repeated after him, and as soon as I said it myself, something inside me clicked. "Mama?"

"Mama." Sonny nodded. He staggered backwards, like he'd lost his balance. He put his hand on the back of his neck and ran it up his hair. Then he suddenly burst into tears. His nose dripped down the front of his shirt, but he seemed not to know enough to wipe it.

"Cole," I said. "We got to get this boy home."

"What's wrong?" Cole had moved along down the room with the rest of his crew, still looking at the pictures.

"*Now*," I barked, and when Cole finally turned and saw Sonny crying, he said, "Settle up, will you, Leroy?" And he took Sonny by the shoulders and led him out the door.

After settling the tab, I walked over to the spot where Sonny had broken down and peered at the faces of the people in the picture he'd been staring at. Fortunately it was getting late and the supper crowd was clearing out, and the barkeep, Charlie, who was still tending bar in spite of the change of ownership, wasn't busy yet with the drinkers, so I took the photograph off the wall and brought it over to the bar with me.

"Hey Charlie," I said. "Let me ask you something."

"Shoot," Charlie said.

"Do you recognize the girl at this table?"

"Sure do. She used to live up top," he said, pointing above him.

"When?" I asked.

"Twenty years ago, must've been."

"You wouldn't happen to remember her name, would you?"

"Lorna Lovett," he said.

"Lorna Lovett?" I asked. "Are you sure that's her?"

"Would you forget a face like that?" Charlie asked me.

Lorna Lovett, I thought. *Nice to finally meet you.* She was looking right into the camera, so you got the feeling she was looking right at you. All these years I'd never known what she'd looked like, and now I could see that she was not only beautiful, but charming. Sweet-looking. I could see perfectly well how a woman like that could get men to risk breaking the law just to spend the night with her.

"Mind if I borrow this?" I asked Charlie.

"You're the judge," he said. "Just bring it back when you're done with it."

When I got home, Mabel lit into me after Caleb was in bed for leaving her with supper on the table.

"You might have at least called, Leroy," she said. "Caleb couldn't wait to show you his report card."

"He showed it to me before he went to bed," I said. "Five As and one B."

"I know, but it's hard for a child to wait."

"Oh, so it was *Caleb* that was mad at me then," I said, trying to make light. "Not you."

"I'm none too pleased with you either," Mabel told me, and I was about to tease her again when the set of her shoulders stopped me cold. "But you can't be unreliable with him, Leroy."

"I'm sorry, Mabel," I said.

"I know you are," she sighed, but she patted my shoulder. "Just call next time."

After Mabel turned in, I went into my study and rummaged around my briefcase for the magnifying glass I used to read fine print and took out the photograph. But in looking at it again, it struck me as odd that the men were deep in conversation with one another on the left side of the photograph while Lorna was turned to the right facing the camera. She looked surprised, maybe even a little alarmed, now that I looked at her face more closely.

Not that it mattered. I finally had two things I'd needed all those years ago to help me find the missing star witness to Buddy Harper's murder. A positive ID from someone who'd known her then and a boy who might know where I could find her.

That night, as I tried to sleep, I wondered about Sonny's silence. I knew that while some children are born mute, others go silent later on, like a case I knew of in Monette where a child had accidently locked himself inside the trunk of a car while playing hide-and-go-seek in an old barn on the back of his folk's property and wasn't discovered for two days. It's a wonder he survived, but fortunately it was an old car with holes in the floorboards, which allowed for some air to get in, and it happened in October, so it wasn't hot. That boy would have died in an hour if it happened in August. Even so, he'd never spoken a word since.

So the next evening, I dropped by Cole's house on my way home from the office. Nicky Joe and Lulu were playing outside and Sonny was nowhere to be seen, so I sat down with Cole on the porch in the cool autumn breeze.

"How's Sonny doing?" I asked.

"He's a mess. You have any idea what upset him? I never heard anyone cry so loud," he said.

"I don't know for sure, but I think it might have been this." I pulled the photograph from the tavern out of my briefcase and showed it to him.

"Where'd you get that?" he asked me.

"Charlie let me borrow it from the tavern."

"What for?"

"Because the woman in the photograph is Lorna Lovett."

"Who's that?"

"She was a prostitute that used to live over the tavern," I said.

"What's that got to do with Sonny?" Cole asked.

"He called her *Mama*."

"Leroy, the boy's mute, for God's sake."

"You just said yourself you never heard anyone cry so loud. He's not mute," I said. "And I heard him say *mama*. I even asked him to be sure. That's when he started crying."

Cole looked stunned. He sat back in his chair for a while and stared into the distance. Finally he said, "Leroy, if you don't mind my asking, why do you care? You've never seemed to like the boy much."

"Because Buddy Harper was killed the same day Lorna Lovett went missing. She'd have been the star witness of the hearing to determine if there was enough evidence to charge Sheriff Slocum for murder. If Sonny knows where she is, she might finally be able to clear up some questions I still have about the case."

"Like what?"

"Like the fact that Sheriff Slocum probably murdered Buddy Harper in cold blood after all. I just don't know why."

"Then why'd you represent him?" I could tell Cole's anger was gathering steam. Cole could not stand injustice or politicking, and more than once since I'd worked with Wiley I could tell he didn't approve of the man, even though he never said so.

"Because I couldn't prove it," I said, and kept it at that. "But Sonny might know where I can find Lorna, if you'll let me question him."

"Look, Leroy, I'm as curious as you are about where Sonny came from. But I've always been fairly certain it's not because he left behind a nice set of parents somewhere. So I'm not letting you drag Sonny into something just to settle some old score with some old boy based on some old hunch you got going, even if you're right about who his mama is. Even if we did ask him, there's no guarantee he'd even be able to answer."

"He said *mama*," I told him. "That boy can talk."

"Don't matter," Cole said. "I'm not going to let you wind him up with a bunch of questions he's too upset to answer right now."

"All right," I said, and it was enough for me that Cole hadn't said I couldn't question Sonny. He'd said I couldn't question Sonny *right now*.

BIG EARL

When I saw Caleb Harrison playing with my son in Cole
Harrison's backyard, I was so grateful to that young boy
I didn't stop to think about who his father was or what he'd
done to Coralee's family or to mine. Hearing my Little Earl's
laughter again that afternoon, well, I'd have forgiven anyone
who could put a smile back on my son's face. Besides, Caleb
wasn't responsible for who his father was, even though everybody knew that he was really Cole's child. But even if he had
been the judge's son, I did not care.

Which was lucky, because I started to see an awful lot of Caleb in the months that followed. Little Earl was getting to the
age where I didn't have to watch him quite so much—he was
old enough to stay home when I worked late, and sometimes
Caleb would be with him. They'd pick pecans from the trees
in our backyard, or head out to fish in Jumper's Hole, or hunt
squirrel in the woods on the edge of town. They were together
so often that they beat a shortcut through the cotton field behind the house that made it faster to get from Caleb's house on
the far edge of the field to ours, as the crow flies, saving themselves a mile each way, and pretty soon it wasn't uncommon for
me to watch Little Earl disappear into the cotton field behind
our house or hear a rustle and see Caleb step out of it into our
yard.

Then one day, when Little Earl was late coming home, I saw

a shiny white car pull into our driveway, and when I walked out onto the porch, I saw it was Judge Harrison. In all the time our boys had been playing together, I hadn't come face-to-face with the man, but now, here he was, walking right toward me.

"Earl Wilkins," he finally said.

"Judge Harrison, sir," I said.

"Call me Leroy."

"Leroy, then," I said.

"I'm looking for my boy. Mabel's got supper ready and he's not home yet. Have you seen him?"

"They should be back soon," I said. Still, I'd held the man at gunpoint last I'd seen him, so I added, "I want to thank you for helping me with my wife."

"You didn't leave me much choice as I recall," he said, but his tone was friendly, like he might be teasing me.

"I also want to thank you for whatever you said to Caleb about my son. He's the only boy will go near Little Earl since Coralee left."

"He just asked a few questions about what was going around at school, and we tried to clear things up."

"Even so," I said, "it takes character to go against the grain."

"I wish I could take credit for that, but I think he gets it from my wife," Leroy said.

"Wherever it comes from, I can't tell you what a difference it's made to my son. It's been hard with Coralee gone."

"I expect it has been," he said. "If I may ask, how is your wife?"

"I'll see her for the first time tomorrow," I told him. "The hospital sent a letter saying she's ready for a visit, but it's been six months."

"They know if she's ready. You wouldn't have wanted to see her before time."

"I'm sure that's true," I said, but just then Little Earl appeared in the side yard. He held up a string of catfish for me to see.

"Where's Caleb?" I called to him.

When Little Earl said Caleb had gone home, the judge turned and eyed the gap in the cotton where Little Earl had come from and said, "I do believe those boys have clean beat a path between our houses."

"One to the creek too. You see how many catfish they caught on Sunday?"

"Mabel can't keep up with them," he told me, but before he got in his car, he said, "Good luck with your wife, Earl. I hope it all goes well."

The next morning, Little Earl and me made the long drive to Little Rock. We had to check in and wait, and the longer I sat there, the more nervous I got. Finally a nurse named Miss Etta came to get us and walked us outside, down the sidewalk to the building where they were keeping Coralee. It was a pretty place. Trees and grass and nice brick buildings, and as we walked I began to feel hopeful that all this might actually be doing her some good.

When we reached the building, Miss Etta said, "Wait here," before she disappeared inside.

Little Earl was looking at the ground. He had hardly said a word on the drive.

"You okay, son?" I asked him.

"Yes," he said, but I could tell by his voice that he wasn't.

And suddenly, there was Coralee, wearing one of the dresses and a pair of shoes I'd packed for her the day Lewis Hopkins took her away.

"I'll leave you now," Miss Etta told her. To me, she said, "Bring her back by half past two."

"Hello, Coralee," I finally said. "It's nice to see you."

"It's nice to see you too," she said, but the words, I could tell, took effort.

"Give your mama some sugar, now, son," I told Little Earl, and the boy hugged her.

"Hi, Mama," he said.

"Hi, son," she said. And even though I could see the hint of a smile on her face when he hugged her tight, and even though she lifted her arms to hold him in return, her reaction was so slow and weak that Little Earl backed away from her then, hurt. But Coralee kept her eyes on him. I could tell she was struggling to say something.

"You've grown," she finally said. "You look like your daddy."

I was afraid she might still be mad at me, so I didn't hug her myself. Instead I put my hand on her back and held up the basket of food Trudy had packed.

"They said we could have a picnic, Coralee." I tried to sound cheerful, but when she turned to look at me, there wasn't anger in her eyes. There was only emptiness, like the Coralee I loved had gone somewhere else and this person who looked like her had come with us instead.

We walked a ways until I found some shade under a pretty tree and spread out the blanket and helped Coralee sit down.

When we were all seated, I said, "Son, why don't you tell your mama about school?"

But instead he said, "Did you get my letter?"

"I surely did. A while back."

When Little Earl didn't respond to this, I said, "Tell her who your teacher is."

When he didn't answer, I said, "He likes Miss Cooper. And tell your mama what your favorite subject is."

But he didn't even look up, so I said, "He likes arithmetic.

And how about those marks on your last report card, son? Why don't you tell your mama how well you did?"

But Little Earl just pretended to scratch at a mosquito bite. "High marks all around, Coralee," I told her. "You'd be proud of him." But Coralee made no answer.

Now, after waiting six months, I could not stand another minute of this. So I started talking and couldn't stop. "Now, then, look at this pretty park you have here, Coralee." And, "See that shiny car parked along the curb, son? That's one of them Buicks Floyd Weatherbee's boy makes up in Michigan." And, "Little Earl here went hunting last week with Shelby's boys and brought home five rabbits, and Trudy cooked them into a stew that lasted us clean through supper last night. Isn't that right, son? Your mama used to hunt, so she knows all about rabbits."

This caught Little Earl's attention, so I said, "Tell him, Coralee."

After a moment, Coralee said, "That's right, son."

But Little Earl only crossed his arms and frowned. Finally he said, "Girls don't hunt."

"They do," I said. "Your mama hunted with her brother, Buddy, when she was a girl."

But Little Earl didn't even nod. He just sighed and looked away, and I felt a flash of anger with him then. He was just a boy, I knew, but I wanted this visit to go well so Coralee would have something to hold on to while she was there, and Little Earl would have some good memories to recall when he got to missing her good. I knew he did, too, because sometimes he'd still call for her in his sleep.

Finally, I let him go off and chase a squirrel up a tree while I pulled out our picnic and served up our plates so we could eat instead of talk, and I was glad to see that even if Coralee didn't have much to say, she still had a good appetite. She'd always been a good eater when she wasn't on some church starving jag.

"Trudy made your favorite rhubarb cobbler for our dessert, Coralee. Wasn't that nice of her?" I said, but she just stared at it while I served it up and then ate what I heaped on her plate.

For months I had waited for this visit. And my biggest fear had been that she'd be too angry to speak to me. But it wasn't anger that was keeping her quiet. Something terrible was wrong with Coralee, and when the time came to take her back, I asked to speak to Miss Etta.

"Something is wrong with my wife," I told her. "She's not herself."

"A lot of folks say that when they first come to visit," she told me kindly. "It's the medication she's on right now. Just to keep her calm until we can get her stabilized."

"Well," I said. "I appreciate your telling me so, but I can't see how this medication is helping her, to be frank with you."

"The doctors know what they're doing," she told me. "We'll see you two again, now."

"Say goodbye to your mama," I told Little Earl.

"Goodbye, Mama," he said, but he didn't try to hug her.

I said, "Goodbye, Coralee."

"Goodbye," Coralee said, but Miss Etta was already taking her up the stairs. And as she disappeared behind those glass doors, I wondered just what in the hell I had done to my wife.

CORALEE

After Earl and Little Earl left me, Miss Etta walked me back to my room and I lay down on my bed and tried to think. I was so fuzzy-headed it was hard to believe they'd been there. I didn't even know how I felt about their visit. When Miss Etta first told me they were coming, I thought I'd feel anger when I saw Earl and joy when I saw my son. But that whole visit had been like watching them from a distance. I could see them, but it was like looking at them through a window. I could hear them, but their voices seemed far away. Now they were gone, and I felt like they'd never come at all. And I tried to pray then, but it didn't help me none. No matter how long I waited, I did not feel His presence. No matter how hard I listened, I could not hear His call.

Then one day, when it was just me and Libby down in the laundry, I asked her something I'd been wanting to know.

"Are you God-fearing, Libby?"

"I'm man-fearing," she told me. "The man who put me here. The doctors who give you the shock. The law. They're the ones who hurt us worse than any hell, inside this place or out of it. Far as I'm concerned, God's got nothing to do with it."

"But do you believe?" I asked.

"I used to," she said.

"But not now?"

"Oh, Coralee," she told me, "when your family is poor as mine, the only choices you have are ones you wouldn't want to make. All the real choices are made by those same men who decide everything. After I'd been locked up for a while, I realized I'd been living in a cage all my life. Bigger, maybe, but it was still a cage. The only difference inside is they want you so drugged up you can't even feel your own fingertips."

Now, I didn't agree with Libby about God, even if I knew just what she meant about cages. I felt like I was in one living in Mama's house. Like I was in one living with Chess's drinking back in Flint. Like I was in one living without justice for Buddy. Like I was in one when Earl took Little Earl to sleep at the gin at night. Like I was in one when Brother Jeremiah turned me away from the church.

But later, after I thought that over, I got to thinking about what Libby said about being drugged up until you can't feel your own fingertips. Now, I had always taken the medicine they brought me, even after she showed me how to hide it, because I decided that to not take it would be deceitful, and the Lord loves truth. But I had not felt the Lord in so long and wondered then if it was the medicine. So the next day when Miss Etta gave me my pill, I tucked it up in my cheek like Libby said to, and when Miss Etta looked into my mouth, she seemed satisfied, walked back to my door, and closed it behind her.

I took that little pill out from between my cheek and gums and held it in my hand. It was so small. Hard to believe something so tiny could make you move so slow and feel nothing at all. Then I put it in my brassiere, and when they came to get me to work the laundry, I didn't even tell Libby. I just took my bathroom break and flushed it like she said. But right away I had more go in me. I could think more clearly. I could see and hear again like I hadn't in months.

I could feel things again too. I could feel my fear of the shock. I could feel my hate of the guards. I could feel my anger looking at the grim line of Doctor Garvey's mouth. I could feel my sadness at being sent away from Little Earl.

I hoped at least by evening I would be able to feel the Lord. I thought I would climb in bed and feel His peace, take comfort in His shelter, see the bounty He had waiting for me if only I was patient. But instead I fell asleep and had the first dream I'd had since I got there. In it, Earl had let me take Little Earl to an ice cream social at Divine Holiness, and the boy was lapping up that good sweet cold creaminess like it was the next thing to heaven, and when I thanked Brother Jeremiah, he said, "You're mighty welcome, Sister." But his voice sounded all wrong, and when I looked up to see why, his smile wasn't right. His teeth were too big and too white and he had a rattlesnake's tongue, and when I tried to run away, he hit me over the head with the collection plate, and the next thing I knew, I was lying in my bed, sweating and panting, and suddenly I began to cry. It was like a lifetime of tears had dammed up inside me and were all coming out at the same time, and I kept a pillow over my mouth so the guards wouldn't hear me.

It was a warm spring night outside my little window, but I felt a chill go through me as I sobbed into my pillow. Because that dream made me remember something I didn't want to know so badly that I had actually forgotten it: Brother Jeremiah and two men whose voices and faces were blurry, carrying me out of the church and putting me in the back of a car.

"Where are you taking me?" I murmured.

"To the doctor's, Sister, don't you worry." That was Brother Jeremiah.

Then the car stopped, and I felt them lift me up. I thought we were at Doc English's office until I felt myself facedown in the grass and heard the wheels of the car spinning on the gravel as they sped away.

I knew the truth then. Brother Jeremiah had dumped me there in case I died. For so long I didn't want to believe it that I'd lied to Doc English. I'd lied to Judge Harrison. But it was really myself I was lying to so I wouldn't have to know the truth: Brother Jeremiah would do anything, even dump the body of a faith-tester, if it meant keeping himself out of trouble. And maybe Earl really had just been trying to protect me by sending me here, best he could. And what I felt then most of all was how badly I wanted to say this to Earl, who was two hundred miles away, and God only knew when I'd see him again.

LEROY

A fter Cole told me I was just going to have to wait until Sonny was ready to be questioned, the only chance I had to observe Sonny at all were those Sunday afternoons when we still had supper at Cole's. Lulu was fourteen by then, old enough to cook the supper herself, but Mabel had been cooking it for so long that the two of them now worked side by side while I waited in the shade of the back porch with Cole, Caleb, Nicky Joe, and Sonny, our mouths watering as the smell of onions frying or pie baking wafted through the kitchen window. For months, I hoped maybe Cole would change his mind and let me question Sonny, but I knew better than to raise the subject even though Sonny seemed just fine to me.

But eventually my patience paid off, because one Saturday night Cole drove over to our place after supper and asked to speak to me privately. Mabel raised her eyebrows at this, but I stepped outside and closed the door behind me.

"What's up?" I asked.

He said, "Leroy, I'm not happy about any of this mess with Sonny. But he hasn't been the same since that night at the tavern. I been thinking. If the woman in that picture really is Sonny's mother, I feel I owe it to him to help you find her if you can. He was so upset after seeing that photograph, I can't help but feel like he misses her."

"All right," I said.

"Bring that photograph with you tomorrow when you come, and after supper we'll head out to the gin and talk to the boy."

"I just want to ask him a few questions is all."

"You bring the photograph," Cole snapped. "I'll ask the questions."

"Thank you, Cole," I said.

"Don't thank me," Cole said. "I'm doing this for Sonny, not for you."

The next evening after supper was over, Cole asked me and Sonny to come out to the gin with him, and we all took a seat in Cole's office.

"Now, Sonny," Cole said, "you're my friend and my employee and you'll always have a job here long as you want. Understand?"

Sonny nodded.

"I just need to ask you something, and I need you to answer me, best you can."

The boy nodded, a short little bob, almost half a nod, which I knew meant yes, but he looked afraid the way a child looks afraid and doesn't know to hide it. For a young man, he had all the guile of a child.

"You're not in any trouble, and you don't need to be afraid of Leroy neither," Cole said. "He just wants to show you something." So I opened up my briefcase, pulled out the picture from the wall of the tavern, and set it down on Cole's desk.

"Now Sonny, Leroy here says you told him the woman in this photograph is your mama. That true?"

Sonny nodded, but his eyes glistened.

"Okay, then," Cole said. "When's the last time you seen her?"

But Sonny started to cry, so Cole handed him his handkerchief so the boy could wipe his face.

"It's okay, Sonny," Cole said. "You don't have to answer that." Then Cole turned to me and said, "I think we're going to have to slow this down."

When the boy had collected himself, Cole said, "Now, I know I've always called you Sonny," he told the boy, "but I've always wondered—did you ever have another name?"

Sonny bobbed his head yes.

"Is it Frank?" Cole asked, but Sonny shook his head no.

"Is it Billy?" Sonny shook his head again.

"Is it Lewis? Garland? Herman?" After each name, Sonny shook his head. "Is it Vernon? Bobby? Dwayne? Elvey?"

This is going to go on all night, I thought. Then I remembered something. Wally Holmes had come to talk business with Cole one Sunday when we were there for supper, and as they spoke, Sonny kept looking up at them with surprise. Sonny generally didn't take much interest in the folks who came and went, but the way he jerked his head up now and then as Cole had talked to Wally had seemed odd to me.

"Cole." I leaned in and spoke low so Sonny couldn't hear me. "There was a man here a few weeks back who Sonny seemed uncommonly interested in."

"Who was it?" Cole asked.

"Wally Holmes," I said. "Earl Wilkins's boss."

Cole turned back to Sonny and said, "You remember Wally Holmes, Sonny?"

Sonny nodded.

"Did you know him before you came to work for me?" Cole asked.

Sonny shook his head.

"Is *your* name Wally?" Cole asked.

Sonny shook his head, but Cole had his attention now. "Wilson?"

Sonny shook his head harder, like he might burst.

"Wesley?"

"Wuh," Sonny breathed.

"What was that, son?" Cole asked, and I was impressed by Cole's composure. I knew he'd never seen the boy speak before, but you'd never have known it.

"Wuh," Sonny said, louder this time.

"Sorry, Sonny, can you try that again?"

"Wuh . . ." Sonny stammered. "Wuh . . . Wuh . . .Wuh . . ."

"There's no hurry, son," Cole said. "Just take your time."

But Sonny had the bit between his teeth now. "Wuh . . . Wuh . . . Wuh . . . Wi . . . ley."

"Wiley?" asked Cole.

Sonny nodded, but Cole stayed calm.

"Wiley. Well, then, son, you did good. You did real good."

Cole smiled at the boy affectionately. But Cole gave me a look that told me he knew what I was thinking, because he was thinking it too.

Now, *Wiley* wasn't an uncommon name in Green County, but you didn't run across it a lot either. And the coincidence that Sonny had identified his mother as the potential star witness who'd disappeared after Wiley Slocum shot a man underneath the window of her room helped me come up with a theory of what might have happened the day Buddy Harper was shot. Maybe the sheriff had been a patron of Lorna's, and when Lorna had witnessed the murder of Buddy Harper, Wiley got her out of town so she wouldn't have to testify against him. She wasn't protected from testifying against him like his wife was. And since nobody had ever once mentioned that Lorna had a child or was expecting, my guess was that she got pregnant after she'd disappeared, and quite naturally she'd named him after Wiley, who must still have been around at the time. Also, she'd obviously raised the boy since he remembered her.

What I needed now was to find Lorna, and Sonny was the only person who might know where she was. But after Cole got him to tell us his name, the boy was so shaken up that when Cole asked if we should start calling him Wiley, the boy started crying again. So Cole told him we'd go on calling him Sonny and told me that was all the questioning we were going to do for a while.

Still, it occurred to me that there might be a birth certificate on record somewhere for the boy, which might at least tell me when and where he was born. But having no last name for Sonny—Wiley'd hardly have given him his own last name—finding one was going to be like searching for a needle in a haystack. I was going to have to work off Lorna's last name and a rough timeline since bastard children generally took their mother's names.

My best guess was that she gave birth to Sonny within a couple of years after Buddy Harper's death, since Sonny looked to be in his early twenties. But in order to prove that, I'd need his birth certificate, which might take me a while to find, though if Wiley Slocum had anything to do with it, I knew it might never have been filed at all.

Another problem was that I didn't know where Lorna had gone after she disappeared, but if Wiley and Lorna were still together at the time of Sonny's birth, which, given the boy's name, I assumed they must have been, it couldn't have been far, considering his wife, Tillie, probably expected him home at night. And although it seemed unlikely that he'd have kept her so close to home, I decided to start with Green County records and cast a wide net from 1927 to 1931. But there were only four children named Wiley born during that stretch of years, all legitimate, with last names and fathers' occupations to prove it. Still, I did the same for all the counties in Arkansas that surrounded Green: Clay, Randolph, Lawrence, and Craighead. But when a search of all four counties turned up nothing after a month, I was ready to give up.

Still, Green County sat on the state line, and it occurred to me that if the sheriff really wanted to bury the birth of his bastard child, the place to do it was across the state line in Dunklin County, Missouri. It was the only bordering county I hadn't checked, and now that I thought of it, the most obvious. Different state, different jurisdiction.

So I drove to the Dunklin County Courthouse in Kennett the next day. As I flipped through the files, I discovered that in Dunklin County there were twelve birth certificates filed for baby boys named Wiley born between 1927 and 1931. The first few were like the others I'd seen before—married mothers and fathers with places of employment listed. Then I noticed one with a mother's first name listed as Lorna, the first I'd seen with a child named Wiley and a mother named Lorna. But her last name was Hopkins, as was the child's. And that wasn't even the strangest part. The strangest part was that when I looked at the name and occupation of the father, it read *Lewis Hopkins, Deputy Sheriff of Green County, Arkansas.*

BIG EARL

One Friday afternoon I heard a knock on my door. I opened it expecting to see Owen Baker, come to deliver our mail, and I hoped that there might be a new notice from the hospital about a visit with Coralee. It had been months since our last one. But instead it was a young boy I didn't recognize.

"Good afternoon, sir," he said.

"Good afternoon," I replied.

"I'm here on behalf of Brother Jeremiah and the Church of Divine Holiness."

"All right," I said. But I felt a rage start to churn in my belly.

"Our number has grown so much that we must expand in order to house all our brethren. We are trying to raise five hundred dollars so we can do the good work of the Lord. Could you spare a dollar or two?"

I stared at him for a long moment. I could not believe my ears.

"Do you know who I am?" I asked.

"No sir," he said.

"That's clear, or you wouldn't be here," I said. "Now get off my porch and don't you or any of those brethren of yours ever come knocking again."

The boy looked surprised.

"Go on, now. Get," I yelled, and the boy turned and ran. I felt bad then, snapping at a kid. Little Earl had problems enough. He didn't need folks saying his daddy was crazy too.

Still, it burned me up that Brother Jeremiah would send anybody to my door after what he done to my wife. And was aim-
ing to do to others. Still, I took comfort in the fact that there
was no way Brother Jeremiah could raise five hundred dollars from a town as small as Paradise, with folks who mostly
worked in the fields or mills or cotton gins like me.

But a couple of weeks later, Mr. Holmes told me he'd read in
the *Daily Press* that Brother Jeremiah had raised that money
after all. People called it a miracle, but I knew it was stealing,
plain and simple. Stealing from scared, weak, desperate people who needed something to believe in so badly they'd let their
children starve. And I tell you, I could not account for it. And
I knew then that Brother Jeremiah just got to folks somehow.

When I thought about it some more, I realized it was hard to
blame Coralee when so many others had fallen for that man's
song and dance. Maybe I just didn't realize the extent of his
influence. Maybe it seemed like Coralee was the only sucker
when it was my pocket the man was picking. But now so many
other folks had all been made to believe they were helping too.
Doing good. Having faith. Maybe it hadn't been a sign Coralee
was crazy after all.

And the more I thought about this, the more I wished I
could say this to Coralee. But bringing up Brother Jeremiah
might get her worked up. Then too, I had the problem of Little Earl. He hadn't behaved very well on our first visit. Almost
mean to Coralee, if you ask me. So when the notice finally came
that we could visit her again, I sat Little Earl down and said,
"Son, is there a reason you were mad at your mama when we
went to visit her?"

"She didn't answer me," he said.

"That's because of her medication, son. It makes her quiet."

"No," he said, "she didn't answer my letter."

Now this stopped me in my tracks. And I felt terrible then. I had always known that Coralee wouldn't write back to him. All this time he'd been angry at Coralee for something she wasn't even able to do.

"Son," I said, "your mama and me had to leave school to work in the fields. We don't know how to read or write much. I know my numbers and your mama knows some of the Bible. And I'm sure she wanted to write back to you. She just don't know how. So it's me you should be mad at, because I didn't know you'd expect a letter back. And I'm real sorry."

He took this in for a while, and I let him. I wanted to be sure he understood.

Finally, I said, "We can go see her again. Think you can be nicer to her this time?"

"I guess," he said.

"Now, son, you don't have to come, but it'll be a while before you get the chance again."

He was only eleven, and maybe I should've been making the decision for him. But truth be told, I couldn't handle a sick Coralee and an angry Little Earl again, so I had to ask.

But he surprised me by saying, "I'll go."

"Don't come because you think it's what I want."

"I'm not. I want to see her," he said. Then he said, "I miss her."

"I miss her too, son," I said, and I scruffed up his hair. And when the day came to set off for Little Rock, I was hopeful as we drove south together that this time it would be a good visit.

CORALEE

A fter my dream about Brother Jeremiah, I took those pills eagerly when Miss Etta brought them to my room each day. But one morning Miss Etta told me that Earl and Little Earl were coming for another visit, and I thought about the last time they were there. About how I couldn't really see them clearly. Couldn't hear them. Couldn't feel them. So when she handed me my pill, I tucked it up in my cheek, swallowed, opened my mouth for her to see that it was gone. Then she left me to eat and dress.

"I'll be back to get you at noon," she said. "You'll have a picnic lunch with them, just like last time."

But already it was not like last time because I understood then that Earl had sent me here to protect me from Brother Jeremiah, who left me to die of that snakebite, and now I'd have a chance to tell Earl this.

"Somebody looks happy," Miss Etta said when she came back to lead me outside.

When I saw Earl and Little Earl standing there, I did not wait for Miss Etta to lead me over. I went right to them. Earl was watching me like he didn't know what to expect, and I don't know who reached for who first, but soon we were hugging, and it felt so good to have his arms around me.

"Hi, Coralee," he said as he held me, and I could hear the smile in his voice even though I couldn't see his face.

"Hi, Earl," I said, and I could feel tears burn my eyes.

And when I turned to hug Little Earl, I said, "Hi, son," and he let me put my arms around him, and slowly, he hugged me back. He was near as tall as me and looked even more like his daddy than he did the last time. It was a feast for my eyes just to look at him.

When Earl got us settled on the picnic blanket, he said, "How are you feeling, Coralee?"

"All right," I said. "Better now." And I reached out then and ran my fingers through Little Earl's hair, and he smiled when I did it.

"How's school?" I asked him.

So he told me about his friend Caleb, and about catfishing and baseball and how many runs he'd brought in, and even though I didn't know who or what he was talking about, I was just happy to listen. He still sounded like a little boy, but I realized that before long, he'd start sounding like a man.

Finally, he seemed all out of talk, so Earl said, "Son, why don't you open up that picnic basket and show your mama what we brought her to eat." So he unpacked ham sandwiches and coleslaw and fried pies, and we sat there in the sunshine and ate all that delicious food and drank it down with the sweet tea that Earl brought in a thermos, and I was just so glad to be able to really see them, to really hear them speak, to feel how happy I was that they were there.

When we finished eating, Earl said, "Son, why don't you go see if that squirrel is still around here somewhere?" So Little Earl went off to play in the park again, and after he'd gone Earl said, "Coralee, I've got something I need to say to you."

"What's that?"

"I owe you an apology."

"For what?" I asked.

"It's about the church. Now, you recall how upset I was about you donating the grocery money to Brother Jeremiah's funds drive."

"I surely do," I said.

"Well, the church has grown since you left, and Brother Jeremiah just raised five hundred dollars from folks in Paradise to expand the church. Five hundred dollars."

I nodded then, but I didn't know what to say.

"What I'm trying to say, Coralee, is I was tough on you for something Brother Jeremiah gets lots of folks to do. And I'm sorry. I was scared of running out of money."

I took a deep breath then and looked into his blue eyes that were clear and honest and loving. I knew then that that man would never've hurt me intentionally, that he would never've sent me to this place if he wasn't trying to help me.

"Earl," I finally said, thinking of Brother Jeremiah dumping me off in that ditch. "I have something to tell you too."

LEROY

Now, I'd been so absorbed trying to figure out the connection between Sonny and Wiley and Lewis and Lorna, and so busy trying to keep up with my cases at work when I wasn't chasing down leads on Wiley's case, that I'd all but forgotten it was the start of an election year. This wasn't something I was worried about since my seat on the bench had gone unchallenged in the two terms I'd served since my first election ten years earlier, so it came as something of a surprise when I learned that for the first time I'd have someone running against me this year, a man named Cal Overton.

I wasn't overly concerned about this—the man was a newcomer with not much experience. It wasn't until I started seeing his campaign signs in yards that had once displayed mine that I understood that this was what Wiley meant when he said I was making a mistake. Telling Caleb who his parents were, ostracizing Mabel from the Junior League, steering business away from Cole's cotton gin—those were just the start.

How Wiley managed to persuade people was something I never thought much about when he was behind me, but now it seemed to me an incredible feat that he could turn the tide of an entire county somehow. Pretending not to hear any kind word someone said in my defense. Saying, "I must admit, I do like that Cal Overton fellow." Telling someone who was friendly with me, "I'm sure you'll make the right decision." And I understood his power in a fresh way then and knew that I wasn't the only fool who'd fallen for his charm when I took him on as my client all those years ago.

When the election was over, it took me a while to recover from the blow. All I'd wanted in my career was to remain judge of Green County, and I'd never considered a different path since I was a much younger man. Now my only real option was to return to private practice because moving somewhere new to start over again was out of the question. After almost two years of living in Paradise, we couldn't move away from Cole or ask Caleb to start over in a new school. And although I felt humiliated at first, once I got past that, what I mostly felt was relief. I had only a couple more months left of my term, and then I wouldn't have to wonder if I was somehow doing the sheriff's bidding on my cases anymore. Besides, there were two senior lawyers in the area who were looking to retire and promised me they'd send any new clients my way, so I was hopeful I'd soon have a few cases of my own. Mabel and I weren't hard up for money, so I could take my time building up a new practice.

All I had to do was finish up the cases I'd started since Cal Overton would be handling any new ones, so in my considerable free time I started packing up my office at the courthouse, going through old files one by one, dating years back, which I'd moved into my chambers with me when I became judge. Truth be told, I didn't do a very good job keeping things organized. Ten years I'd been in those chambers and there were still files I'd never unpacked. But I didn't want to get rid of anything that I didn't take a look at first, just in case. You never know when something could be useful on down the line.

I went in chronological order, dating back to my first cases. It was funny looking at each one and remembering how each had consumed me. And it made me sad too, looking at those early cases and thinking how much I believed I was doing right back then. I still cared about doing right, of course, but those early cases were divided from the rest of my career by one case, the file for which I found in the bottom of the second box I looked through. It was a plain folder with *Sheriff Wiley J. Slocum* written in my young scrawl.

I held it in my hands a long while. I knew I shouldn't look at it, that it would only stir me up. But I couldn't help but wonder if, twenty years later, presented with the same set of facts, it would look any different to me, so I unclasped the band that held the file together and looked inside.

There was the contract I'd signed to represent Wiley. There were the witness testimonies. There was my letter withdrawing myself from the case due to a conflict of interest, a letter I'd never sent because Mabel had lost our second child that very day. And there were the coroner's report and photographs of Buddy Harper's body, which I had no desire to see again, but they fell out when I opened it. I tried not to look at the images as I collected them, had only really seen them out of the corner of my eye as I gathered them up, and I was just about to close the file when something flickered in the back of my mind.

I did not know Buddy Harper at the time of his death and had only seen him in the photographs that I was sifting through now. I was trying to figure out what was bothering me. A photograph of his hand with the bullet hole in it. His arm, with an exit wound, taken from the back. His chest, a direct shot to the heart if I ever saw one. And finally, the photograph of his face documenting the shot to the left eye, which was mostly covered by the boy's flagging eyelid. But nothing I saw helped. It was something else that was bothering me, but no matter how long I looked at those photographs, I couldn't figure out what it was.

I finally closed the file and moved on, case by case. For days as I loaded boxes and moved them by the trunk load to the new office I'd rented out in downtown Paradise, those coroner's photographs of Buddy Harper kept nagging at me. Finally, I decided it had just been the grisly nature of his death that was bothering me. A thing like that stays with you, I realized, even without you wanting it to, so quite naturally a photograph of the boy whose death I might have let go unavenged would bother me. At least I had tried to do my best by his sister, I thought, even if that hadn't turned out the way I'd hoped it would.

By Sunday morning, I had moved fully into my new office, so when my term as judge was up I could hit the ground running. Then Mabel and me and Caleb headed over to Cole's as usual. Mabel and Lulu were closing in on supper being ready and sent me to fetch Cole and Sonny from the gin out back where they were dealing with some problem or other.

It was dark inside the gin, and I could hardly see a thing after stepping inside out of the sun, but I could hear Cole on the phone in his office.

"Supper's ready," I called out. Then I heard footsteps.

"Hey there, Sonny," I said as he walked toward me. But as he got closer, I finally understood what had been bothering me so much about those autopsy photos. I was staring at the spitting image of Buddy Harper.

BIG EARL

Now, annoyed as I was about that big fundraiser Brother Jeremiah had run, I was still curious to see when the building on the church would start. Every so often I'd even ask around. One day down at Merle's, Charlene told me that she'd heard that Brother Jeremiah had discussed the project with several builders, looking for the right man for the job. Another day Wilber Higby mentioned that Brother Jeremiah was down at the lumberyard in Stillwater, comparing prices with the one in Kennett, across the border.

Then one day I heard a rumor that services at Divine Holiness had been cancelled. Even Laverne Bishop hadn't shown up to let folks in for Bible study like she normally did if Brother Jeremiah was sick, so someone went to her house, which was just down the street, but she didn't answer the door. So some folks drove out to Brother Jeremiah's house, which was so far from Paradise that hardly anybody had seen it, but the door was locked and his car was gone.

At that point the congregation got worried and checked with Doc English, but Doc English said that he'd never heard a word from Brother Jeremiah about his health. Then a few days later, a neighbor needing flour knocked on Laverne Bishop's door, and when she didn't answer, the woman walked around to her backyard. Laverne's garden was getting tall with corn, so she walked over to see if she wasn't out there doing some gardening, and that's when she found her, facedown in the corn rows with a snakebite in her hand.

How long she'd been there was anybody's guess, but by then folks were starting to get suspicious, wondering less about Laverne Bishop's death and more about where their contributions to expand the church had gone. I suspected the congregants all knew Laverne had been bit testing her faith, but of course they denied knowing anything about it. I also suspected everyone in town knew their money was gone for good.

Still, I thought maybe they'd catch the man. He'd only been gone a week when they'd found Laverne Bishop and put the pieces together, and I knew the sheriff's office was on it because Lewis Hopkins had stopped by to speak to me while he was looking for answers.

But a week later when I ran into Lewis on the street and asked how the investigation was going, he said it was over.

"You mean you found Brother Jeremiah?"

"I had a lead," Lewis said. "But he slipped away."

"He wasn't there?"

"It's complicated, Earl," Lewis sighed. "I know you and all the folks that man swindled deserve justice, not to mention Laverne Bishop's folks, but I don't think you're going to get it."

"I'm sorry to hear that, Lewis," I said. "But thank you for trying to get that bastard."

But Lewis said, "I'd like to say you're welcome, Earl, but in this case I can't accept any thanks because I failed you all. I'm real sorry."

But my worries about Brother Jeremiah were soon replaced by new ones when I reported for work the next day because Mr. Holmes asked me to meet him in his office when I finished my shift. The end of the harvest is usually a relief, but it is also the time when cotton ginners are most often laid off, and something about the seriousness in Mr. Holmes's voice made me nervous. So when my shift ended, I walked to Mr. Holmes's office and knocked on the door.

"Earl," he said, "take a seat."

When I was settled, he said, "Buelle Fisher is moving up to Flint to work at General Motors. Nothing's been the same for him since Esther died, and I think he wants a fresh start."

Now this was sad news. I'd worked with Buelle for a long time. I couldn't imagine a better manager. In fact, I worried whoever Mr. Holmes had in mind to replace him wouldn't be near as good as Buelle.

But he said, "So, considering Buelle will be leaving, I've decided to promote you."

"To what?" I asked.

"Earl, are you stupid or just so modest you don't know you'd make a good manager?"

"You want to make me manager?" I said.

"Yes." Mr. Holmes laughed. "That's what I wanted to tell you. I'm promoting you."

"But I can't read," I said. "Or write. You know that."

"But you've got a head for numbers. Besides, you know all the fellows here, and exactly what they do because you've done it yourself, and they all respect you for it. We'll figure the rest out. Now what do you say?"

"I say yes," I told him, and we both smiled and shook hands. And then he explained the position, and that it came with a bigger salary, and sent me on my way.

Well, I was thrilled about the raise, of course, I'd been living so close to the bone all my life. But more important than that raise even was that I had never known what it felt like to have someone say you're good at something. Value what you do. See you're important in your way. Neither did I know that good news can make you cry, but the tears that fell as I drove home felt different than other tears. They felt like relief, and I didn't even try to wipe them away, just let them drip onto my overalls in the wind, I felt so good.

But when I got home, I wiped my face and blew my nose and prepared to walk into the house. And when I stepped inside, Little Earl was bent over his homework at the table.

I said, "Hi, son."

"Hi, Daddy," he said.

"How was school?"

"Good," he said. "Caleb's coming over in a few minutes. We're going fishing."

"They should be jumping by now," I said, looking at my watch.

Now, Little Earl was too young to think about asking how my day went. He was just a boy. But this promotion was the biggest thing that ever happened to me, and here I was home with nobody to tell. So I poured myself a tall glass of sweet tea Trudy had left in a pitcher in the icebox and sat down on the porch, trying to take it all in. But having nobody to share my good news with, I felt lonelier in that moment than I had since Coralee left.

I was still sitting there when Leroy Harrison pulled into my driveway to drop off Caleb, and those two boys took off so fast down the path through the field out back that neither of them bothered saying goodbye, which left Leroy and me on our own.

"Want some tea?" I asked.

"I'd love some," he said, and when I came back with a glass for him, he'd taken a seat on the porch.

"I was sorry to hear about the election," I told him. "It don't make no difference, I suppose, but I voted for you." Mr. Holmes had shown me how to fill out the ballot, and I figured it was the least I could do for a man who'd done so much for my boy.

"I appreciate that, Earl," the judge said.

"What comes next?"

"I'll go back to the law. I can't tear Caleb and Mabel away from Cole and his family in any case, even if I wanted to move."

"Makes sense," I said.

"Speaking of family, how's your wife?" he asked me.

"Hard to say," I told him. "Our first visit, they had her on some kind of drug that slowed her way down, but she was a little better this time. She also told me the truth about what happened to her when she was bit by that snake."

"Which was what, exactly?" he asked me.

"What I thought. She was testing her faith. And when she got bit, Brother Jeremiah and his boys dumped her in Wilber Higby's ditch."

"That's quite a turnaround from her testimony," he said.

"It is," I said. "But I always knew that's what happened."

"Why did she lie on the stand, then?" he asked.

"She says she couldn't recall it, but she woke up one night and it all came back to her. She said it after I told her about Brother Jeremiah's fundraiser."

"Hard to believe he got folks to give so much when most of them make so little," he said. "It doesn't make sense."

"I know it," I told him. "But it got me thinking. I thought Coralee was crazy to give him so much money, but maybe she's no crazier than the rest of these folks who did the same thing."

"What are you saying, Earl?" he asked.

"It all got me thinking that maybe Coralee is a little more together, you might say. More there. To do something so many other folks have done."

"How does she seem to you otherwise?" he asked.

"Well, she remembered the truth, for one thing. Admitted she was wrong, for another. You don't know my wife, but Coralee don't like being wrong."

The judge sat for a while just drinking his tea. Finally he said, "Earl, I need to ask you a favor, and it's no easy thing considering my history with your wife's family."

"I'm happy to help if I can."

"I need a photograph of Coralee's brother, Buddy. Do you have one?"

"What do you need it for?" I asked.

"I'd rather not say yet, if you don't mind. But I promise I wouldn't ask if I didn't think I might be able to do some good for your wife's family."

"Coralee has an album inside," I said, and went to get the one she kept in her bedstand. I flipped through the photographs until I came to the one of Buddy.

"Here it is," I said.

Leroy looked at the photograph for a long time. Finally, he said, "Look, Earl, would you mind if I borrowed this for a few days?"

"Just don't lose it," I said. "Coralee would kill me."

"I'll take good care of it," he told me as he stood to leave. "And I'll have this back to you as soon as possible."

CORALEE

After Earl and Little Earl left, the echoes of Earl's loving words and Little Earl's happy chatter hurt me so much I cried all night. So when Miss Etta finally brought my medication the next morning, I snatched up that pill and swallowed it without any water, I was so eager for the nothingness to take me.

I honestly don't know what I'd have done in that place without Libby. On top of always being so kindly to me, she taught me all kinds of secret things I needed to know to get by inside that place. Not just how to hide my medication when I didn't want to take it, but also to say please and thank you to the doctors who I met with, even the ones who had given me the shock, and to never, ever let them see you cry.

But Ruth and Ester were with us almost all the time in the laundry, so these talks were few and far between. Mostly we all talked about who we knew in common and who'd arrived and who'd gone home. We talked about the guards and the orderlies and the doctors. But we did not talk about ourselves unless it was just me and Libby, so I always waited and hoped and prayed for those moments when it was just the two of us down there.

One day when it was, I asked her where Ruth and Ester were.

"Ester's sick," she said. "But Ruth went home. I'm sorry to have to be the one to tell you, Coralee. I heard they didn't even tell her until this morning. That's how they do it," she said. "They don't like folks talking about going home. It just works everybody up."

"How long was she here?" I asked Libby.

"You know, I have no idea," Libby said. "How long you been here, Coralee?"

I had to think. I could only really measure time if I thought about Earl's visits.

"About a year and a half, I think," I said. "Maybe more."

"A year and a half." She whistled, and she must've thought that was a long time. Then she said, "I been here almost six now. And before that, I was in Jacksonville for two."

I must've looked sad, because Libby touched my arm. "It ain't so bad, Coralee. My life wasn't much to begin with. I wasn't like you, with a husband and a child to go back to."

"Why'd they move you here?" I asked.

"They got overfull."

"Isn't Jacksonville for criminals?" I asked.

"It is," she said. "But I'm no criminal."

"How'd you end up there?"

"I was arrested for disturbing the peace. Later, I found out there was a long list of other charges on my intake form, things I never even did. I tried to tell the doctors, but nobody listens when they think you're crazy."

"Did you really disturb the peace?" I asked. Libby wasn't one to make a fuss.

"I'd had a letter from my sister. I hadn't heard from her in so long, everyone thought she was dead. But some neighbors saw me crying by the mailbox, and by evening word had spread and folks were standing around my yard rejoicing. Someone opened a bottle of moonshine, and the next thing I knew, I was in the back of a police car, on my way to Jacksonville."

"Where you from, Libby?" In all the time I'd known her, I realized I'd never asked.

"Dodgeville, born and raised. You?"

"Paradise," I said. "It's pretty small. You might not have heard of it."

"My sister lived there for a while."

"Maybe I knew her," I said.

"I doubt it," she said. "She didn't live there more than a year, but the man she was engaged to lived there all his life."

"I must know him," I said. "What's his name?"

Libby said, "Did you ever know a man named Buddy Harper?"

———————

Now, this news about Buddy and Libby's sister, Lorna, like to knock me flat. It took weeks for me to get my arms around it. But Libby and me talked about them whenever we got the chance to be alone, and finally it began to sink in. Then one morning, Miss Etta came in with a dress and shoes and said, "Coralee, you've got a visit from your husband today." And when she handed me my pill, I hid it again instead of swallowing it. Later she came back to lead me out to where Earl was waiting. He was holding a picnic basket in one hand and a bouquet of flowers in the other.

"Where's Little Earl?" I asked him.

"He's got school today," he told me. But I was disappointed not to see my boy.

Earl hugged me close, then handed me the flowers.

"Coralee, do you know what these flowers are?"

"I surely do," I told him. "They are beet flowers."

"They're from your garden," he said. "I looked out there and saw a line of leaves coming up, all in a row. You didn't sneak home and plant those beets on me, now, did you?"

"No," I said.

"You sure?" He grinned.

"It was me," I told him then, but I couldn't help smiling. Earl might've known everything there was to know about cotton, but that man never understood the mystery of a garden.

"You're pulling my leg," he said.

"The flowers come after two years if you don't harvest beets."

"Coralee, you got to get well so you can come home and tend your beets."

"Too late for tending," I told him as he spread out the blanket. "Just save the seeds."

"Maybe you'll be home to save them yourself," he said. "You seem better to me."

"I feel better," I told him. "I even have news."

"That so?" Earl said.

"There's a girl here from Dodgeville named Libby. She told me her sister, Lorna, was engaged to Buddy."

I could see Earl's face fall as I talked. Finally, he said, "Coralee, wouldn't you know if your own brother was engaged?"

"Folks said Lorna was a fancy girl," I told him. "Mama would've died. She was mad at him as it was."

"Well," Earl finally said, "how about that." Then he opened the picnic basket, but I knew it wasn't because he was hungry. It was because he knew I couldn't talk about Libby or Buddy with a mouth full of cornbread. Oh, he talked about Little Earl's marks at school and Mr. Holmes having trouble with a couple of folks he'd hired at the gin, and said again how much he hoped I'd be home in time to plant my beets. But I knew better than to bring up Libby or Buddy, even if it was the only thing I wanted to talk about, and after feeling so good when he first got there, by the time he left, I felt all alone with my news, almost as if Earl hadn't heard a single word I said.

LEROY

After Earl Wilkins loaned me the picture of Buddy Harper, I didn't stop and think. I drove over to Cole's and knocked on the front door.

"Leroy?" he asked, but Lulu and Nicky Joe were standing there so I said, "Can we speak privately?"

A look of annoyance crossed Cole's face.

"Five minutes," I said. "I've got something I want to show you."

He led me out onto the back porch and sat down.

"This better be good, Leroy," he said.

I handed him the photo Earl Wilkins had lent me of Buddy Harper, and I saw Cole start.

"Why, that's Sonny," he said.

"No," I said. "That photograph is too old to be Sonny."

"Who is it, then?"

"It's Buddy Harper," I said. "The man the sheriff shot when I represented him. I think he's Sonny's father."

Cole stared at the photograph for a long time, and although I expected him to dismiss this the way he dismissed most things I said about Sonny, he surprised me by saying, "Couldn't be anybody else."

"No, I don't think it could be," I said. "Which means that Lorna Lovett was Sonny's mother and Buddy Harper was his father, and if Sonny's given name was Wiley, I've got motive for why the sheriff shot Buddy Harper in cold blood."

Cole took this in for a while. Finally he said, "Let's say you're right, Leroy. I don't have to be a lawyer to know that you can't prove Wiley murdered Buddy Harper over Lorna Lovett based on a photograph."

"No," I said, "but if Sonny knows where Lorna is, she might be able to confirm it."

"Listen, Leroy, I didn't even know that the boy could speak, and he's still shaken up. He slept for three days straight and hasn't made a peep since. We need to back off for a while."

"How long should we wait?" I asked.

"Until Sonny starts talking on his own. He's got to come to it in his own time."

"All right," I said, because I knew Cole had a point. "We'll wait." But I didn't like it one bit.

We stood up then and Cole saw me out the front door. But as I said my goodbyes and started down the steps to my car, Cole stepped out onto the front porch after me.

"Leroy," he said. "I got a question for you."

"What's that?" I asked.

"If Sonny looks so much like Buddy Harper, how come nobody else has noticed?"

I had to think about this. Finally, I said, "Do you remember what Daddy looked like?"

"Sure," Cole said.

"No, I mean, really, exactly what he looked like. Can you picture his features?"

Cole was silent for a moment. Then he said, "Not exactly."

"Me neither," I said. "I can only remember him well if I look at that photograph of him Mama used to keep on her dresser. And photographs are few and far between for anybody who can't afford them. I expect most folks have forgotten exactly what that boy ever looked like."

"Fair enough," Cole said. Even so, his question gnawed at me as I drove home that night, and by the time I reached the house, I realized why.

He won't talk to me, Coralee Wilkins had told me the night Earl held me at gunpoint and drove me to the field where I sat with her while she cried. *My own brother won't talk to me.* And at the time, this made no earthly sense to me. But now I had to wonder if perhaps she wasn't quite as crazy as she sounded, because I understood then that maybe it wasn't her brother's hallucination that wouldn't talk to her. Maybe it was her brother's son, and maybe the reason he wouldn't talk to her wasn't because he didn't want to. It was because he didn't know how.

I needed to return those photographs of Buddy Harper and Lorna Lovett if I didn't want to raise any suspicions around town. But I also needed them for evidence. And I couldn't exactly go waving them around Green County, asking for copies. So I'd called across the state line until I found a photographer in Kennett who specialized in reproductions.

"How old are they?" he asked me when I told him what I needed.

"Pretty old. Twenty years, maybe."

"Depends on the quality of the film, then." But when I made the long drive to his shop and handed them across the counter, all he did was eyeball the photograph of Buddy and peek under the frame on the photograph of Lorna to look at the paper stock.

"I'll try my best," he said.

"How long before they're ready?"

"Couple of weeks?" he'd said. But it was a month of worry

before he finally called to tell me they'd come out perfectly, which was such a relief I left work that very morning and drove over to pick them up. They were packaged up nicely and waiting for me on the counter along with the originals, and although the bill was even more than I'd bargained for, I paid it gladly. I was thrilled to be able to return the photos to Earl and Charlie and planned on doing it as soon as I got home.

I stopped by the house first and put on my raincoat, hot as it was, because I wanted to hide the photograph of Lorna inside it in case Charlie's new boss at the tavern was around. I didn't want to get him in trouble for lending it to me. But when I stepped inside the tavern, I noticed something more alarming than Charlie's new boss. It was Lewis Hopkins, the man listed as Sonny's father on Sonny's birth certificate and Wiley's first in command. So instead of hanging the photograph, I sat down next to him and ordered a beer.

"Isn't it kind of hot for that raincoat, Leroy?" he asked me.

"Isn't it against the law to drink in uniform?" I shot back.

"Don't matter," he said sadly.

"Bad day at work?" I asked.

"Last day at work," he said.

"Don't tell me you quit. You're the finest officer in Green County."

"Not according to the powers that be."

"Slocum?" I asked.

He took a long slug from the glass in front of him. "You know, I always knew the man was a real shit. How I worked for him for so long is beyond me."

"You don't have to tell me," I said.

"No, Leroy, I expect I don't. He sure got you good."

"He did," I said. "Time was I thought the man made me."

"The sheriff giveth," Lewis said, "and the sheriff taketh

away. When does that Cal Overton fellow take your seat, anyway? A week?"

"A little less than two," I said. "Then it's back to private practice."

"I'll be joining you there myself," Lewis said.

"You got something lined up already?

"You are looking at the future Lewis Hopkins, Private Eye. Gonna start slow, go off on my own line."

"I might have something for you," I said.

"You got a job for me already?" He leaned toward me so far I thought he was going to fall over, and that's when I could smell the bourbon on his breath.

"Maybe," I said. Wiley and Lewis could still make it up, and then I'd be high and dry. If not, my guess was that Lewis would be a wealth of information about both Wiley and Lorna.

"How about that," Lewis told Charlie. "Haven't even put my shingle out yet, and Leroy here wants to hire me."

"Sounds like you're in business," Charlie said.

I drained my glass. "I'll be in touch," I told Lewis.

"You do that," Lewis said, then drained his own glass and turned to Charlie. "I need another."

"That's up for debate," Charlie said.

But by the time I'd settled my bill, Lewis had put his head down on the bar and was snoring softly, so on my way to the door I took the photograph from inside my jacket and hung it on the wall as I slipped out.

My next stop was Earl Wilkins's house. He was sitting on the porch when I pulled in his driveway, and he stood to greet me, then invited me up for a glass of sweet tea.

"I wanted to thank you for lending this to me," I said as I

gave the photograph of Buddy Harper back to him. "Sorry I had it so long. I had a copy made, and the photographer took a while to get it back to me."

"Was it any help?" he asked.

"Yes, it was," I said. "I think it might be helpful to your wife's family at some point."

"Helpful how?" Earl said.

"Do you know the mute boy who works for my brother? Cole calls him Sonny."

"I've seen him before, sure."

"Well, he looks exactly like your wife's brother here."

Earl looked at the photograph. "He does look like him, now that you mention it."

"The reason I asked to borrow the picture is because I think he's Buddy's son."

Earl looked surprised. "With who?"

"Do you remember a girl named Lorna Lovett? Used to live over the tavern?"

"Funny," he said, "my wife just mentioned her."

Now I was itching to leap on this nugget, but instead I asked, "How is your wife?"

"Better in some ways," he said. "But she still talks nonsense about Buddy."

"I thought you said she was talking about Lorna."

"She tried to tell me Buddy was engaged to Lorna. Seems to think she's locked up down there with Lorna's sister. Some girl named Libby who got a letter from Lorna years after she disappeared. I figured it was one of Coralee's made-up folks. But if Lorna and Buddy had a child, maybe she's telling the truth."

Buddy Harper was engaged to Lorna Lovett was all I could think. I wanted to jump off Earl's porch then and throw my hat in the air. I wanted to shout to the world that I now had proof of motive. But instead I said, as calmly as I could, "Why don't you give me some time to look into this for you, Earl? Meantime, I'd appreciate it if you kept this under your hat."

"Don't worry," he told me as I stood to go. "I'd like to forget the whole mess."

I pulled out of his driveway real slow, until I was far enough away that he couldn't see me anymore. Then I burned rubber all the way to Stillwater to dig around in the county records. I'd been in the basement of the courthouse nearly two hours when I finally found a 1944 citation for a Libby Lovett from Dodgeville for disturbing the peace. And at the bottom of the citation was the signature of the arresting officer: *Sheriff Wiley Slocum.*

It was a long drive down to Little Rock the next day, so I left without waking Mabel. This was my chance at charging Wiley with the murder of Buddy Harper, and I was not going to let it slip through my fingers. But I was only judge of Green County a few days longer, and if I was going to pull some strings, I needed to act fast.

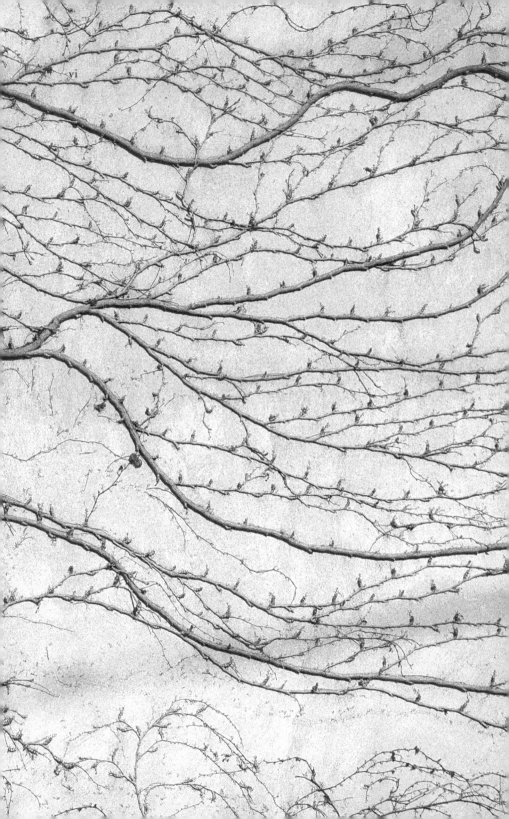

PART III

BIG EARL

One day shortly after my visit with Coralee, an envelope arrived from the hospital. It looked just like the ones that I usually got when it was time for a visit, but that made no sense. I'd only just been. Still, I took it to Mr. Holmes the next day to have him read it for me. Little Earl could read most things, but anything to do with Coralee I wanted to know first myself, in case something went wrong. But when Mr. Holmes opened the letter, a smile spread across his face. He said, "It's good news, Earl. Coralee is coming home."

Now, you could've knocked me over with a feather when he told me this. Every time I drove down to visit Coralee in Little Rock, I thought maybe Miss Etta might give me an update, but not one time in over two years had she ever said a word to me about how Coralee was coming along. So I could not believe my ears when Mr. Holmes told me the news. I had no warning. Wondered, sure. Hoped, of course. But when it finally sunk in, I felt lighter, walked faster, did my work that day with a smile on my face.

But by the time I got home that night, I realized there were things I had never told Coralee to protect her. One thing was that Coralee's mama was real sick, and although she was holding on still, Doc English said it was only a matter of time. Then there was the possibility that Cole's mute boy, Sonny, might be Buddy's son. Not to mention Brother Jeremiah's fraud and Laverne Bishop's death.

Then, of course, there was Little Earl. Now, I knew how much that boy missed his mama, but I didn't know what he'd be like with her when she came home for good. So that night, I told Little Earl over supper that I had some news.

"What news?" he said.

"Your mama's coming home on Friday," I said.

"For a visit?" he asked, and I realized that's how he thought things worked. All we'd ever done was visit Coralee. Maybe he thought she could visit us too.

"Not for a visit," I told him. "For good."

When he didn't say anything, I said, "How do you feel about your mama coming home?"

"Is she really better?" he asked.

"They say she is," I said.

When he still didn't answer me, I said, "It's okay not to know, son. We just got to take it as it comes."

When the day came for me to go pick her up, I asked Little Earl if he wanted to come with me, but he just said, "I'll see her soon."

Now, this was true enough. And maybe it was better I went alone. But it made me sad to know what all this had done to Little Earl. He'd loved his mama so much as a boy. And he'd been so sad when she went away I didn't think he'd ever smile again for a while, until Caleb Harrison came along and cheered him up.

So that Friday, I drove down to the hospital alone. Miss Etta met me in the building where they told me to go.

"Where's Coralee?" I asked.

"She'll be along shortly," she told me. "Right now, I'm going to take you to meet with Doctor Garvey."

Now, I'd never been inside the building where Coralee stayed, and as Miss Etta walked me to Doctor Garvey's office, I heard a terrible wail coming from the end of a hallway. Down another, someone was shouting words that made no sense. I passed a room where a woman gripped the bars on the door and shook it, and I shuddered to think this was where Coralee had been all this time.

When we finally reached Doctor Garvey's office, I felt nervous. The only doctor I'd ever talked to was Doc English, who was so much like the rest of us that I never worried he'd think I was simple. Now I felt ashamed of my overalls and work hat. Embarrassed that I couldn't read. Frustrated that I hadn't been able to help Coralee, which is why she came here in the first place.

"Mr. Wilkins," he said, and stood to shake my hand across the table. "I thought we might discuss what needs to happen once your wife is home."

"Okay," I said.

"She's going to need rest. Not too much activity, not too many folks around. She'll need time to adjust to the change of environment. If you can help make her transition as peaceful as possible, that would be a great help to her."

"It's just me and my boy," I told him. "We don't have a lot of visitors. Maybe her mama will want to see her, and her sister."

"That's fine. Just not every day, and not for too long."

"Can she leave the house?"

"It would be good for her to get some fresh air."

"She has her garden," I told him.

"That's fine as long as she doesn't overdo it."

"All right," I said, and I thought we were finished.

"There's one more thing," he said. "Your wife must take her medication every day, but you'll have to check her mouth to see if she's swallowed it."

When I didn't say anything, he folded his hands and said, "I can see you're having some trouble with this."

"It just seems," I said, "well, it kind of seems liked I'd be accusing her of doing something wrong even if she ain't."

He smiled then and nodded, like he'd had this conversation before.

"What you have to understand, Mr. Wilkins, is that the only way your wife can stay out of here for good is if she takes her medication. We've found a good drug for her. But she has to take it or she'll end up right back here. I'm sure you don't want that."

"No sir," I said. "And I will make sure she takes it."

"Good, then," he said. "I'm glad we understand each other." He stood then and opened his office door. "Now, if you'll follow me, we can go meet your wife."

———

Coralee was sitting on a bench outside with Miss Etta. And my god, did she look beautiful. Maybe it was because I knew she could come home with me now that I could see it. Maybe I couldn't let myself see how beautiful she was on those short visits because it would've hurt so much knowing I had to leave her behind. But now, sitting there with the sun shining down on her hair, knowing I'd be driving home with Coralee by my side, I'd never seen a woman look so good in all my life.

"She's ready to go," Miss Etta told me. "Have a good drive now." Then Miss Etta and Doctor Garvey said goodbye to Coralee, Doctor Garvey shook my hand, and they left me and Coralee alone. It was the first time I'd been with her knowing I didn't have to return her to nobody. And I couldn't wait to get out of there, but Coralee didn't stand up when she saw me, so I sat down beside her.

"Are you glad to be coming home?" I asked her.

"Yes," she said, and smiled faintly.

"Then what's wrong?" I asked. "I figured you'd have made a run for the truck by now."

"They didn't let me say goodbye to Libby."

"Why not?"

"Libby says they never let anybody know until the day they're leaving. She says they don't want folks making a fuss."

"I'm real sorry," I told her. "That's a shame."

When she didn't answer me, I said, "You ready to go now, Miz Coralee?"

She smiled then, and I took her hand. I could tell by the way she held mine back that she was ready, so I helped her into the truck, climbed in beside her, and finally drove her home.

CORALEE

Outside, everything moved so fast. From the minute Earl picked me up, I noticed it. I hadn't been off the grounds of the asylum in probably two years, and I swear during that time everything sped up. The highway was full of cars that zoomed past us. Even Earl seemed to drive faster than I remembered. And Little Earl talked with amazing speed when we pulled into the driveway.

When Earl got me unpacked, I went to the kitchen window to look out at my garden. Earl was right that it had gone to ruin while I'd been away, but I saw the green and purple shoots growing in a row and leaned in to take a closer look.

"Those're them beets I told you about," Earl said behind me. "Now you're here to save the seeds yourself." And he seemed so happy that it was hard not to feel happy too.

Even so, I couldn't think of anything to do. Nothing growing in my garden. Trudy had done the cooking and laundry for days, Earl said, so I'd have time to settle in. And Little Earl was so big now. That little boy who sobbed on the porch watching Lewis Hopkins haul me off had learned to do most things for himself now. And Earl had told me about Laverne Bishop and Brother Jeremiah driving home, so I couldn't have gone back to church even if I'd wanted to.

When Little Earl left to go fishing, Earl came to sit beside me.

"How are you feeling, Coralee? Is it good to be home?"

"It is," I said. "But I don't know what to do with myself."

"Well," Earl said. "I wondered if maybe you'd like to see your mama tomorrow. I didn't want to tell you before now because there wasn't anything you could've done about it, but your mama's sick. She's been sick for some time with the cancer. Doc English says she probably don't have much time left."

I thought about this for a while. I didn't know how to feel about Mama being sick. But I said, "Does she still go to First Baptist with Shelby?"

"She does," he said. "But Shelby's got a new baby, so she's too busy to do more than walk her there. I thought maybe you'd like to go with her tomorrow."

"Mama can't walk?"

"She can," he said. "She just needs a little help."

Now this was something I could do. I was needed.

"I'll go," I told Earl. "I'll take her to church."

I didn't sleep well that night, but the next morning after my bath, I opened up my closet and saw all those clothes I'd clean forgot about. Dresses I hadn't worn in two years. But when I took them down, they looked like dresses that belonged to some other woman, so I put on one I'd had with me while I was away because it felt familiar. And just then, everything around me—my husband, my child, my life—felt so strange that anything familiar was a relief.

Little Earl had gone off to play with some school friend of his, so Earl drove me to Mama's on his way to the gin, which was open on Sundays during harvest. I told him he was breaking the Sabbath and the Lord would not approve, but he just said, "Coralee, if the Lord wanted us to rest on Sundays, he wouldn't make it rain Wednesdays during harvest." Then he said he'd see me later at home. When I knocked on the door,

Mama opened it, and I was shocked. She looked sickly. Her skin was almost gray. She smiled when she saw me, but she didn't try to hug me. Mama was never one for comfort. And I made up my mind to try harder with Little Earl, to make sure he knew how much I cared for him.

"Coralee," Mama said when she saw me. "Earl told me you were home. Thank you for coming to walk me to church. Shelby's so busy with them kids she just don't have the time anymore. After all those boys, she finally has a baby girl. I don't know how in the world the child keeps going."

I realized as Mama chattered away that she was never going to ask me how I was. She was acting just like she did when I came home from Flint all those years ago, like I was just back from a jaunt somewhere and she didn't want to know about it. I also knew that this was how Mama had always been, and I couldn't decide if I was relieved or sad. Not that I would've talked about it. But it hurt that she seemed not to care.

Even so, she took my arm as we stepped off the porch, and we started to walk to First Baptist. It felt strange not to be walking to Divine Holiness. It felt stranger knowing Brother Jeremiah had skipped town, and that it might've been me that died instead of Laverne Bishop. And it felt stranger still when we got to the church and I stepped inside. It was so different than Divine Holiness. It had real pews and a pretty altar and lectern. By the time I got Mama seated and sat down myself, a preacher appeared and said, "Welcome, welcome. So glad you could all be here today."

He was so different from Brother Jeremiah. Younger by a little. Quieter by a lot. Brother Jeremiah had a booming voice you felt in your chest. This one had a voice that was softer. Which made it seem like he cared less, felt the Holy Spirit less, called forth the Lord less. And because of this, I feared we might feel Him less at first.

But as I sat there listening, I saw that in his quiet sort of way, he was leading us to a God I hadn't known before. As he read from the book of Job and talked about Job's crops being destroyed, his children killed, his boils and sores, and how Job took it all because he had so much faith, there was a kind of music in his voice, and I felt something for the first time that I had never felt in church. I felt calm.

I did not know that God could feel so calm. I thought God was fierce. I thought you had to shout when the Holy Spirit moved you. I thought you had to let Him roll you. But in this church nobody rolled, and I have to admit that I was glad of that, because after getting the shock, I did not want nothing to run through my body again. Folks called out on occasion, but after Pastor Samuel's sermon was over, I noticed my nerves weren't all jangly like they always were after one of Brother Jeremiah's.

On our way out the door, Mama introduced us.

"Pastor Samuel," Mama said. "This is my daughter, Coralee."

"It is nice to meet you, Coralee," he said, taking my hand. "Glad you could join us today." And when he smiled, I could tell there was nothing but simple gladness there.

I thought about the difference between Pastor Samuel and Brother Jeremiah as Mama and I walked home. Pastor Samuel stood aside and showed you the way to the Lord. But Brother Jeremiah blocked your view. And I realized then that all that time I'd spent at Divine Holiness, I'd been breaking the first commandment. The whole time I'd been at Divine Holiness, I had been putting Brother Jeremiah before the Lord.

LEROY

When I got home near midnight after my drive down to Little Rock, I was surprised to see Mabel sitting up in the living room when I walked in.

"What are you doing up, Mabel?" I asked her.

"Waiting on you," she said, and her voice was so hard I knew trouble was coming.

"Sorry I'm so late," I said. "I had to go to Little Rock today."

"What for?" she asked.

"An old case," I told her. "Something important's come up." I'd never told her about my suspicions about Sonny or that I was on Wiley's tail because I wanted to have all the facts before I did.

"Well, Leroy, it must have been important because you missed Caleb's birthday."

"Oh, God," I said. I had completely forgotten. I'd been out the door too early that morning for Mabel to remind me, but the truth is I should have remembered it myself. The week before I'd even driven to Stillwater and bought Caleb a new fishing pole he'd been wanting, with a tackle box full of fancy lures. And I'd looked forward to seeing his face when he opened it. But I'd missed it all. I'd missed everything.

"You know, Leroy, if I didn't know you better, I'd think you had a woman on the side."

I sat down next to her and reached for her, but she pulled away.

"There's no woman on the side," I said.

"I know there isn't," she said. "But there might as well be for the amount of time you spend out at night. Now, what is going on with you?"

"What do you mean?" I asked, but I knew damn well what she meant.

"You don't eat. You don't sleep. You forget Caleb's birthday. And even when you do grace us with your presence, you're so preoccupied you may as well not bother. On top of which," she added, "you look like something the cat dragged in."

"I'm not as young as I used to be," I said.

"You're also not as old as you look. Now, something's going on, and you better tell me what it is."

Right then, I felt the weight of all the months of chasing after Wiley catch up with me, and suddenly I felt unbearably tired. And I knew Mabel was right. I felt terrible. I looked worse. And I hadn't been a good father or husband or even lawyer lately either, something that hurt me more than I could say to Mabel.

"I haven't told you because you'll think I'm crazy."

"I already think you're crazy, Leroy. Your new job seems to be the full-time observation of Cole's mute boy, Sonny."

"It is in a way," I told her. "But I'm doing this for us."

"Now how's that?" she asked.

"It has to do with an old case."

"Something to do with Sonny?" she asked.

"Something to do with Wiley," I said.

"That is an old case, then," Mabel told me.

"Wiley was guilty. I'd have dropped out as his lawyer, but I couldn't."

Mabel sat right up. "You could have cited any number of reasons to get out of it."

"That wasn't the only reason," I said. "I've never told you because I did it to protect us. To protect you."

"What have I got to do with Wiley Slocum?" she asked.

"I'll show you," I said.

I had my briefcase with me, with all my files on Wiley in it. I'd begun to carry them everywhere with me, I was so afraid of losing them, so I opened up the old file on the Buddy Harper case and found the letter I'd written all those years ago but never sent, withdrawing from the case. It was yellowed and faded with age.

"Read this," I said, handing it to Mabel.

When she was finished, she said, "Why did you never send it?"

"Look at the date," I told her. It hurt me to have to do this, but it was the only way for her to understand.

"So what?"

"Look again," I said, and this time I could see it register in her face. She set the letter down, and I could see her fighting mightily against tears, but she couldn't beat them.

"I got the call from the doctor just as I finished typing this up," I told her gently. "And I couldn't drag you through the scandal. Not after having seen you lose the first baby. I was afraid we'd have to move away, and I just didn't want to uproot you at a time like that."

Mabel cried so long I realized she was still grieving for those lost babies. I thought Caleb had filled that hole for her, but I understood then that even though those babies had never breathed a single breath, had never cried or laughed or smiled one time, Mabel had shaped a whole person out of the idea of each of them and seen our life play out with them as they grew up, long before she lost them.

Mabel's voice cracked when she finally said, "Leroy, why does this even matter anymore?"

"Because I think I've found motive that Wiley was guilty."

"What's that?" she said.

"I think Sonny was the motive."

"Does Wiley even know Sonny?"

"I think he used to know him really well. I think he thought he was Sonny's father."

"How can you possibly know that, Leroy?"

"I don't know it for sure," I said. "But Sonny's started talking a little, and when Cole asked him what his real name was, he told us it was Wiley."

"Oh, Leroy," she said, looking at me like she honestly felt sorry for me. "There are a hundred boys named Wiley. That's not proof of anything."

"Look here," I said. I opened my briefcase and took the packaging off the box of copies the photographer in Kennett had made. The one of Buddy was on top, and it was a good copy too, I noticed, so clear it could have been the original if the paper stock wasn't so new.

When I showed it to her, she looked surprised. "Is that Sonny?"

"It's Buddy Harper."

Mabel took in this news slowly.

"And you think . . ."

"Yes," I said. "That's what I think."

"And the mother?"

"The prostitute who used to live above the tavern, Lorna Lovett. She went missing the day Buddy Harper was shot."

After a while, Mabel said, "It's certainly an odd coincidence that the boy's name is Wiley and he looks just like the man Wiley shot."

"It's more than a coincidence," I told her. "That's what I've been trying so hard to prove."

"Oh Leroy," Mabel sighed. "What difference can that possibly make now? Buddy Harper's dead and gone over twenty years, and nothing you do will bring the boy back."

"I want to put Wiley away for it. I want him to pay for all he's done to Coralee Wilkins's family, and to us too, to you and Caleb."

Mabel stood up then and wiped her eyes. "If Wiley is guilty of killing Buddy Harper, then his family deserves that justice. But don't sit here and expect me to believe that you're doing it for me or Caleb. You're doing this for yourself."

She went off to bed then, leaving me with the uncomfortable feeling that she was right. Finally, I put the letter back in the file and went to replace the photograph of Buddy Harper in the package from the photographer. And that's when I noticed something I hadn't seen in the photograph of Lorna Lovett.

When I'd gone to have those pictures copied, the photograph of Lorna was still in its frame. I didn't want to damage it since I had to return it, so I'd just handed it to the photographer the way it was when I dropped it off. But when I picked up the photographs, he'd put the frame back on the original of Lorna, and he'd wrapped up the copies so nicely that I'd never opened the package, just paid up, drove home, and dropped them into my file.

But what I saw now in the unframed copy of the photograph of Lorna made me freeze. There was a man to the right of Lorna who'd been hidden behind the frame. I'd always noticed that Lorna was turned to the right, with her back to the men on the left in the photograph. But now I could see why. The man to her right was gripping her forearm, trying to pull her away. And even if I hadn't recognized him, I'd have known who it was, because there on the table in front of him was a cigarette lighter with the initials WS standing out clear as day.

I got in bed next to Mabel and lay there all night long, thinking about that photograph, and about Mabel knowing the truth now, and about all those lost babies and how much hurt she still carried around inside her over them. In the morning, her eyes were puffy from her crying, and mine were bloodshot from exhaustion, but I got up when she did, shaved and cleaned myself up, and sat at the table with her and Caleb to eat breakfast.

"Son, I'm real sorry I missed your birthday yesterday," I told Caleb. "I got hung up with some business in Little Rock, but I know that's no excuse."

When he didn't answer me, I said, "Do you like your new fishing rod?"

"Yes," he said. Then, "Thanks."

And as I watched him eat in silence, I realized how long it had been since I'd really looked at the boy. He'd turned thirteen the day before, and he'd grown so much in just the months I'd been off chasing leads on Wiley. But I hadn't even noticed. So I asked him if he'd like me to help him work on casting those new lures that evening, but he said he had baseball practice. Even so, I was rewarded with a touch from Mabel, just her hand on my shoulder as she passed me clearing the table, but it was enough to know that if I was willing to try, she was willing to be patient.

After breakfast I told Mabel I was leaving for work and even drove out like I was headed to town, but then I looped around a back road and raced to Cole's to show him what I'd seen on the edge of the photograph of Lorna.

"I'll be damned," Cole said when he saw the photograph. "That son of a bitch."

"I know it," I said. "Sitting there in my pile of evidence all this time. He's so young," I said, knowing I couldn't ask Cole to question Sonny again. Still, I prayed that Cole would pick up on my drift, thinking all the while he never would.

To my surprise, Cole said, "He probably looks a lot like he did when Sonny knew him, if you're right."

"Maybe," I said. "Maybe."

"Well," Cole said. "Let's find out." And he stood and headed for the barn, and I was so surprised it took me a second to follow him.

"Sonny," Cole called to him where he was working. "Come over here for a second, will you?"

Sonny came over right away. He'd been more comfortable around me lately, maybe because I was around more often, or maybe because he somehow thought I was connected to his mama.

When we were settled in Cole's office again, Cole said, "You know how we asked you recently if the woman in that photograph was your mama?"

Sonny nodded.

"Well, Leroy found something else in the photograph that was hidden behind the frame." Cole slid the photograph across the desk. "Do you know who that man is?"

Sonny nodded, but he turned pale as a ghost.

"Is he your father?" Cole asked. Sonny nodded again but started up with the coughing, and suddenly the coughing turned into wheezing, and then the boy was hyperventilating.

"Get him, Leroy," Cole said, but by the time I grabbed hold of him, Sonny had lost consciousness. "Help me carry him up to the house." We each took an arm. He was heavy to lift, but we made it inside and laid him out on the couch.

"Sweet Jesus," Cole said. "What the hell was that about?"

"Different altogether from showing him his mama's photograph," I said.

We waited for Sonny to come to. After a few minutes he blinked, but when he saw us, he started up with the wheezing again. Cole got a paper bag from the kitchen and tried to get Sonny to breathe into it, but Sonny fainted again. When it happened the third time, Cole said, "I'm calling Doc English."

While we waited, Lulu came out of her bedroom on her way to school. But when she saw Sonny, she ran to his side. "What happened to him?" she asked.

"Something upset him," Cole said.

"*You* upset him," she said, glaring at me.

"Me?" I said.

"You always upset him," she said. At seventeen, she looked and sounded so much like Bess it was hard not to wonder if it hurt Cole to look at her sometimes.

Lulu turned her back to me then, almost protectively, like she was trying to shield Sonny from my view, so I got up then and walked out onto the porch to wait for Doc English. Lulu was the second female to give me a piece of her mind in twelve hours. I suddenly wanted a beer, and it wasn't even nine in the morning.

Cole and Lulu and Nicky Joe had moved Sonny into Lulu's room and laid him down on the bed by the time Doc English arrived. I wanted to hear what he had to say about Sonny, but Lulu glared at me when I looked in the door, so I slunk into the living room and waited there.

Cole and Doc English finally came out, leaving Lulu to tend to Sonny.

"Something upset that boy good," Doc English said.

"Yes," Cole said.

"Care to tell me what?" he asked. Cole looked at me.

"We just asked him a question," I said.

"What kind of question?" Doc English asked.

"It's part of an ongoing investigation."

"Well, you're not going to get much out of him now," Doc English said. "That shot will keep him calm for a while. If he needs another when he comes to, call me. In the meantime, I wouldn't ask him any more of those questions if I were you."

"Let me ask you something, Doc," Cole said. "You ever seen

a case like Sonny's before? The boy can hear. He understands everything you say. He can even say a word now and then, but it's hard for him. Are there doctors who can help him?"

"Used to be a specialist in Jonesboro dealt with cases like this," he said. "I could look him up if you'd like."

"I'd be mighty grateful if you could," Cole said.

But even as I tried to thank Doc English while concealing the urgency I felt, I knew that specialist in Jonesboro was likely our best hope. If Sonny could never tell me where Lorna was, my chances of ever getting Wiley Slocum for murder were slim. But I had proof nonetheless. Even Lulu's glares couldn't suppress my excitement. Sonny's positive ID of Wiley Slocum as the man he'd known as his father was enough to move forward on the case.

What I needed now was for Coralee Wilkins to talk.

BIG EARL

One of the strangest things about having Coralee home again was the fact that I had to give her that medication every day. That would've been bad enough. But what Doctor Garvey said was that I had to check her mouth afterward, and although I'd promised him I'd do this, it made me feel like she'd think I didn't trust her. But I was willing to do anything to keep Coralee out of that hospital if I could, so after handing her that first pill, I said, "Coralee, I hate to have to do this, but Doctor Garvey told me I have to make sure you've swallowed your medicine. He says if I don't check your mouth, you might end up back in the hospital, and I don't want that for you."

Now I could tell she didn't like this one bit, but she didn't fight me on it. She said, "I don't want that neither, Earl."

"All right then," I said. But I didn't know what to say after that. How do you ask to look into somebody's mouth? So I said what Doc English always said when he looked down our throats when I was a boy.

I told Coralee, "Say ahh."

Which must've sounded funny to Coralee too, because she smiled a little when I said it before she opened her mouth. And pretty soon it became a kind of joke. Which was such a relief. Coralee had never been one to laugh much. So it surprised me that the hardest part of my job looking after her became a time for us to share a smile. We'd even get to giggling. Sometimes she even said it back to me. "Say ahh," she'd say, making fun.

Then I'd open my mouth and let her look down. Then we'd smile again and go on about our day.

Now I figured this was a good sign if we could laugh about something that was not one bit funny. We couldn't even do that before she left, and it was such a relief to me to think that Coralee was really better. For all our laughing, every time she opened her mouth, that pill was gone. And every time it was, I felt like I'd done my best to do what Doctor Garvey told me to do.

Now, there were folks who wanted to see Coralee, like Wilbur and his wife, and Charlene and Sherwood, but I figured walking her mama to church was about all the people Coralee could handle, so I had to ask all those decent folks to stay away awhile. Leroy Harrison said Little Earl could come to their house or go over to Cole's cotton gin any time he wanted. Said it'd keep Caleb out of Coralee's hair that way. And I was grateful to him for being so considerate of Coralee's need for privacy.

So when he pulled into our driveway one night looking for Caleb, I was happy to see him.

"I know Caleb isn't supposed to be over here, but I thought I'd check," he said.

"Little Earl's not back yet," I said. "Fishing must be good."

"Must be. They get back later every night, I swear."

"Growing up," I said. "Guess they're not as worried what we think these days, but I suppose that's natural."

"I suppose it is," he told me. But when he didn't turn to go, I asked if he wanted to sit down.

"I don't want to disturb your wife," he said.

"She's inside. She won't come out, don't worry," I told him. "She's only been out for church with her mama."

"I expect it will take some time for her to adjust," he said.

"It will," I said. "I just wish there were something I could

do to help her find her way. She used to garden, but she hasn't
been out there once since she's been home."

"Well, Earl," he said, "I might have something she could do,
but I worry that it's too much for her just now."

"What is it?" I asked.

"You remember that photo of her brother you lent me?"

"Course," I said.

"Well, I've found a photograph of Lorna Lovett with Sheriff
Slocum. What would really help me now is if Coralee would be
willing to talk to me about what she knows about Buddy and
Lorna. With a statement from her, I might finally be able to get
justice for your wife's family."

I really wanted to tell him yes. I owed that man so many
things. But I said, "I'm not sure now's the time."

"I can understand that, Earl. And don't think another thing
about it."

Now, I didn't want to wind Coralee up. But I also knew getting justice for Buddy might make her feel useful and finally
put his case to rest. And I knew it still ate at her, even after all
these years.

"Look," I told him, "let me sit on this a while. Maybe I can
get a sense from Coralee how she's feeling. If she seems okay,
I'll ask her if she'd be willing to talk with you."

"All she'd have to do is make a statement," he said.

"All right then," I said. "I'll let you know."

Little Earl still wasn't back by the time he climbed into his
car to go look for Caleb, and as he pulled out he said, "I don't
know about you, Earl, but I'm looking forward to hunting season. I've had about all the catfish I can stand."

CORALEE

Now, even though it had been over twenty-two years since Buddy's death, Mama still had never told me why she was angry with Buddy before he died. And I could already tell she had one foot in that other world and was almost there. So after I walked her home from church on our third visit there together, I was glad when she asked me if I'd like a glass of sweet tea. I said yes, and she went into the house to get it, and we sat on the chairs on her porch in the warm morning air, drinking down that good cold tea. Mama always did make good tea.

I waited for Mama to talk after she sat down, but when she didn't say anything, I said, "Mama, what do you pray for in church?"

But Mama just said, "That's between me and the Lord, Coralee."

"I know that," I said. "But do you pray for people?"

"I pray for all my kin," she said.

"Did you pray for me while I was gone?" I asked.

"Every day, Coralee," she told me, which made my eyes prick with tears.

And even though I knew I was pushing my luck, and even though I couldn't ask her what I really wanted to know, I said, "Do you pray for Buddy?"

"Especially for Buddy," she said. And that was enough. Maybe next Sunday I could ask her more, I thought. But when I'd finished my tea and it came time for me to leave, Mama had some trouble getting up, so I helped her stand and set her down in the armchair inside.

"You're a good girl, Coralee," she said. It was about the kindest thing she'd ever said to me, but even as she said it, she patted my hand in a way that meant she was ready for me to leave.

"I'll see you next Sunday," I told her, and before I was out the door, she was fast asleep. But she might've been more than just asleep, I realized later, because when Shelby went over later to take Mama supper, Mama was right where I left her, already gone.

I didn't go to Mama's funeral. Earl thought it would be too much for me. But I felt bad about it, like it was just about the kind of thing Mama would've expected of me. So when Shelby asked Earl if I wanted to help her clean out Mama's house, I told him I would. I hadn't been inside it for so long, except to set Mama on the armchair that day. And I was amazed at how just walking around that house I could see things I hadn't seen in years. I don't mean furniture and windows and crosses on the wall. I mean Daddy, sitting in his chair by the window with a drink in his hand. I mean Shelby and me, giggling ourselves to sleep on Christmas Eve when we hoped Santa would leave us a candy stick. I mean Buddy, lounging on the back porch with me after I'd come home from Flint.

I could hear their voices echo through the house—Mama scolding Buddy for sneaking cracklings she was frying up for cornbread. Shelby shouting for me to come downstairs and tie up her hair. Buddy teasing Shelby by holding her shoe over his head where she couldn't get to it. And they didn't feel like memories somehow. They felt alive, like everything was happening all at once, the now and the then and the yet to come, because I could also see this house empty soon, and a new family moved in after that.

There wasn't much left in the house by the time Mama died. Mama had already given Shelby all the beds but her own for Shelby's kids, something I was sad about when I looked in the room that was once Buddy's and remembered seeing him sleeping in his bed the night before the sheriff shot him. And since I didn't have room for any of Mama's furniture in our little house on Oak Street, when it came down to it, it was just a few dishes and some silverware I wanted, so I packed them into a box.

"I guess that's all," I said, looking around one last time.

But Shelby said, "Something's missing."

"We've been all over this house," I said.

"There was Mama's necklace."

"Mama had jewelry?"

"She sold her and Daddy's wedding bands after he died, but she had a cameo necklace Elbert gave her when they was first married."

"Maybe she sold that too," I said.

"Mama would never've sold that necklace," Shelby said. "She still loved Elbert."

"How do you know?" I asked.

"When I was about fourteen, I was putting away laundry and found it in her bottom dresser drawer, and when she come into the room and seen me trying it on, she started to cry."

"Mama cried?"

"Then she snatched it off my neck and told me to never touch it again. And I didn't, but later that year when money ran short, I asked if she mightn't sell it so we could eat, and she slapped me clean across the face. I even asked if I could wear it just once, on my wedding day, but she said no."

"Well," I said, "she couldn't have taken it to the grave."

"Mama was so stingy, I wouldn't put it past her."

Shelby started digging through drawers again, muttering how she'd like to give that necklace to her baby girl one day, but all I could think was that I finally knew the right word for Mama. Stingy. Not with her things. With her feelings. She could've shared her own young love of Elbert with Shelby the day she got married, or her own young pain of losing him with me when I divorced Chess. She could've told me she understood. She could've told me she'd been there. It would've made all the difference. Instead, she made me feel ashamed, like I'd just gone and made another stupid mistake.

There wasn't much else to say after Shelby gave up looking, so I picked up the little box of dishes and silverware, and Shelby locked the house. But when I turned to look back for the last time, I saw Mama standing on the porch. She didn't look sad. She just looked like she was watching us go like she sometimes had when we'd gone off to work the fields, or to an ice cream social, or to Bible study back when we all went to Divine Holiness.

"Come on, Coralee," Shelby said. "I got to get home."

Well, we talked about the weather and the crop reports and when Shelby's husband could borrow Earl's truck to pick up the furniture from Mama's house, and pretty soon we were at Shelby's house and we said goodbye.

It had turned into a pretty night, all cool and quiet and peaceful, and I felt aware of a kind of freedom I'd longed for when I'd been in the hospital and the guards would walk alongside us. And for the first time since I'd been home, I felt good just being outside in the fresh air. With most folks tucked away in their houses eating supper, it was like having the whole town all to myself. I could hear the song of a lark. I could see the

pink and yellow of the sky as the sun sank behind a bank of
clouds. I could smell the fresh green grass. I could hear my
shoes crunching the gravel with each step.

I felt so good that it took me a second to realize something
wasn't right. I didn't know what it was at first. Just a feeling I
had. But as I walked I began to hear a footstep, then a whisper,
then more footsteps, and picked up my pace. I was only a couple of blocks from home. But the noises got closer, and finally,
I looked over my shoulder and saw three boys on my tail. At
first I thought they just happened to fall into step behind me
and that their whispers were nothing special, just things boys
talk about. But as their footsteps got closer, I sped up too. I
was a block from home when I heard their voices clearly: *Loo-
ney bin. Crazy lady. Go back to the asylum.* And it was then that
I started to run. But that medication made me so slow. And
when I could feel them closing in, I dropped the box of Mama's dishes and didn't stop running until I had the door of the
house locked safely behind me.

LEROY

While I waited to hear from Earl Wilkins about whether Coralee would be willing to give a statement about her brother's engagement to Lorna Lovett, I put the rest of my evidence together. The photograph of Buddy Harper. The photograph of Lorna Lovett and Sheriff Slocum. Sonny's identification of Lorna as his mother. Sonny's identification of Wiley as his father. Sonny's admission that his given name was Wiley despite his resemblance to Buddy Harper. And my own theory that Sheriff Slocum had shot Buddy Harper because he was about to marry Lorna, who the sheriff believed was carrying his child. I sat back and looked at the file I'd put together with satisfaction. I was going to bring Wiley Slocum down. All I needed was for Coralee Harper to go on record.

Still, there was one thing that needed clearing up, and that was Lewis Hopkins's name on Sonny's birth certificate. Now, I knew that Lewis Hopkins was not Sonny's father. But it's hard to argue with a legal document, so I had to track down Lewis, which wouldn't be hard since word was he'd spent most of his time in the tavern since he was fired.

When I walked in, he was sitting on the same barstool where I'd last found him, looking like he might have been there ever since.

"You're back," he said.

"You're still here," I said.

"In case you forgot, Leroy, I got no place to be at the moment."

"So it's really over between you and Slocum?"

"Bastard wouldn't even honor my last paycheck."

"You must be looking for work, then," I said.

"You still got that job for me you mentioned?"

"You want to take down Slocum?" I asked.

"You got a job for me taking down Slocum?"

"Maybe," I said. "It all depends."

"On what?" he asked. I got up then and took down the photograph I'd hung back up on the wall of the tavern and set it down in front of him.

"Did you know that girl, Lewis?" I said. When he didn't answer, I said, "She was the prostitute that lived upstairs here."

"Don't call her that," Lewis said. He drank down the rest of what looked like bourbon and said, "She was never a prostitute. Wiley just told people that so it would look like police business if anybody saw him coming or going."

"So that's why she never had a record," I said.

"You won't find a man in Paradise slept with that woman for money, and the only one besides Wiley who did got himself killed.

"Then I just have one more question for you, Lewis," I said. "Were you married to her?"

Lewis looked at me for a long moment. Then he said, "I'm going to need another drink."

I'd never known where Lorna had disappeared to the day Buddy Harper was shot, but Lewis admitted that Sheriff Slocum had instructed him to get her out of town before dawn that morning.

"Where'd you take her?" I asked. We'd walked down to my office by then, and I'd poured Lewis a tall glass of Wild Turkey I kept hidden in my bottom drawer. I wanted to keep his tongue loose in case he changed his mind the next morning.

"Middle of nowhere," he told me. "Wiley had it set up before he shot Buddy Harper. He'd given me a key to her room over the tavern, and I thought she knew I was coming because her bags were packed. But when I opened the door, she seemed surprised to see me. Later she told me she was expecting Buddy Harper."

"So was she still with Wiley or wasn't she?" I asked.

"I thought it was all over between them," Lewis said. "Wiley had women all over the place. I couldn't understand why he suddenly cared so much about this one again. It wasn't until she started showing a couple months later that I realized she was expecting."

"How often did you see her?" I asked.

"More than Wiley did after a while," he told me. "He used to send me out there with food and clothes long after he lost interest."

"For how long?" I asked.

"I don't know," he said. "Years."

"Still?" I asked.

"Not anymore," he said. "I went out there one day, and she was gone. Took the boy with her. Tell you the truth, I was glad. I'd thought of driving them up to Cape Girardeau or over to Memphis, dropping them someplace where Wiley'd never find them. But I was too afraid he'd find out. I was too afraid to even tell her that she could hitch a ride with a delivery truck that I always passed on my way. Only traffic I ever saw out there."

"But you didn't?"

"Closest I came was mentioning that when I drove out on weekdays, I saw that truck pass me by about noon, and that the fellow who drove it was friendly, always waving or stopping to exchange niceties after a while."

"You think she took the hint?"

"I did at the time, because she asked me exactly where I'd seen the truck. All she'd needed to have done is walk to the end of that long drive, turn left, and keep walking, which I explained like I was just answering her question in case Wiley caught wind of it. But I don't think she'd have made it otherwise, forty miles from anywhere and she was such a tiny little thing."

"How'd Wiley take it?"

"You know, I thought he'd be mad when I came back and told him they were gone, or blame me for it somehow, but he just seemed relieved not to have to bother with them anymore."

"What about you?" I asked. "You must have known her well."

"Not like that," he said. "Don't think it didn't cross my mind, but even if I hadn't been married, she got so thin and pathetic after a while that it wouldn't have been right. Anyway, it was clear that she was still hung up on Buddy Harper."

"How do you know?"

"She started asking after him once Wiley stopped coming."

"She didn't know he was dead?"

"Wiley never told her," he said. "I figured if he hadn't told her, he had his reasons. Besides, she had so little to hold on to. I didn't want to destroy her hopes. Without that child, I don't know what she'd have done."

"What was the boy like?"

"Sweet little thing," he said. "A chatterbox. He used to run to my car when he saw me coming and beg me to stay for supper the minute I opened the door."

"You ate with them?"

"Sometimes. Lorna was so lonesome for company that I couldn't say no. But I have to tell you it tore me up that they thought I was their friend. Confused the hell out of me that they were always so damn happy to see me."

Now this got me thinking. "Do you think the boy would recognize you if he saw you?"

"No telling," he said. "It's been twelve years at least since he saw me last. But he might, if only because I was the only other person besides Wiley they ever saw."

I thought about this for a while. Finally, I said, "What'd Wiley have over you?"

"My mother needed surgery," he said.

"He paid for it?" I asked.

Lewis nodded. "And I was so grateful, I did whatever favors he asked."

"Then why'd he fire you?"

"I refused a bribe from Brother Jeremiah Cassidy when I caught up to him outside Jonesboro one night after he skipped town. Slocum told me to take the money if he offered it to me. But I couldn't. Laverne Bishop was a friend of my mama's, so I brought him back to Paradise and booked him, but in the morning, the record was gone and so was he. And a few weeks later," Lewis added, "so was I."

"That's Wiley for you," I said, thinking of my original verdict in Coralee Harper's sanity hearing.

"Sure is," Lewis said. "I didn't know until that day that the favors he asked of me weren't favors, even if he made it sound like I had a choice."

"Favors like marrying Lorna Lovett?" I asked. "I saw the birth certificate."

"He never asked me to marry Lorna. Wiley had that birth certificate forged and filed it in Missouri so the boy would have an ID when he got older. He thought the boy was his son, after all. Guess he had plans for him."

I sipped my Wild Turkey, thinking about this. Finally, I said, "Lewis, I need you to testify as a witness against Wiley for murdering Buddy Harper."

"I wasn't there when Wiley shot Buddy," he said. "I'm not a witness. Sometimes I think Wiley sent me off with Lorna early that morning just to make sure I wasn't there to see it. But I can't prove it."

We sat there for a while, finishing our drinks. I'd never known how much I had in common with Lewis before that, or how much I probably had in common with plenty of people I'd worked with every day when I'd been over in the county courthouse.

"Where do you think Lorna is now?" I asked.

"No telling," he said. "I thought she'd have come back here to find Buddy, but she must have learned he was dead and moved on."

"Where was she from?"

"Dodgeville, I think," he said.

"She tell you that?"

"No, but the last time I saw her she gave me a letter to mail to her sister there."

"You took a big risk for that woman, Lewis," I said, but I didn't let on that I already knew about the letter. "Were you in love with her?"

"It wasn't such a big risk," he said. "I read it before I sent it, just to make sure she didn't give anything away that could get back to Wiley."

"No return address, I presume."

"That place Wiley kept them wasn't on any map."

"Let me ask you something," I said. "When's the last time you tried to find them?"

"A year ago, maybe," he said. "Maybe two."

I did the math on this, and said, "You must have been in love with her."

"No." Lewis shook his head. "I just felt . . . responsible, I guess. Guilty, you know. I felt guilty." Finally, he said, "That job offer still on the table?"

"Indeed it is," I said.

"I'll take it," Lewis said, and we shook on it.

"Now, how about another drink for your new private eye?" he asked.

It was a quiet evening by the time Lewis and I walked back to my car so I could drive him home. Mabel would be fussing if I was late for supper, and according to my watch I could just about make it if I hurried. But as we passed the tavern someone was walking up the sidewalk, and when we got closer, I realized it was Wiley, dressed in plain clothes. As surprised as I was to see him, I was struck again by just how ordinary he looked out of uniform. Vulnerable, even.

Lewis must have thought so too, because before I could stop him, he said, "Well, well, well," and his voice was loose and amused and angry with bourbon. "If it ain't the King of Green County himself."

"Shouldn't you be in the unemployment line, Lewis?"

"Oh, I got a job," Lewis told him.

"Warming barstools doesn't count."

"Matter of fact, Wiley," I jumped in, "Lewis is working for me now."

"I tell you what," Wiley scoffed. "That must be one sorry operation you're running out here these days, then, Leroy. Damn shame about the election. Real sorry to hear it."

"How's Cal Overton working out?" I asked. "Does he need me to show him the ropes?"

"The ropes?" Wiley asked.

"The ones he'll be swinging from if he doesn't follow all those *suggestions* of yours."

Wiley opened his mouth to say something, but Lewis staggered between us, and I suddenly realized just how much he'd had to drink.

"Hey," Lewis told Wiley, "I'm a private eye now."

"You're a drunk, Lewis," Wiley spat.

"And you're a crook," Lewis shot back.

"You haven't got one shred of evidence on me, Lewis, and you know it."

"I got more than you think," Lewis said, and at that Wiley grabbed Lewis by the collar.

"You breathe one word—one word—to anyone about me, I'll slap you into Little Rock so fast it'll make your head spin."

"I got a lot of friends down there, given how many trips I made on your behalf. We might all have a lot to say to one another, come to think of it."

"Nobody listens to lunatics," Wiley snorted.

Lewis said, "I mean *staff*." And at that Wiley slammed Lewis into the wall.

"Never seen you lose your composure before, Wiley," I said. "What would Tillie think?"

"You leave my wife out of it," Wiley said.

"Like you left my son out of it?" I said. "Now look, why don't you let Lewis here go, and then Lewis can let you go. Isn't that what you taught me?"

Wiley turned and looked at me then, and for the first time I caught a glimpse of what lay behind the mask I always wondered if he was wearing, and what I saw chilled me to the bone. He let go of Lewis then, who staggered toward me.

"That's mighty gentlemanly of you, Wiley," Lewis said, and I hoped we'd be on our way when Lewis added, "Considering you normally finish the job." Lewis spun to punch Wiley then, but he missed the mark, and Wiley twisted his arm and bent him over in pain.

"I will finish the job if you don't keep your mouth shut, Lewis," he hissed. "You know better than to mess with me. You know better than anyone." But just as quickly as he'd lost his temper, we heard footsteps in the distance, and he let Lewis go. Wiley's hat had fallen off in his scuffle with Lewis, and he picked it up, settled it back on his head, and said, "You boys have yourselves a fine evening, you hear?" Then he walked to the door of the tavern and stepped inside.

Now, if you'd been the passerby whose footsteps brought the matter to a close, you'd have thought we were just folks exchanging pleasantries in passing. But I recognized something in Wiley's voice I'd never heard before in all the years I'd known him. It was the unmistakable rattle of fear.

BIG EARL

I'd felt hopeful when Coralee went to clean out her mama's house with Shelby because it was something she finally seemed to want to do. But she came home after that and just sat. I'd try to get her out to her garden, knowing she used to say she'd just be a minute weeding carrots, and two hours later the whole damn garden would be clean as a whistle. But she wasn't interested.

Worse yet, Little Earl now ducked under her hand when she tried to ruffle his hair, never looked up at the dinner table, stayed out of the room if she was in it. And I wanted to help them both. I just didn't know how. I'd asked Little Earl to help Coralee peg out the laundry, shell a bowl full of peas, clean out the icebox with her, thinking they'd begin to talk naturally. But they never did. Mr. Holmes just told me I had to give them both time.

Finally one evening I asked Coralee why she'd been so quiet lately, and at first she didn't seem to know. Eventually she said, "I miss Libby."

"Would you like to send her a letter?" I asked.

"Oh," Coralee brightened. "Could I?" And just that little spark of interest gave me hope.

Little Earl was out in the toolshed when I went to ask him, and I didn't know for sure what he'd say, he'd been so offhand with her. But he went straight to his room and got paper and a pencil. He was all business. He sat down at the table with

Coralee and said, "Daddy says you want me to help you write a letter."

Coralee said, "I'd be most grateful, son."

"Who's it for?"

"My friend Libby," Coralee said, and Little Earl mouthed *Dear Libby* as he wrote.

"What do you want to say?" he asked.

"Tell her I'm real sorry I didn't say goodbye. Tell her I miss her." Little Earl scribbled this down.

"Tell her it is good to be home," Coralee said. "Tell her it is nice to be with my husband and my boy." So Little Earl wrote some more.

"Say my boy's as tall as his daddy," and I could see a smile tugging at Little Earl's mouth. "Tell her he is so smart, he's writing this letter. Tell her how proud I am to be his mama," Coralee said. And I knew that smile was winning, so I turned my back on them and washed my hands because it felt like such a private moment, even if I wouldn't have missed it for anything.

"Anything else?"

"That's all," Coralee said, and so Little Earl read out, *Regards, Coralee Wilkins.*

"Thank you, son," Coralee said.

"You're welcome, Mama," Little Earl said, and when she reached to ruffle his soft brown hair, he let her.

Regards. Now where did the boy come up with a fancy word like that? He was always surprising me. Even the way he talked was real proper-like. He already ma'am'ed and sir'ed everyone in town, and when you asked him if he wanted cornbread or biscuits, he didn't just answer "Cornbread" or "Biscuits." He said, "I'd like the cornbread, thank you." Manners. Nobody in my family or Coralee's ever had time for them. My mama once told me manners were only for folks who could afford them, and I could see why that might be, but my heart about busted with pride whenever I overheard Little Earl use them so easily. He didn't get that from me and Coralee. Those manners he'd picked up were the influence of Leroy and Mabel Harrison on Caleb, who in turn passed them on to Little Earl.

That boy was starting to remind me of Mr. Holmes's son Bobby Lee, who had graduated college now and had gone on to become an accountant in Stillwater, which Mr. Holmes was pleased as punch about because he got to see his boy so often with him living nearby. One day Bobby Lee even turned up at the gin and like to knock my socks off in his starched white collar and tie. I could just see Little Earl in a tie like that. I could just imagine my son walking with that kind of nerve. And I knew watching him write that letter for Coralee that he was not going to wear overalls for the rest of his life, even if they suited me just fine.

CORALEE

W alking to church on my own turned out to be a lot harder than walking with Mama. I thought maybe in the sunshine I'd be safer than I was at dusk when those boys almost caught me after cleaning out Mama's house, but instead it only made me see more clearly how children giggled as I walked toward them, then ran as I came near. Women looked down at the sidewalk or up at the trees, but they might as well have looked right at me for all the trouble they took to hide it. But men were different. Men stared. Boys too. They weren't ashamed of it. And the look in their eyes was so cruel that it took all I had not to bust out crying right there on the street. So I was relieved when I climbed the steps of the church and Pastor Samuel took my hand and said, "It is good to have you back with us, Sister Coralee."

But it was only an hour later that I felt those eyes on me walking home, and I prayed to the Lord to see me home safely and help me remember that all my trials were His way of reminding me how much I needed Him. But I could still feel those eyes on me, and I tried to walk a little faster to get home. But when I could hear gravel crunching under tires behind me in the distance, I sped up. *Just a few more blocks*, I thought, *and I'll be home*. And I felt sure I was in the clear when the car started to pass me until a boy shouted "Lunatic!" from the window and I heard some others cackling inside the car as it drove away.

I was near tears when I heard another car in the distance

behind me and tried to speed up again. But that gravel kept crunching and I kept walking faster, and the next thing I knew, that car had pulled over and I was sure that this time those boys were going to get me when a woman's voice called out my name. And when I turned, I saw what must've been one of God's own angels walking toward me. She was fair and slim with hair the color of honey, wearing a pretty yellow dress, and I felt relief flood through me at the friendliness in her smile.

"Mrs. Wilkins," the woman said again. "I'm Mabel Harrison, Leroy's wife," she said, and she offered me her hand.

"I'm Coralee Wilkins," I said, and as we shook hands, I saw that being beautiful must not've made her happy because up close she looked sad.

"Can I offer you a ride home?" she said. "It's awfully hot today."

"It is hot," I said, trying to stop my hands from shaking. "And I'd be most grateful." But I was so relieved to have someone speak kindly to me that I began to cry, and she took my arm and walked me to the door of the car.

Inside, it was cool on the leather seat, and I sank into it gratefully as I wiped my tears with a handkerchief I'd fetched from my purse.

"Are you all right?" she asked me.

"I'm fine now," I told her.

As she started to drive again, she said, "I'm so glad to have the chance to finally meet you. My son, Caleb, is good friends with your Little Earl."

"I haven't met Caleb," I said. "I've been away a long time."

"Little Earl was Caleb's first friend when we moved here, and moving is so hard on kids. So me and Leroy are both so grateful to your boy for making Caleb feel welcome in town," she said.

"I'm glad," I said. "Little Earl's a good boy."

"He is a good boy. It must have been hard to be away from him for so long," Mabel said, and her kindness touched me deeply.

"It was terrible," I told her.

"Well, he's awfully glad to have you home," she said, but there was no time to say more because we'd pulled up to the house by then.

"Thank you for the ride," I said.

"It was nice to meet you," she said, and her smile was so kindly that I knew she meant it. I even stood on the porch watching her pull out of the driveway in that shiny white car and waved as she drove away.

But the minute her car was out of sight, I felt that fear come right back. I looked up and down Oak Street, but I didn't see those boys. I listened for their laughter but only heard the leaves rustle in the trees. Even so, when I went inside, I locked the front door behind me, then the back. I closed all the windows and the curtains and found a place to hide in my closet. When Earl and Little Earl got home that night from the gin, Earl said the temperature in the house was so high we'd get heatstroke if we didn't open some windows, so I let him, because having him there made me feel so much safer.

But the next morning when he gave me my pill, I tucked it up in my cheek before he checked to see if I'd swallowed it, and after he went out to the work shed, I flushed that little pill down the toilet. Those boys could chase me if they wanted. They could even chase me faster. But I was never going to let them catch up to me again.

LEROY

In the end it wasn't me or even Cole who got Sonny talking. It wasn't Doc English or his specialist down in Jonesboro. And it wasn't until Cole and I saw him standing out beside the gin smiling with Lulu that we even realized it was possible. When we first saw them one Sunday afternoon before supper, Cole stood up and walked to the edge of the porch to get a better look. He said nothing for a while, just leaned against a porch rail and watched.

Now, Sonny had always had a soft spot for Lulu—even when she was a little girl, he'd been kind to her in his silent way, was more protective of her, treated her gentler than he treated Nicky Joe or Little Earl or any other kid who happened to come around the gin. And Lulu had always been kind to Sonny in return, even now that she was older and the kids at school didn't understand her friendship with a mute boy who worked for her father. But standing on the porch watching the little scene unfold between them, the truth began to dawn on us both.

"I'll be damned," Cole said at last.

"Women," I said. "I swear." And I think we both understood in that moment that all it took to get that boy talking was falling in love.

When Lulu came inside to start supper, Cole said, "Lulu, I saw you out there laughing with Sonny."

"Uh-huh," she said as she mixed up the biscuits while Mabel battered the chicken.

"About what, if you don't mind me asking?" he said.

"Sonny said Nicky Joe looks like you when he gets mad." She smiled, but Cole didn't rise to the bait.

"Sonny's talking?"

"Sure," Lulu said.

"How long's this been going on?"

"I don't know," she said. "A little while."

"What else did he say?"

"None of your business," Lulu said, in a tone of voice that made it plain that Sonny's interest in Lulu wasn't one-sided. But Cole took this in stride.

"That's fine," he said. "But it must be kind of specific, what he says to you, if it's none of my business."

"Sometimes," Lulu said.

It wasn't long after that night that Cole asked me if Lewis would come by to meet Sonny, and when I asked, Lewis said he would and picked me up on his way. When we arrived, Cole called to the boy, and as he walked toward us his expression changed. Sonny's face seemed to say he just needed confirmation, and so Cole said, "Sonny, this here is Mr. Lewis Hopkins. He says he used to know you."

"Nice to see you, son," Lewis said. "It's been a long time."

Sonny took a step forward, then another. Then a smile spread across his face that nothing could stop, and before I knew it Lewis and Sonny were clapping each other on the back. Sonny shook Lewis's hand for so long I thought he might just throw his arms around Lewis and hug him. He didn't, but I can't say that watching their reunion wasn't just about the most touching thing I'd ever seen. And it wasn't just me. When I looked at Cole, his eyes were misty too.

Cole said, "Lewis here's come to catch up with you after

all these years. Why don't y'all come into my office and make yourselves comfortable."

It was one of the hottest days of the year, and Cole's office was close and stuffy, but at least not in the sun. And once we got settled, Cole nodded to Lewis, and Lewis said, "So what have you been up to since I last saw you, son?"

Sonny looked at Cole, who nodded, and Sonny said, "Wuh-work."

"Here?" Cole said.

Sonny nodded.

"I always wondered what happened to you. I went out to visit you and your mama one day, but you were gone. I went back a few more times, but I never did see either of you again. And I only just learned that you were working for Cole from Leroy here."

Sonny waited.

"Did your mama come with you?"

Sonny shook his head.

"Did your daddy—did Wiley—ever come back to see y'all?"

Sonny nodded.

"Did he bring you here?"

Sonny shook his head, no.

"Did he take your mama somewhere?" *Now we're getting somewhere*, I thought, and my stomach lurched at the thought of a testimony from Lorna.

Sonny shook his head again, no, but slower this time.

"Do you know where she is?" Lewis asked.

Sonny didn't nod or shake his head.

"Does Wiley know where she is?"

Again, nothing. But tears had begun to stream down Sonny's face, and Cole handed the boy a handkerchief.

"Let me ask you something, Sonny," Lewis said. "Did he

hurt her again?" Lewis had never mentioned Wiley had been violent with Lorna, but I can't say it surprised me one bit.

Sonny nodded.

"How bad?" Lewis asked.

But Sonny broke down sobbing, and I think we knew the answer to Lewis's next question before he asked it.

"Did he kill her?"

Sonny nodded, tears rolling down his face so fast they were bouncing off his overalls.

"I'm real sorry to hear that, son," Lewis said, and he sounded really sorry. "I'm so sorry." And he reached over and put his hand on Sonny's back in a gesture so natural I could see the bond that had once been between them was still there.

Cole said, "I think we better wrap this up here."

"Just one more question, Cole?" Lewis asked, and Cole nodded.

"Do you happen to know why?"

Sonny took some deep breaths. He opened his mouth and said, "Mmm . . . me."

"You?" Lewis said.

Sonny nodded.

"Why you?"

Sonny touched his cheek.

"He slapped you?" Lewis asked, but Sonny shook his head no.

"He hit you?"

Sonny shook his head no again, but finally, he spoke. "Muh. Muh. My face."

"Your face?" Cole asked.

Sonny nodded, and I can't say I've ever seen someone look as sad as Sonny did then.

Lewis said, "Was it because you looked like somebody else?"

Sonny nodded.

"Somebody named Buddy Harper?" Lewis asked.

But Sonny started to cough, that terrible wheezing sound that meant he was about to hyperventilate, and Cole ushered us out of the office fast.

"Thank you, Cole," I said.

"Send Lulu down here on your way out," Cole told me. "And call Doc English." So I stopped at the house and told Lulu to get down to the gin. Then I put in that call to Doc English, and Lewis and I walked back to the car.

"So Wiley killed her," I said. "And Sonny witnessed it."

"I always wondered when Wiley would notice how much that boy resembled Buddy Harper, but by the time they were gone, I didn't think Wiley'd been to see them for years."

"Well," I said, rubbing my temples. I had a headache coming on, but from the disappointment or the heat I didn't know. Maybe both. "There goes my testimony from Lorna."

Lewis thought about that for a while. Then he said, "Maybe not."

"What do you mean?" I said.

"What if we could get Wiley for murdering Lorna? We have an eyewitness."

"But we don't have a body," I said. "And Wiley could have put her anywhere."

"He could have," Lewis said. "But I bet he didn't. He couldn't have hid her any better than that place he had her stashed."

He backed out of Cole's driveway then and pointed the nose of his Chevy east, and that's when I realized he wasn't dropping me at work. We were going to find Lorna.

BIG EARL

Now, after Coralee and Little Earl wrote that letter to Libby together, things got a little better between them. When Coralee asked him how his day was, Little Earl told her about his spelling test or math class. And when Little Earl got hungry between meals, Coralee got right up and buttered him some cornbread. These were simple things, I knew. Things that happen between mamas and their boys every day. But in my house it felt like a miracle every time.

So when Coralee mentioned that Mabel Harrison had given her a ride home from church one Sunday, I decided it might be time to ask her if she'd give a statement to Leroy about her brother, Buddy. I wasn't ready to tell her that Buddy may have a son until it was for sure, and even then, I worried it would wind her up. But just asking her to talk with Leroy didn't seem like asking too much.

"Mabel's nice, isn't she?" I began.

"She surely is," she said.

"Well, she and Leroy have been awful good to Little Earl. I'm glad you got to meet her."

"Me too," she said.

"You know, Coralee," I said, "Leroy would like to talk with you too, if you're feeling up to it."

"I don't want to talk to Leroy Harrison," she said.

"I think you might, Coralee. Leroy's a good man. He's been

trying to clear your brother Buddy's name, and he thinks you can help him do it."

Coralee perked up then, with a kind of clearness I hadn't seen in her since she'd been home. "I will gladly talk to him about Buddy if it can help clear his name." And she went off to church the next morning with a spring in her step, and at first I thought I'd done right to ask her.

But it wasn't long after that she stopped sleeping as well, didn't eat as much of her supper as usual, started locking the doors and windows so often I had to bang on the door to get her to let me and Little Earl in when we came home at night. And I felt like it was my own fault that I'd asked her to speak to the judge about Buddy. I'd been afraid it would be too much for her, and I must've been right.

Still, she took her medication every time like always, which is what Doctor Garvey said was the most important thing, and every time I looked in her mouth it was a relief to me to see that she'd swallowed it. But it was like the joke about saying *ahh* had worn off, because she didn't laugh anymore when I said it.

But when Little Earl started ducking whenever she tried to ruffle his hair again, I knew it wasn't just me who noticed the difference in her. And I was really grateful for Leroy's offer to let Little Earl spend time at his place because that's where Little Earl was most of the time if he wasn't at school or helping me at the gin, and knowing it was okay with Leroy made me worry about everything less.

Still, it occurred to me that maybe I should talk to Doc English. Maybe I should get Mr. Holmes to call Miss Etta or write a letter to Doctor Garvey down in Little Rock. But I was too afraid to say anything at all. Because now that I had Coralee home with me again, I knew that I could never send her back to that hospital after seeing those folks inside it when I went to meet with Doctor Garvey. People wailing and screaming and shaking their bars. Coralee did not belong in a place like that. So I already knew that if I had to, I would find some other way. But she was never going back to that hospital again as long as I lived.

CORALEE

Now, when Earl asked me if I'd be willing to speak to Leroy Harrison about Buddy, I was thrilled at the chance to get justice for Buddy at last. And I felt so happy at the thought of clearing my brother's name that the next morning I put on my best dress and headed down to First Baptist to say thank you to the Lord personally for this opportunity. I was so happy I didn't even stop to worry if those boys were following me, and I made it all the way to the church steps without any trouble.

And when the service was over, I headed home in the hot sunshine and felt like maybe things would turn out after all, and I was only sorry Mama wasn't alive to see Buddy's name cleared. I was so caught up thinking of justice for Buddy that I didn't realize a young man had fallen into step beside me, asking me questions like "How are you today?" and "Isn't this a fine September Sunday?" And although at first I was afraid, his questions were so easy and natural that I finally agreed that it was a fine September Sunday. And he said it was only after the summer haze cleared that you could ever really see the sky, and I had to agree. I was feeling so good that I didn't realize that underneath his friendly words was something cruel until I turned and saw his friends laughing at me behind us. I sped up then, but he sped up too and kept asking me those questions, but I stopped answering and just tried to get myself home as fast as I could. I was so glad I'd stopped taking that medication or he might've just caught me. And I had almost reached the front steps of the house when I felt a hail of stones pelt me hard on my back.

Tears were streaming down my cheeks by the time I slammed the front door of the house, and I knew then that the Lord had abandoned me. My hands were shaking so hard that I had trouble fastening the locks on the doors and windows. I closed the curtains then and locked myself inside the bathroom to wait for Earl to get home. I knew too that it was the last time I would go to church. If the Lord wasn't going to help me, I was going to have to help myself. And I was never going to let those boys hurt me again.

LEROY

L ewis drove for a long time, stopping only to buy a couple of shovels from a farm goods store before we crossed the state line into Missouri. Eventually we turned off Route 108 onto a slim lane of gravel, where we drove again for miles. We were hell and gone from Paradise by now. Cotton and rye fields gave way to shrubs and clumps of trees, and after about five miles of this, Lewis turned into what looked like some brush.

"This way?" I asked.

"It used to be a two-track," Lewis said. "It's grown over now."

Most of the road had washed away, and the car was bouncing up and down so much my head hit the ceiling. I kept thinking we were going to get stuck, miles from anywhere on the hottest day I could remember, but suddenly Lewis cut the engine.

"I can't go any further in the car," Lewis said. "We're going to have to walk the rest of the way. That rainstorm last year must have washed the road out."

"Where the hell are we?" I asked Lewis.

"In Dunklin County," he said. "Wiley's father owned this land, all of it, but after he died, Wiley never bothered to farm it. Before he set Lorna up here, he was running a still."

Lewis walked easily through the brush like he knew exactly where he was going, which was good because there was no sign of any road left, but I thought I was going to die of heatstroke if I had to take one more step. And that's when I saw it. A tiny little building, like a work shed, almost caved in.

"Was that where they lived?"

"It was in better shape in those days," Lewis said, and when he opened what was left of the door I said, "Holy smokes."

Inside, there was a table and a little gas stove and what looked like mattresses on the floor, only so rotted and mouse-bitten that this was just a guess. There was also some kind of shelf holding a pile of canned goods with the labels faded and peeling with age. Everything was covered in years of dust and dirt.

We stepped out again, and Lewis said, "Just look around. It might be hard to identify a grave, but any place that looks hidden might be a place to start." He opened his trunk and handed me one of the shovels.

"Don't dig anything up yet," he said. "If we find anything, we have to be real careful. We'll need a coroner to remove the body, or it won't hold up in court."

Lewis sent me off to the right of the little caved-in house, and he went left. I looked at grass and weeds, at places where, years ago, dirt might have been disturbed. I checked and double-checked, kept widening my circle, but found nothing. I was starting to lose heart. I was also sweating through my clothes. I'd spent most of my working life indoors, and I wasn't used to the midday summer heat.

"Find anything?" Lewis called over to me.

"Nothing," I said. "You?"

"Not yet."

"I'm starting to feel sick in this heat, Lewis. I hate to say it, but this is looking like a wild goose chase."

"Get yourself a drink. There's a well over there. We need to keep looking."

I found the little brick well in the tall grass, lifted the lid, and unspooled the bucket into the well. But it stopped only a short ways down.

"It's dry," I called to Lewis.

"It's roots," he said. "I used to have to clean it for Lorna all the time. Give me a second."

He went to fetch a flashlight from his glove compartment and shined it down the well while I waited for his verdict. But instead of speaking, he turned his back on me and threw up.

"Told you it was hot," I said, handing him my handkerchief to wipe his mouth.

"It's not heat," he said, handing me his flashlight. "It's her."

And when I looked down the well, I saw what could only be the remains of a human face looking back at me from the bottom of that well. The skull was turned up, looking skyward, but it felt like it was looking right at me.

Lewis sank down in the grass where he was standing. "I'm going to hell for what I did to that woman and her son," he sobbed. "I should have helped them." I didn't know what to say, but I patted his shoulder and walked back to the car to give him some time alone.

We drove to Senath after that, where Lewis called the Dunklin County police from a diner and told them where they could meet us. We drank sweet tea until they showed up with the coroner's vehicle and followed us to the spot, where the coroner set up shop and got down to work.

Lewis hadn't said a word the whole time, but as they began to lift Lorna's body out of the well, he said to me, "I can't help you with the Buddy Harper case, Leroy, but if there's a case against Wiley for Lorna's murder, I'll testify. I'll tell them everything I know."

This gave me some hope, right up until I saw what was left of Lorna's body as they placed her in the bag they'd brought with them. Nothing but bones and dirt, like a skeleton filled with mud, and I felt despondent then, because I knew, looking at what could only have been Lorna, that we'd never be able to prove it was her. Even with Lewis's and Sonny's testimony, we didn't have a case if we didn't have a body. And it burned me up that after all my sleuthing, Wiley Slocum was going to get away with murder for a second time.

It was after eleven when I got home, and Mabel was up with the light on. I knew this was trouble, but I was so exhausted and broken and depressed that I didn't have it in me to fight her.

"Leroy," she started when I walked in.

I cut her off. "It's over, Mabel. I'm done."

We sat together in the lamplight and I told her about finding the birth certificate with Lewis's name on it, and how Wiley had fired him, and how we'd questioned Sonny and found Lorna's body, and how it was too decomposed to be of any use, even with an eyewitness account. She listened while I talked, and when I was finished, she was quiet.

Finally she said, "Leroy, what were you doing down in Little Rock a while back?"

"I had a lead on Wiley and had to question an old friend from law school to see if he might know anything."

"Who?" she asked.

"Fred Jacobson," I told her.

"Doesn't Fred work at the hospital there?"

I nodded.

"I gave Coralee Wilkins a ride home from church last week," Mabel said. "She came home only a couple of weeks after you were down in Little Rock. Does that have something to do with why you went to see Fred Jacobson?"

"I was there to see if I could find a girl Coralee told Earl about, who claims to be Lorna's sister. Fred said the girl was criminally insane and her testimony would be worthless. But I did ask after Coralee. Earl felt she was doing much better, and I asked if Fred could look into her case," I said.

"Oh Leroy," she said, "that poor woman is sick. She was so terrified of something she was crying when I stopped to offer her a ride, and she shook the whole way to her house. Now, are you going to tell me she wouldn't still be in that hospital if you hadn't been down there poking around?"

"Fred told me they wouldn't let her out if they didn't feel she was ready."

"If you say so, Leroy," she said, but I could tell she didn't believe me.

I followed her to bed and collapsed beside her, so tired I could hardly keep my eyes open, but I couldn't fall asleep either. My mind kept turning to the photograph of the beautiful woman in the tavern who was nothing but a skeleton now, and how Wiley was going to get away with it all, and that my work had been for nothing until I reached out and put my hand on Mabel's back. She was already asleep, but the rise and fall of her breathing calmed me, and finally I slept.

For the rest of the week, I was at the breakfast table every morning with Mabel and Caleb. None of us said much, but I was so tired from running around that even if I couldn't stand the fact that Wiley was going to get away with it all, it was also a kind of relief. I didn't know until then that losing could be such a relief, but it was. I was sleeping better than I had in years, but I knew settling back into things at home wasn't going to be easy. I could tell by the set of Mabel's shoulders that she was still angry, and would be for a long time.

Worst of all, though, Caleb had no interest in me. When he got up from breakfast to head off to school one morning, I remembered that he'd made the football team at school and said, "How about we throw that football around after school today?"

"I've got practice after school," he said.

Another night after supper, I said, "Hey, son, want to drive over to Stillwater and look at that new shipment of hunting rifles on Saturday?"

But he said, "Me and Earl are working on target practice Saturday. Deer season starts soon."

I'd forgotten this. I'd seen them practicing on a bale of cotton with a target fastened on it behind Cole's house. Those two boys were joined at the hip. And until now I'd even been glad he had a friend to fill in the void I'd left behind, chasing after my leads. But now Caleb's voice had no curiosity in it about anything I said. Even worse, it was so much deeper than I remembered.

"Have some patience, Leroy," Mabel said as the screen door slammed behind Caleb.

Now, patience was something I'd never been good at, but over the last two years I had learned to live with it. But patience with a lead is different than patience with a child you love, whose love you want back and, what's more, feel like you deserve for all the work you've done putting a roof over his head and food on the table and clothes on his back.

But when I said as much to Mabel, the look she gave me was sharp enough to cut through me.

"Who do you think you are, Leroy? You thought you could bring Wiley to justice single-handedly. You thought you could keep Coralee Harper out of that institution, then once you put her there, you thought you could take her out again. And now you think because you put food on this table, you deserve the kind of love and respect you've done nothing to deserve for a long time. But I'm going to tell you something, Leroy. You're not God. You're not even a judge anymore. And your child is not some client of yours. You have no right to expect loyalty from a boy you've neglected for years."

I slunk out the front door the next morning and drove to my office, feeling bruised and alone and defeated. I was already struggling with an emptiness inside me without the thrill of every new lead on Wiley to fill me up, and it had only been a week since we'd found Lorna's body. And nothing else in my life felt solid. Where I thought I had a family, I found a gaping hole. Where I thought I had a business to return to, I found a list of phone numbers of clients who'd moved on to someone else. And Mabel was right. These were not things I could force. I was going to have to work hard, bide my time, and hope for the best.

Now, I knew there wasn't much I could do about the mess I'd made of my own life, or Mabel's or Caleb's, or even Coralee's and Earl Wilkins's, but after all that had happened, there was one person I thought I might be able to do some good for. It occurred to me that Sonny might want to bury his mama properly so he'd have a place to visit her. And that coroner had no reason to call me. As far as he knew, I'd randomly found the body with Lewis trying to get a drink out of that well while passing through the area. It was also Dunklin County, Missouri, not even in Arkansas's jurisdiction, so any news about the body wouldn't show up in the *Daily Press*. But I had to act fast or Lorna would end up buried in an unmarked grave. So on Monday, I put in a call to the coroner and identified myself.

"Listen," I told him. "I know you might not be able to tell me this, but I wondered what you found out about the body we ran across out in that well last week."

"It was a woman's body. Looks like someone beat her to death."

"How do you know?" I asked.

"Fractures and breaks that never healed," he said. "Whoever put her in that grave really must have wanted her dead, because I've never seen so many broken bones before. A bullet would have been kinder."

I could see the scene he described so vividly, and what was worse was knowing that Sonny had witnessed it. And I knew then it was the reason he had gone mute, like the child locked in the trunk of the car over in Monette.

"What will happen to the body?" I asked.

"We'll keep it in the morgue for a couple of weeks, and if nobody can ID her, we'll bury her with the other Jane Does."

"There was nothing left to identify as I recall," I said.

"We did find one thing," the coroner told me. "After they washed the dirt off her, they found a necklace lodged in her ribcage. Some sort of cameo. If someone can verify it was hers, that'd be enough to settle it."

"I can do better than that," I told him, feeling around for my magnifying glass and pulling out the photo of Lorna at the tavern. "I've got a picture of her wearing it."

I wasn't there when they arrested Wiley Slocum for the murders of Buddy Harper and Lorna Lovett, and Lewis Hopkins wasn't either, which I'm sorry about because I know he'd have loved to have been the one to take him in. But we sat together at the trial and gave our testimonies one after the other.

For weeks, I had worried that Sheriff Slocum and his machine would finesse things the way they always had and he'd come out clean as a whistle. But it turns out Lewis and me weren't the only people Wiley had in a vice-grip, because when news got around of Sonny's eyewitness testimony and the photographic evidence, those who had all been bullied into doing the sheriff's bidding for years were only too happy to corroborate an old story it appears they'd known all along in exchange for immunity: Buddy Harper had been planning to elope with Lorna Lovett the morning he was killed by Sheriff Slocum, but the sheriff had caught wind of it and whisked her away before Buddy could make an honest woman of her. Which is what got Buddy killed, after he had found her room empty. Buddy Harper had never even broken into the tavern or taken a crowbar to Wiley. Wiley'd simply laid in wait and shot him.

By the time it was all over, they were able to get Sheriff Slocum for the murders of Lorna Lovett and Buddy Harper, not to mention kidnapping, extortion, witness tampering, destroying legal records, forgery of documentation, and bootlegging. Lewis had even tracked down Brother Jeremiah Cassidy out in Oklahoma, put him behind bars, and added a bribery charge to the long list of Wiley's crimes. In the end, he was given the equivalent of nearly three life sentences, but the one he received for the murder of Buddy Harper was the one I found most gratifying.

But it was funny, because after all my chasing after him, what peace I felt knowing Wiley Slocum would die in prison was short-lived. I couldn't figure out why until I finally realized all my fear and hatred of Wiley had been holding me up, and when they were gone, I was as limp as a glove without a hand in it. And as the days wore on, I was left with the sense of my own responsibility in some of those misdeeds, and I knew they'd eventually catch up with me, because by then I understood that nobody gets away with anything. Not really. Not for long. I was already paying for them with a wife who turned her back to me in bed and a son who didn't want me around. And mostly, I just tried to wait it out.

But one evening my impatience got the better of me. Mabel

was cooking supper when Caleb appeared in his hunting gear, and I was so tired of him running off I couldn't stop myself.

"Where do you think you're going?" I said.

"Hunting with Little Earl," he told me.

"Your mama's getting supper ready," I told him sternly. "Put that rifle away and eat."

I expected to get a rise out of him, but Mabel told me, "Caleb is waiting on Little Earl, but he's late. It's opening night of deer season, Leroy. You'd know that if you'd been paying attention."

"Can I go now, Mama?"

"What about Little Earl?" Mabel asked.

"I'll find him," he said.

He never even looked at me that whole time. He didn't ask for my permission. And as he walked out the door, I realized that in a few years he'd be off to college. And with Wiley behind bars, I could finally see what Mabel had been trying to tell me, which is that all this time, I hadn't been paying attention.

BIG EARL

Now, I was anxious to finish up the harvest. It had been a cooler season than usual overall, the cotton coming off at different times in different places, and although harvest was always an exciting time, it was especially exciting because it was my first harvest as manager. Of course I wanted to do a good job for Mr. Holmes, but I was also ready to be done with it and get home to look after Coralee more closely. I was worried about her. She still hadn't been back to church.

I knew Mr. Holmes knew this, but he also needed me too, and he needed Little Earl, who was the all-around gofer for the gin by then. And at least the work gave me some relief from my worry about Coralee. I could sometimes even forget while I was busy welcoming farmers, working the scales, unclogging the gin. But when each day was done and Little Earl and me went to head on home, all my worries about Coralee were waiting for me, like they'd been sitting around the parking lot wondering where I was.

But I was also hopeful again for the first time. Coralee might've been acting a little strange, but she was home at last, and the harvest had been a good one, and I felt I'd done my best as the new manager for Mr. Holmes. And it occurred to me that this was the best my life had been in a long time. Maybe ever. My wife and boy at the dinner table at night. My job done well. Even a little more money coming my way. It was as much as I'd ever hoped for.

But on the last day of the harvest, when the final farmer had come through and Mr. Holmes shut down the gin, there was still a lot of cleaning up to do, and we were running behind, something that really stuck in Little Earl's craw. He'd started fussing the day before because the last day of the harvest just happened to fall on the opening day of deer season, and he was planning to meet Caleb at his house to make tracks for the woods. It was all he'd talked of for weeks.

"Don't worry, son," I told him. "Caleb knows you're coming."

"But we want first crack at those bucks," he said. "Plus it's a fifteen-minute walk."

"Listen, son," I said. "I'll drive you. We'll stop at home so you can pick up your gear and then I'll drop you at Caleb's. That should save you those fifteen minutes."

Well, that seemed to settle the boy down, and when we finally finished up at the gin, I could see the relief written all over his face as we drove home. But when we pulled in the driveway and climbed out, Coralee had locked the front door again. I knocked and knocked. And when she didn't come to the door, Little Earl was in such a hurry to meet Caleb that he jumped off the front porch and said, "I'll check around back."

As he disappeared around the side of the house, I looked in the window. The lights were off, but I could see Coralee rocking back and forth in the front room, holding Little Earl's gun. *Oh, no,* I thought. *Oh, god.* And I knew I needed to be gentle with her. Someone could get hurt.

I rapped on the window softly, then rapped again.

"Coralee, it's me," I told her. "It's Earl." But just at the moment she turned and saw me, Little Earl screamed.

CORALEE

In the end I never did get to give my statement about Buddy to Leroy Harrison. It turned out he didn't need it. But it was funny when Earl sat me down and explained they had cleared Buddy's name. I thought I'd feel relief, and for a few days I did, but then I realized that I'd already known he was innocent and no court saying so made it any more true than I already knew it was. And no matter how long that sheriff sat in jail, it couldn't bring Buddy back to me. It didn't help Mama to know he was innocent. It didn't mean Buddy could marry Lorna and have the life he wanted. And I wondered why I ever thought it would've made a difference.

Only thing that could make a difference for me now was that Earl told me the harvest season was finishing up and I wouldn't be alone all the time, day and night. And on the last day, when Earl and Little Earl were running late getting home, I decided to unlock the back door and go out and look at my garden. I already felt safer just knowing they would be there with me for a good long while to come.

I hadn't been outside except to hang laundry on the line by the back porch since those boys hit me with the stones, and the fresh air felt nice, and the sky was a pretty pink as the sun began to set. I hadn't touched my garden since I'd been home from Little Rock, and now, up close, I could see what a wreck it had become. Only good thing was that some of those beet seeds were still in their shells, and I decided on a lark to surprise Earl by shelling them. He'd wanted me to do this since I got home, but I just hadn't felt up to it. The thought of how happy he'd be to see I'd been out to my garden got my fingers moving, and those seeds slipped into my apron pocket as I worked, and before I knew it I was halfway down the row and thought maybe I could even finish by the time Earl got home.

I was almost done when I heard something moving behind the house, and I stopped and looked out over the cotton field. It was a quiet night, and without my noticing it, the pink sky had turned to dusk, and it would've been peaceful if I had not felt so afraid. *Maybe it's a dog*, I thought, and peered through the dying light. But the sound got closer this time, then closer still. And when I could finally make it out, I could see it was a young man with a gun out there in the cotton field, coming straight for me.

I ran into the house and locked the back door behind me. Then I ran into Little Earl's bedroom, which was the closest place I could hide. I hunched down on the floor and started crawling under the bed. And that's when I saw Little Earl's gun tucked beneath it.

Now, I knew the Lord said to turn the other cheek. But I also knew the Lord was not going to help me now. He'd failed me too many times, and I wasn't leaving it up to Him. I wanted to live even if He didn't want me to, and I was going to make sure I did.

I picked up the gun then. I hadn't held one since I was a girl. I was so small back then the kickback used to knock me over until Buddy showed me how to lean my shoulder into the stock so I'd keep my balance. But it all came back to me with that gun in my hands, like my fingers remembered how it worked even if my mind didn't. I slid the cylinder open. One bullet inside. I closed it up again, took off the safety, and cocked the gun. Then I unlocked the back door and walked right out onto the porch. I was done being afraid.

LEROY

I don't remember much of what happened the night Coralee Wilkins killed my son. Maybe it's because I can't. Maybe it's too painful. Or maybe I just don't want to because I'll have to remember the moment Earl Wilkins's neighbor Wilbur Higby showed up at our door and Mabel started screaming.

What I do remember is that after Cole showed up with Lulu to sit with Mabel, I got in the car and drove over to Earl Wilkins's house. There was something I had to do. But when I arrived at the house, the sheriff's deputy who'd replaced Lewis Hopkins had Coralee in the back seat of the police car and was trying to pull out of the driveway through the crowds that had gathered around the little house. And I understood then that even as I had lost my son, Earl and Little Earl were losing Coralee too. Probably forever. And when Earl Wilkins saw me pull into his driveway, the anguish on his face made me so angry at myself that I got out of the car and turned to the crowd and said, "Get out of here, all of you. Now! Leave these poor folks alone."

Maybe it was because they recognized me that they vanished into the darkness outside the streetlight in front of Earl's house. Maybe they thought what was left was between me and Earl. But when they were gone, I stepped onto the porch and sat down next to Earl, whose face was buried in his hands.

"Leroy," he choked out. "I'm so sorry."

"What happened?" I asked.

"Little Earl was supposed to meet Caleb at your place, but

we were late getting home from the gin. Caleb must've come to find him when he didn't show up."

"Where's Little Earl?" I asked.

"Doc English sedated him." He was quiet awhile. Finally he said, "This is my fault, Leroy. I knew something was wrong with her. I thought about calling the doctors but I was afraid they'd take her away again, and now . . ." His voice broke off then, and he couldn't finish.

It was hard for me to speak just then too. But I said, "Listen, Earl. It's not your fault. You couldn't have known it would come to this." I had never told him that I'd passed on his assessment of Coralee's state of mind to Fred Jacobson at the hospital in Little Rock after Fred told me he couldn't release Libby Lovett—that I'd tried to use my last bit of power as judge to convince him because I needed Coralee out of the hospital for my own purposes—and I knew then that I never would. But there was one thing I could still do.

I said, "Earl, your wife is going to need a lawyer. I want to represent her."

"You want to represent the woman who killed your son?" he asked.

"Coralee doesn't belong in prison. If I'm the one to say she's not guilty, they won't charge her. She'll just go back to the hospital."

"We can't afford you, Leroy," he said.

"I won't charge you a dime, Earl. Please let me represent her. It's the only thing I can do now for anybody."

"All right," Earl choked. "Thank you, Leroy. And I'm real sorry. I'm just so sorry." He broke off then and began to cry. And even though the reality that Caleb was gone hadn't hit me yet, I could feel it coming, like storm clouds gathering on the horizon, and I knew I needed to get off that porch before they rolled in.

CORALEE

In the mornings, they brought me my pills. More than I'd ever taken before, but I didn't fight them, and I knew then that I never would again. I'd have swallowed any number of them just to blot out the sound of my boy screaming after he saw I killed his friend, the look on Earl's face when he realized what I'd done, the fact that Little Earl didn't even say goodbye when they put me in the police car. But I went gladly. I didn't know they were taking me to jail that first night, but the truth is I felt safer there than I had since the day I came home.

And when they drove me the whole long way from Stillwater to Little Rock and we pulled onto the grounds of the hospital, my first thought was that I'd get to see Libby. But they put me in a different building, with more bars on the windows and more guards around me. And even if the medication made it easy not to think about much, taking it always reminded me of Earl saying *say ahh*, only instead of making me laugh, it made me sad. I wasn't even allowed visits, which was fine because I couldn't have faced Earl or Little Earl anyway, I was so ashamed.

Eventually there were fewer pills I had to take, and without them I started to feel a little more in ways I didn't like. I couldn't block out what I didn't want to remember. But what came to me most often was the moment I decided not to trust the Lord to take care of me. I gave in to despair. I did not believe He would protect me. I did not let Him decide if I should live or die. I took matters into my own hands. And I knew I would never doubt Him again.

I don't know how long I'd been in that place when one morning, Miss Etta came in just like she always used to. I hadn't seen her since she'd seen me and Earl off when he'd come to get me that day and bring me home. Must've been years.

"What are you doing here?" I asked.

"They're sending you back to your old building," she told me. "I'll be your nurse from now on." And she walked me freely through the halls without the handcuffs they'd been putting on me to move me from place to place, and I was pleased to see my old hallway and to discover that the room they had for me was just across from my old one, and it was nice for something to feel familiar.

They changed my pills again, and after months of nothing but eating and walking and lying on my bed, Miss Etta came in one morning and said I could have my job at the laundry back. And when she walked me down there and I opened the door and saw Libby, Libby gave a little cry and about knocked me over with a hug, she was so glad to see me.

"Is it really you?" Libby asked.

"It's me," I said.

"I knew you was back, but they said you was in a different building now. They said something bad must've happened to you. Are you okay?" And her kindness was so welcome that even through the medication I started to cry. I wanted to tell her right then about Buddy and Lorna and the sheriff going to jail and Little Earl's friend and what I done to him, but she stopped me cold.

"Hush now," Libby said. "There's plenty of time to talk. But you can't start crying. They'll take you away again." Then she hugged me again and said, "I missed you so much. Is it wrong that I'm glad you're back? Is it selfish?"

I didn't know the answer to that question, but in that moment I was glad to be back too. And as it turned out, Libby was right. There was plenty of time to talk, and as the weeks and months passed we had a few minutes now and then when I was finally able to tell her everything, even if it was in bits and pieces. But I started with what I knew she'd care about most, which was that her sister Lorna's body had been found and the sheriff had gone to jail for murdering her. Libby cried then, even after saying I couldn't. But when I told her the old judge got Lorna buried next to Buddy, she smiled through her tears and said, "She'd have liked that."

"Buddy would've too," I told her.

"Where'd they find her?" she asked.

"Down a well, someplace over the state line. It's where the sheriff kept her."

"Are they sure it was her?"

"They found a necklace on her that she was wearing in some picture," I said.

"The cameo," Libby said. Then she smiled at me. "Buddy gave that to her, Coralee."

And after all these years, I finally understood. This was why Mama was so mad at Buddy when he died. Buddy had stolen the cameo Elbert had given her when she was a girl. But even if my brother had been a thief for stealing Mama's necklace, when I thought about how Mama wouldn't even share her feelings with us, it seemed like she was the real thief, holding back the things we needed most that would've cost her nothing. And thinking about it that way made me feel all right with it after a while.

For a long time after that, Libby didn't want to talk about Lorna. But I guess she'd been thinking about Buddy stealing Mama's necklace too, because one day she said, "You know, Coralee, your brother gave my sister a necklace, and that necklace is the reason they were finally able to lay her to rest beside Buddy. That's quite a present, if you ask me." And I understood then that you couldn't know the meaning of a thing when it happened. You just had to bide your time and wait to find out what it all meant.

After that, there didn't seem much else to tell Libby. But we always found things to talk about. Sometimes we'd get to wondering about Buddy and Lorna and what their life together might've been like. And one day, Libby said, "We was almost family, Coralee. Just imagine."

But as I lay in bed that night, I realized that Libby and me had become family anyway. And I knew then that men could do what they would, and do what they might, but there were some plans God had that men could not change no matter how hard they tried.

BIG EARL

A fter Coralee left, only one thing mattered to me, and that was Little Earl. I knew he'd never be the same after Caleb's death. And I knew he'd never feel the same about his mama, because when they finally transferred her out of that maximum security building after a few years and sent me a letter saying we could come visit her, he didn't offer to go, and I didn't ask him. He still worked at the gin during harvest, and I think it kept his mind off things, but I let him spend most of his time on homework and didn't bother him too much, even when we were short at the gin.

And I really felt in spite of everything I'd done my job well when Little Earl graduated from high school as valedictorian. I tell you, watching him graduate at the top of his class was one of the proudest moments of my life. One of the happiest. But one of the saddest too, sitting through the ceremony without Coralee beside me, and listening to the principal read off the names *Phyllis Gilbert* and *Clyde Johnson* with no *Caleb Harrison* in between. Still, I made sure to take the program from the ceremony with me to show Coralee the next time I went to visit.

But proud as I was, it was also a hard time for me, because all those years earlier when Mr. Holmes had promoted me to manager, an idea began to take root about what I might do with that raise, and I had saved almost all of it to send Little Earl to college. I knew he needed to get out of this town and go live in the world, someplace that wasn't so full of sad memories.

Bad enough for me every time I walked out the back door and saw that spot where I'd found Little Earl hunched over Caleb's body. But I knew for Little Earl, it must've been unbearable.

I thought maybe he'd go to the University of Arkansas down in Little Rock, but I think that was too close to his mama, so he decided on Arkansas State, which took some of the sting of losing him away because he would only be in Jonesboro, just an hour away. So even if the house was empty something terrible after he left, he came home on summer breaks and at the holidays, and I got to see him more than I expected to.

He even worked alongside me on those vacations until the year before he graduated, when Mr. Holmes closed down the gin. Lots of cotton gins were closing now that the machines were taking over. Those machines could do in an hour what it took twenty-five men and a cotton gin to do in a day, right there in the fields. But I sure was sad the day we ginned our last, and Mr. Holmes shuttered the place, and we all went our separate ways. Half my life. Hell, more. It was all in that gin, and even if it had been hard work, and bad seasons had left us all down in the mouth, it was the place where my life had unfolded, and I didn't want to let it go.

Lots of folks had left town by then, migrating north for jobs, and it was sad to see the empty shops along Main Street. Vernon Hartsoe's barbershop was still there, and the credit union too, and Merle's, though word was that Merle's was probably closing soon enough with the new highway making the drive to Stillwater so quick. And I'd have been worried sick about a job if it hadn't been for Cole Harrison, who came to my house the day he heard about the gin closing and said he'd hire me on since so many folks were heading north he needed the help. It was a demotion, but I didn't care one bit. I had spent the raise I'd saved to see Little Earl through school, and now I didn't need many more years before I could take the Social Security and retire.

Now, I was sure this was as good as my life would ever be again, and I'd accepted it, when something happened I never expected. Coralee'd been locked up more than ten years when I got a call one day from the hospital saying it was shutting down most of its facilities. At first I thought they were transferring her somewhere else and got to worrying if my old truck could make a longer drive if they sent her further away. But eventually I realized they were telling me about a new medication that was so effective, they were releasing most of their patients.

"Don't get me wrong," I told the woman who'd called. "I want my wife to come home more than anything, but do you think it's safe?"

"Long as she takes her Thorazine, she'll be just fine, Mr. Wilkins."

"What happens now?" I asked.

"You can come pick her up," she said. "We're sending her home."

LEROY

In the months that followed Caleb's death, I tried to locate the exact moment when I'd lost my way. All the strings I'd pulled trying to settle an old score. Taking the photo from the tavern. Badgering Sonny to get information that traumatized the boy every time. Dredging up Lewis's guilt about Lorna. Getting Coralee Wilkins an earlier medical review just so she could make a statement that, in the end, I never needed. And for all my hatred of Wiley Slocum, I realized I had more in common with him than I ever realized, letting my pride run roughshod over folks' lives to get what I wanted. Coralee Wilkins's actions had been pure and unintentional, but vanity and vengeance shaped every single decision I made that led up to Caleb's death, and I knew that even if she had pulled the trigger, it was me who killed my son.

I knew Mabel knew this too. She never said so, but then she didn't say much after Caleb died. She didn't smile much either. In fact, I only saw Mabel smile a real smile, the old smile I knew so well, one time after Caleb's death. It was at the christening for Lulu and Sonny's baby boy, whom they'd named Buddy after the father Sonny had never known. And I have to say it was really something to see my family lining the pews of First Methodist in Paradise right alongside Buddy Harper's to watch the pastor pour holy water over the child that now linked our two families forever by blood.

It was after Lulu handed the child to Mabel so she could

collect her things that little Buddy looked up at Mabel and let out a squeal of laughter, and that's when I saw it—the great big smile I used to see on Mabel's face when she looked at Caleb or me back in the old days. I suppose in time it's possible I might have seen it again if I hadn't found her slumped on the porch swing after driving home from work a few years later. At first I thought she'd fallen asleep there, but as I got closer I could see her stillness, the unnatural angle of one of her hands, and that's when I knew. And I really have to hand it to Earl Wilkins. When word spread about Mabel, he was there almost as fast as Cole was, and checked in on me for months. So I couldn't have been sorrier when, a few years after that, Sonny found Earl face down inside the gin with a plug stick still in his hand.

It was at Earl's funeral that Little Earl finally introduced Coralee to Sonny, and I watched her closely for any confusion that Sonny might be Buddy. But she just seemed glad to meet her brother's son at last. It was the first time I'd seen Little Earl since he'd moved north for a job with an engineering firm, but I knew he'd been back for a visit with his wife and baby girl recently because Earl had talked of little else before he died. But a week after Earl's funeral, Little Earl flew back to Minnesota, and I wondered if I shouldn't look in on Coralee until Cole told me that her sister Shelby's daughter kept an eye on her, so I stopped worrying.

Then a few years on, I saw Coralee alongside the road, dressed for church. She was having trouble walking, so I offered her a ride. When we pulled up to the church, I walked her up the steps to get her seated inside, but by the time I did, the service was starting and it was too late to walk out. And when it was over, I offered her a ride the next week, and pretty soon it wasn't unusual to see the two of us sitting together in church on Sundays.

People sometimes asked me how I could sit in church with

the woman who shot my son, and the truth is I can't account for it. I suppose it was because I was hoping it might bring me some of the peace I knew she found there, but later I understood, after a sermon on forgiveness, that this was what I really wanted. Not from God, mind you, though I had respect enough for Him by then, but from Mabel and Caleb, who I'd loved so much and whose lives, one way or another, I'd taken from them.

Then one evening, driving her home after a carol service in December, Coralee mentioned that Little Earl was bringing his family down for Christmas.

"Well," I said, "it'll be nice to see your boy again."

We'd just pulled up to her house when she said, "I see your boy now and again too."

I didn't know what to say, but since I saw no point in correcting her, I said, "Where?"

"On your front porch swing," she said. "Mabel's always with him."

I couldn't think of an appropriate response to this, but still, it took me a moment to be sure my voice wouldn't tremble.

"Well," I said at last. "I'll see you next Sunday."

I drove home then, pulled into my driveway, and cut the engine. I'd dreaded coming home ever since Caleb died, but with Mabel gone too, the emptiness of that house was almost too much to bear. Then I noticed the old porch swing swaying in the cold winter breeze, and I felt silly when I caught myself wondering whether it was Mabel and Caleb sitting there just like Coralee said it was, so I got out of the car then and walked up to the house. But I didn't sit down on the swing when I reached the porch, not that day or any other. I just hoped when the time came, there'd be room enough for me.

ACKNOWLEDGMENTS

I am so immensely grateful to everyone who helped me bring this novel to life. First, my agent, Ann Collette, who helped me find my way back to this subject, offered encouragement along the way, and found a very happy home for it at Blair. To my editor, Robin Miura, and my publisher, Lynn York, I cannot thank you both enough for your early feedback and support of this book, your enthusiasm and attention to detail, and your willingness to take a chance on a native Michigander who lacked a southern accent. To Arielle Hebert, thank you for your patience and swift responses to my too-frequent emails and for keeping things moving forward, and to Laura Williams, for the absolutely beautiful cover you designed. To everyone at Blair, your support for this book has been everything a writer at the end of a long journey could hope for. Thank you, thank you, thank you!

I also want to thank my group of "writing ladies" who helped me get the first half of this novel written—Lee Hope, Meg Senuta, Faye Snider, and Robin Stein. Our Wednesday evening meetings kept me going for a long time, and I am so grateful you helped me set and meet deadlines and offered such wonderful and supportive feedback. This book would not exist without you.

This novel is inspired by the lives of my paternal grandparents, and I want to thank my father, Joe Pope, for his stories about growing up on the southwestern border of the Missouri Bootheel, just across the St. Francis River from Arkansas, and for all those seventeen-hour drives we took from Michigan south to visit my grandparents. In particular, I am grateful for the trips I took with just my father to visit my grandmother while staying in Monette, Arkansas, with my Aunt Tootie and Uncle Tommy Gathwright, particularly the trip in the summer of 1990 when we cleaned out my grandmother's house after she moved into a nursing home. Cleaning out someone's home is a deeply personal and unintentionally intrusive way to get to know someone, but I learned just as much about my father on that trip too, not the least of which was just how wide the cultural gap between his upbringing and mine really was. In sorting through papers, I ran across a formal 8 × 10" black-and-white photograph of a beautiful dead girl lying in a coffin smothered in flowers. Shocked, I shoved it in my father's face and said, "What the hell is *this*?" Unfazed, my father peered over his glasses at the picture for a moment, then said, "Why, that's Bobbie Jean."

I would also like to thank my mother, Betty Pope, who was not only the earliest and fiercest supporter of my writing, but having grown up in New England, never took things like photographs of corpses for granted. My father was in the military when my parents married in 1969, but he retired shortly thereafter and returned to his alma mater, Arkansas State University, for graduate school. My mother was hired to teach third grade in the local school district in Jonesboro, where a senior administrator warned her she'd have a boy in her class that year who "wasn't right" because when his mother had been pregnant with him, she'd looked at a crazy person. It was my mother's observations of the social context my grandmother had to navigate bearing the stigma of her illness and years in a mental hospital that helped me understand the sad outcome that might have been, which inspired this novel.

I also owe a huge debt of gratitude to my father's relatives, both living and dead, whose voices, cooking, and company gave shape to the characters that appear in this novel. When mechanized cotton picking and ginning did away with so many jobs in the South, my father's relatives migrated north for work in the auto industry in Flint on what was known as the "hillbilly pipeline." Having grown up in Michigan myself, I spent a lot of time with these transplanted Missourians and Arkansawyers. My thanks to Stella Tate, Bud and Tootie Tate, Tootie and Tommy Gathwright, Jerry and Barb Tate, Pistol and Joyce Tate, Vicki Jane and Nathan Puckett, Jimmy Dale and Clarice Tate, Judy and William Tate, and L. B. Defoe on my grandmother's side. On my grandfather's side, to Gerold and Nancy Pope and their children Kathy, Judy, and Kevin, as well as Harlan and Betty Pope and their daughter Kim, and also my Aunt Etoile Hooper, cousins Tink and Sonnyboy, and all the children on both sides of my father's family with whom I ran around both the greater Flint area and the Missouri/Arkansas border. A very special thanks to my Uncle Jerry Tate, who, sick as he was, allowed me to interview him about growing up in my father's hometown on my parents' front porch in Michigan just weeks before he died. Some of his answers to my questions that day appear word for word in this novel.

I also owe a special debt of gratitude to my father and grandfather's barber, the late Vernon Hartsoe, whose own father had been my great-grandfather's barber as well. After Vernon appeared in the Kentucky Headhunters' music video for their version of "Oh Lonesome Me," my father took me down to Vernon's barbershop to meet him on our next visit south in 1992. Over the heads of his patrons, Vernon told me stories about my family and his own, and showed me the framed obituary of his twin brother, Max June, who died aboard the USS *Arizona* in the bombing of Pearl Harbor. I remember realizing that in 1992, it had probably been hanging there for fifty years. At some point that afternoon, I asked Vernon where he was born.

He walked me to the door and pointed down the street. "See that big tree?" he asked me. "There used to be a house there. That's were I was born." I understood in that moment that a life lived in the space of a few square yards could be every bit as large as a life lived anywhere else, and Vernon's answer to my simple question is the true beginning of this novel, though I didn't know it at the time.

I also have many professors, teachers, and mentors to whom I am immensely grateful—Robert Root, Jr.; Susan Schiller; Kathleen Stocking; and the late and much-missed Michael Steinberg, as well as Marge Sheppard and Rosie MacFarlane from Kinney School in Mt. Pleasant Michigan, Pat Seiter from Mt. Pleasant High School, and Sr. Thaddeus Kowalinski from Sacred Heart Academy, all of whom helped me recognize that I was a writer. I must also thank my high school religion teacher, Father Don Henkes from Sacred Heart Academy, who first introduced me to Edgar Lee Masters's poetry collection *Spoon River Anthology* in a unit called "Death and Dying." It was Masters's ability to see profundity in seemingly ordinary lives that helped me understand the truth that came to me standing in the doorway of Vernon Hartsoe's barbershop, but without exposure to Masters's work first, I might just have missed it.

Finally, I do not even know how to begin to thank my wonderful husband, Matt Elliott, for his extraordinary support of my writing and for his general good humor, patience, and kindness these past seventeen years. One afternoon he wandered into my study while I was crawling around on my hands and knees laying out chapters of this novel on the carpet when, behind the door, he noticed the floor-to-ceiling chart of manuscript pages, sticky notes, and arrows covered in my wild, serial-killer scrawl. "What's this?" he asked. I looked up from the floor and said, "It keeps the plot straight in my head." We had been avid watchers of the first two seasons of Showtime's

Homeland, in which CIA agent Carrie Mathison loses her grip on reality tracking down a terrorist called Abu Nazir. I knew Matt feared I was straying into dangerous territory when he crossed his arms, eyed the mess on the wall, and said, "Okay. But if a picture of Abu Nazir shows up, I'm calling someone." He never did call anyone, but what he did do was read the manuscript of this novel in at least twenty different iterations. Asking someone to read a draft of your novel once is a big ask. Anyone who says yes twenty times is either nuts or really loves you. It is my great good fortune that my husband is the sanest person I know.